SIGN YOUR FEARS AWAY

SIGN YOUR FEARS AWAY
THE AGENT OPERATIVE™ BOOK 1

MARTHA CARR
MICHAEL ANDERLE

DISRUPTIVE IMAGINATION

This book is a work of fiction. All of the characters, organizations, and events portrayed in this novel are either products of the author's imagination or are used fictitiously. Sometimes both.

Copyright © LMBPN Publishing
Cover by Fantasy Book Design
Cover copyright © LMBPN Publishing
A Michael Anderle Production

LMBPN Publishing supports the right to free expression and the value of copyright. The purpose of copyright is to encourage writers and artists to produce the creative works that enrich our culture.

The distribution of this book without permission is a theft of the author's intellectual property. If you would like permission to use material from the book (other than for review purposes), please contact support@lmbpn.com. Thank you for your support of the author's rights.

LMBPN Publishing
PMB 196, 2540 South Maryland Pkwy
Las Vegas, NV 89109

Version 1.00, November 2022
ebook ISBN: 979-8-88541-849-2
Print ISBN: 979-8-88541-988-8

The Oriceran Universe (and what happens within / characters / situations / worlds) are Copyright (c) 2017-22 by Martha Carr and LMBPN Publishing.

THE SIGN YOUR FEARS AWAY TEAM

Thanks to our beta readers:
Malyssa Brannon, John Ashmore, David Laughlin

Thanks to our JIT Readers:

Christopher Gilliard
Diane L. Smith
Wendy L Bonell
Dave Hicks
Jan Hunnicutt
Peter Manis
Billie Leigh Kellar

If we've missed anyone, please let us know!

Editor
SkyFyre Editing Team

CHAPTER ONE

Norah watched the flame dancing across the man's fingers with the sinking realization that she was mesmerized. The fire, a candle's worth, flickered over his fingernails, which were crusted with half-burned grease. She tried to look away, but her neck was stiff, and what could be better to look at than this captivating blaze? Her corneas stung, trapped unblinking in the cool Los Angeles night air, and she snorted.

The man in front of her was supposed to fall into *her* trap, not the other way around. Rude! Half-dwarf and half-elemental, he was short and almost as wide as he was tall. With his tight black jeans tucked into dainty-heeled cowboy boots embroidered with flowers and skulls, he looked like a triangle balancing on its point. Her old friend Stellan, a dwarf who worked in the props department of the latest superhero blockbuster, had told her a teamster named Vince was not-very-subtly offering to sell information about some ex-Silver Griffin agents in the Bay Area who sounded like Norah's parents.

Now, Vince was here. Through Stellan, Norah had passed a message to him that she was interested in buying whatever he had to sell. She'd said the Silver Griffins had imprisoned her father in Trevilsom, and she was out for revenge. A decent cover story. No one would find out Lincoln was quietly tending goats in Northern California.

Something had been off when she'd arrived. Normally, the grid of 202 lampposts in front of the Los Angeles County Museum of Art was lit all night, controlled by an astronomical clock that turned them off at dawn. Instead, she'd found them dark, except for the one Vince leaned against as he coolly manipulated a small flame with his hands.

Now she was fucking mesmerized. This was why she hated art. She sighed internally and painted a dazed smile on her face. "Pretty," she said, doing her best brain-dead ingenue impression.

Vince grinned, his eyes cold beneath eyebrows so thick she half-expected birds to fly out of them when he scratched his face.

"That's right, princess. Look at the lovely lights." The flame brightened, and its arabesques accelerated. She had to move fast.

She reached into the pocket of her vintage 1980s windbreaker. Thankfully, her fingers were still under her control, and she wrapped them around her trusty blue gum eucalyptus wand. Without pulling it from her pocket, she traced a one-inch circle in the air, then slashed through it with a violent stroke—a simple spell for breaking an enchantment.

The magnetic tug of the flame on her eyes released with

a soundless pop, and Norah blinked. Her poor eyes were grateful for the moisture. She pulled her wand out of her pocket and pointed it at Vince's chest. The hair of one bushy eyebrow undulated as it quirked up. Norah looked down. The tiny flame flickering in Vince's hand hopped to the tip of his middle finger and stayed there. *Fuck you too, Vince.*

"Nice stick. Hand it over," he directed, his low voice unruffled.

His middle finger flickered and the candle flame roared into a fire rope and slithered through the air. Norah ducked behind the nearest lamp post, which sizzled when the flame hit it.

"This is iconic LA art!" she screamed, running between posts to escape the elemental flame.

"I hate art!" Vince shouted after her. Norah agreed with him about *Urban Lights*, which struck her as a sterile bastard forest.

The fiery rope gouged halfway through a lamppost behind her, sending sparks toward the electric wires at its core. Her occasional glimpses of the flames blinded her, bright orange against the deep blue night.

She raised her wand again, intending to cast a stunning spell, but she was forced to improvise an energy shield to divert the fire.

She needed a better view of the battlefield.

"Fly, my pretties," Norah murmured, and the soles of her white-and-orange Hermes sneakers, a gift from a grateful popstar siren, glowed dark green. She bent her knees and jumped, soaring away as a tentacle of flame snuck up behind her and snapped at the empty air at her feet. What self-respecting witch wanted a broomstick when she could have couture?

Hanging in mid-air, it was easy for Norah to forget she couldn't fly. It was just aggressive jumping. As she landed on a lamppost, she saw Vince dead center in the grid. His fingers traced complex patterns to control the fire around him. The air rippled with the heat radiating from his body. Every hex she knew would burn before it touched him. Except... Maybe she didn't have to touch him.

Norah swiveled a quarter-turn to the light post Vince had gouged with fire moments ago. She fed more energy into her shoes and hopped across the tops of the other poles. When the movement caught Vince's attention, his hands gestured so fast they disappeared. The fire rope shot up between two posts to her right, twisting into a massive lasso.

Norah focused on her wand. Abandoning any pretense of spells or hexes, she shot pure power out of the tip to the half-severed lamppost. She wanted to yell, *"Timber!"* as her magic sheared the streetlight off its base. It toppled toward Vince, the fraying electrical wires in the exposed core sparking.

A thud and a scream echoed through the air, and Norah floated back to the ground, sneakers dimming. When she reached Vince, she understood why he had shrieked.

He had tried to melt the post coming down on him with fire. That had worked, but being hit by globs of molten metal wasn't much better than being hit by a two-ton post. There wasn't enough Elemental DNA to withstand the superheated metal.

Dwarves' burns healed quickly, and the red welts on his

body would feel like a bad sunburn in a few days. For now, he was in a lot of pain.

He'd used his hands to shield his eyes, and they were now raw and useless on his lap. Norah stood over him and drew an icicle in the air with her wand. Vince froze. She took pity on him and sent a wave of blue light cascading over his hands. Blue gum eucalyptus was finicky on offense but more than made up for it with its healing power.

She tapped Vince's mouth with her wand. His face unfroze and cracked like ice.

"You can't kill me, or you'll end up in Trevilsom like your old man!" His lips wobbled.

"Give me your info, and I'll let you go."

"Let me go, and I'll tell you," Vince countered.

"Tell me, and I'll pay you. At a steep discount, of course. Say, seventy percent off."

"That's not fair!"

"Fine. Eighty percent. Call it a fire sale. Now choke up the goods before we have to explain ourselves to Interpol's art crimes division." Norah didn't know if Interpol *had* an art crimes division, but it sounded threatening.

"Look, all I know is that two former Silver Griffin agents live in Oakland. They run an organic apiary."

"What are their names?" Norah demanded.

"I don't know! How many organic apiaries can Oakland have?"

In Norah's experience, the answer was "more than he'd expect." Vince didn't have the details right. Her parents ran a goat farm, not an apiary, and lived near Berkeley rather than Oakland. It was still too close for comfort.

"What else can you tell me?" Norah asked.

"Not much. They took a couple of relics with them when they fled."

Norah inched back. She'd never taken her folks for looters. Maybe he was lying. Still, she filed the information and peered at Vince. His eyes watered in the smoke blowing off the broken lamppost.

"The icicle hex should wear off in about ten minutes. I suggest you repair the damage and hightail it out of here."

As promised, she tucked two crisp hundred-dollar bills into the tops of his boots. Twenty percent of her original offer.

"If you sell any more information about *any* Silver Griffin agents, I will find you and do things to you that make these burns look like a hot-rock massage. Understand?"

She moved to poke him in the chest, stopping before her finger touched his burned skin. Vince winced and nodded.

"Hey, you're not hiring, are you?" he asked, looking at the hundred-dollar bills. She shook her head.

As she ran across the LACMA courtyard, her feet left glowing forest-green streaks.

CHAPTER TWO

Norah cracked open a bottle of Floe and placed it on the desk in front of Daniel, a B-list drow with a chip on his shoulder. She still wasn't sure he'd been the right choice for First Arret, her talent agency. For one thing, he drank an ungodly amount of water. Floe, which claimed to have been captured from Icelandic glacial runoff, cost eighteen dollars a bottle at the nearest natural foods store.

Norah had found a significantly cheaper source: fish the bottles out of the recycling, wash them, refill them with tap water, and reseal the caps with magic. She expected someone to catch on, but her clients gulped the cheap stuff like suffocating fish.

The drow, for instance, who went by the stage name "Daniel Night Lewin," was on his fifth bottle. He took huge gulps between frenetic sentences. Norah struggled to listen attentively to his rant, which was identical to the one from last week. She worked hard to ignore the alert on her phone from her assistant Madge, who had texted her twenty times in the past fifteen minutes.

Daniel went on. "...I shouldn't have to play *dark* roles because I'm a dark elf, you know? I'm sick of auditioning for Tim Burton! Believe in my range, Norah. I can be the boy next door! Literally! I will move next door to Spielberg.

"Would that help? Imagine the block parties. Do you think he knows his neighbors? No more fantasy shit, either. I want hardcore dramatic roles. Or a surf movie. Hardcore drama or a surf movie. Or a hardcore dramatic surf movie. Has anyone done a Laird Hamilton biopic? Because I'll go blond."

He drained the Floe and glared at Norah until she placed another bottle in front of him.

Two more texts from Madge, then a third. Norah smiled. "I love you for Laird, but you'd have to train. Are you prepared to spend the next six months on a beach?"

"I'll spend a year on a beach. I am fully committed."

Norah nodded gravely. "Drama. Surfing. Got it. You better buy sunscreen in bulk, Daniel, because your future will get much brighter. SPF seventy. Buy the stuff that won't rub into your skin."

Daniel grinned. "You're the only one who understands me, Norah."

He took a last sip of his Floe and chucked the almost-full bottle into a nearby metal trashcan. Glass shattered, and a damp stain spread out under the wastebasket. Great. Another eighteen dollars down the drain.

The instant the door closed behind the drow actor, a sliding door covering a four-foot section of the bookshelf behind Norah burst open, and a tiny, fat pixie flew out. Madge, who had started shopping at a high-end Victorian dollhouse store in Larchmont, looked chic in a navy romper. Her tiny fingers were tipped with pointed acrylic nails, which she affixed with the tough dwarven glue typically used to shore up subsurface construction.

"Did that asshole break another Floe?" The pixie's wings flapped fiercely to keep her aloft, and the breeze blew Norah's bangs into her face. She brushed them back into place and stared at her tiny office. The centerpiece was an acid-pink desk swiped from a Barbie dreamhouse. It irritated the eyes.

"Are you sure you won't let me buy you a new desk from that dollhouse place? What's it called again?"

She walked over to the corner of the room, where an enormous number of dominoes floated in the air. Domino trains branched out from a central tile in all directions, and the structure looked like a contemporary sculpture of neurons. Norah placed a tile.

Madge, sensing Norah's distraction, called after her, "It's called Small Hollywood." Norah had gone with Madge to the store once, and the pixie had spent hours staring at a three-inch tall 1920s rolltop whittled from real mahogany. It had cost more than the IKEA desk Norah was sitting behind. The pixie flitted back to Norah's eye level. "I don't need a new desk. Unless it's a magic desk that forces you to answer my texts when Sal Glicker calls."

"Sal Glicker? *The* Sal Glicker? Why didn't you tell me?" Madge alit on Norah's cell phone.

23 Missed Messages

She stamped her foot so hard on the notification that it looked like she was auditioning for a revival of *Stomp!*

Norah sighed. "Undivided attention is the keystone of the First Arret Experience."

"Are you reciting that from some brochure I don't know about?"

"We're a small company. Our services have to be personal."

After breezing past Madge, Norah sat. Sal was one of the most important producers in Hollywood. If you looked at the IMDB page of any box office hit from the past twenty years, his name was on it. She dialed the number, and an assistant put her through.

"Miss Wintery, it is a pleasure to hear from you." Sal was affable, and if he was annoyed at being unable to reach her the first time, nothing in his voice showed it. "I don't wanna beat around the bush. I'm looking for an actor for a project. Seven names have fallen through. I think the thing is cursed."

Norah frowned. She was an agent, not a curse breaker. She almost told him that, but he kept talking. "Sorry. Was that offensive? I'm not talking about a literal curse. It's one of those movies where there are two fans pointed directly at one another, and the shit hitting one flies into the other, back and forth to infinity."

It was a vivid metaphor, and as Norah stared at the slowly spinning blades above her head, it made her want to get central A/C.

"Long story short," Sal continued, "I need an actor who won't blow anyone up. Or is explosion-proof. CAA is tapped out, and the kid at Gersh's front desk has been instructed to put me off. He was so scared. Anyway, I thought someone of a magical persuasion might fit the bill, and..."

"I'm the only game in town. For out-and-proud magicals, anyway."

"Your client list is scattered, but everyone raves about you."

Norah felt a spark of pride but decided not to grill him about who "everyone" was. "What's the role?" she asked.

"Michael Bay is doing an adaptation of *Pride and Prejudice* set on a cold war submarine. We need a villain, a guy. Kind of a Mrs. Bennett type."

Norah rolled her eyes but stopped when she realized *she* would spend twenty dollars at the Arclight to see that movie.

"Would you call it 'hardcore drama?'" Norah asked. Silence filled the line.

"No." Hm.

"Can you set a scene on a beach? Maybe they wash up after a daring escape?"

"If you've got someone, we'll shoot a scene on the fucking moon. Can't promise it'll survive the edit, though."

"I'm emailing you a headshot now," Norah told him.

As she finished the call, Madge gave her a huge thumbs-up as she took two overjoyed laps around Norah's head.

"Should we treat ourselves to a celebratory pizza?" Norah asked.

On the way out, she locked the door with a wand flick. She suspected the deadbolt was plenty but had also set protective charms that activated when the door locked.

What was the point of struggling with blue gum eucalyptus if you weren't going to use its protection?

Ji-woo, the owner's son, waved when Norah came in. She had been here so often that she didn't have to order. A slice of cheese, garlic knots, and a container of kimchi ranch. Choosing an office upstairs from Hwang's pizza was one of the best decisions she'd ever made. Ji-woo brought out the food. He placed a pizza the size of a single pepperoni in front of Madge.

Norah had finished her slice and was dipping the crust in kimchi ranch when she was interrupted in mid-bite by a cheerful young male elf who stuck his hand out. A piece of cheese grease dropped onto it from Norah's mouth, and he retracted it. He wiped it on a silk robe that looked like it cost more than her monthly rent.

She swallowed. "Hello!"

"I'm Frondle!" He drew a small rectangle in the air, and a four-photo headshot grid appeared. Frondle in a cowboy hat. Frondle in a toga. Frondle in a lab coat. Frondle in a Speedo.

The last one was compelling. A weaker person might have laughed him out of the pizza place, but Norah had a superpower suited to Hollywood: the ability to take ridiculous people seriously. Fresh-faced kids from Ohio had been showing up in LA since time immemorial. It was only a matter of time before the same thing happened with fresh-faced kids from the Ohio of Oriceran.

When Norah flicked her wand, the headshots disappeared. Frondle drooped like a willow branch. She was about to open her mouth to give him her best "that's not how things in this town work, buck up, bucko" speech when he placed a small dark wood carving of a tiny brown chickadee on the table next to her garlic knot. The wings and tailfeathers formed whimsical curlicues. Familiar workmanship.

"Stan sent you?" Norah asked. Stan Royale was her downstairs neighbor, a retired stunt coordinator who specialized in making things go boom. He was also an elf and a gifted sculptor of small wildlife like birds and lizards, although he insisted it was a silly hobby.

Leaving her garlic knot on the table with a regretful look, she led Frondle up the stairs to her office. They chatted, and she discovered that despite the headshots, the young elf had taken acting classes from an ancient, terrifying teacher who had coached the biggest names in the business. He had a strong sense of himself and realistic expectations. Norah shrugged. "Welcome to First Arret."

They shook hands. No pizza grease this time.

As Frondle, dazed from excitement, walked toward the door, he approached the dominoes floating in the corner. He grabbed one from the pile to contribute and jumped as the tile delivered a slight shock and refused to move. Norah laughed.

"That was a gift from an elemental actor I helped through a tough spot. You have to be invited to play," Norah explained.

"How do I get invited?" Frondle asked.

Norah shrugged. "Let's see how things go with auditions." Once or twice, she'd seen actors abandon their craft the second they got a big audition.

Madge, who hadn't thought Frondle was worth cutting her lunch short for, arrived moments later. She was struggling under the weight of a plastic takeout bag stuffed with extra garlic knots. "A gift from Ji-woo."

As Norah munched, she waved her wand and pulled up the virtual screen she and Madge used to organize their projects. It displayed the names of every First Arret client. Here and there, lines connected names. Norah arranged the clients in groups with her wand.

"We've got many pieces, but they're not fitting together quite yet."

Packages. Deep in her gut, she knew First Arret would live or die by its package deals. She didn't want to be the place producers went to when they needed a twenty-two-year-old with an artsy vibe for a new digital tablet commercial. She wanted to be where producers went when they needed everything—actors, directors, writers. Whatever.

If she could nail packaging magicals, she'd have something truly unique. She and Madge worked on their list for a few minutes before Norah gave up and wandered over to the dominoes game. She plucked a floating tile and placed it near the center of the network, diagonal to the floor. It stuck.

"I've got six new names to check out," Madge told her. "You ready to watch some reels?"

"I'm always ready," Norah replied.

CHAPTER THREE

The atrium was a nice place, with the quintessential casual Los Feliz glamor. Norah wondered if she'd be able to slip the bottle of Floe on the table into her purse before a server whisked it away.

Harry Bing held court in a green velour booth in the corner of the room, near the white birch tree growing from a recessed well in the restaurant floor. The natural beams of the high ceilings gave the place a greenhouse vibe. Norah thought it was misguided. In her opinion, someone who wanted to be in a forest would go hiking, not out to an expensive brunch. Still, the food was excellent. Better than the company, anyway.

Harry Bing had clawed his way to the top of the Hollywood food chain, but not with talent, instinct, or good looks. Instead, he was a human-sized pair of jaws. When he wanted something, he clamped on until he got it.

Norah, knowing how this meeting would go, ordered three appetizers. She was tempted to wash them down with cocktails, but it was noon, and she had an afternoon of work to tackle.

"I'm going to give you a great price for First Arret. You won't have to work for a couple of years. Girl like you could use that time to lock down a man before you age out of the market."

Norah bristled, although she suspected he was pushing her buttons as a negotiation tactic. "How's your wife, Harry? You teach her to drive yet?"

"Please. My useless son is teaching her to drive." He slurped his cocktail loudly and took a bite from a slice of pineapple dried into the shape of a flower. Then he fished a business card out of his pocket and slid it across the table.

"Thanks, but I know how to Google," Norah said. Harry refused to rise to this insult.

"Look at the number on the back."

Norah sighed and flipped it over. There were so many zeros on it that she had to count them twice. Shit.

"Maybe you're not pretty enough to go the trophy wife route, and you want to keep working. That's fine. I'll mentor you my fucking self, or shove you under the wing of one of the desiccated cat ladies who run the TV division. Whatever you want."

Norah's face got hot. It was true that she put in less effort than other Hollywood pros. She wasn't ugly, either, no matter what Harry was insinuating. She had long brown hair that looked straight, which was lucky because hyer hair resisted all attempts to curl it with styling tools and magic.

As a runner, her taste in clothing swayed toward athleisure or well-made basics. She finished a bite of serrano-jam-glazed burrata and almost said something insulting, but Harry was still talking.

"Imagine your new life. No more going home from a shithole pizza attic smelling like fermented marinara. I'll get you a corner office and an assistant who will make you look successful. God, that sloppy pixie of yours makes me want to vomit." He sloshed a few bucks' worth of his twenty-dollar cocktail into his lap.

Norah's face got hotter. If he wanted to take digs at her, that was fine. That was Hollywood. However, she wasn't going to stand by while he slung mud at Madge, who was the only reason First Arret existed.

Before she realized it, her wand was in her hand, and she drew a tiny pictogram of a wild stick figure under the booth table.

Harry went to grab his fork, then sputtered as he realized he was no longer at his table. His feet dragged him to the bar, and his eyes darted helplessly to Norah. "You little freak," he shouted. It was hard to hear him over the crashing glass as he climbed on top of the small circular bar in the restaurant's center. He knocked over bottles of infused syrup and buckets of citrus as his feet performed an unattractive jitterbug.

As Norah breezed into the discreet alley off Vermont that led to the restaurant, at least one of the customers was already live on TikTok. It served the asshole right.

CHAPTER FOUR

Norah pointed her wand, and the tofu sausages on the table leapt to life and assembled themselves into a spider. The meatless beast skittered over a pile of buns to her brother Andrew. He yelped and pushed away from the table.

"Party foul! Party foul!"

Andrew's six-year-old Leaf giggled and threw a Brussels sprout at the spider. Norah's mother Petra snatched the small green orb from the air and stuffed it in her mouth, chewing mischievously.

"You know I hate spiders!" Andrew shrieked. He jerked his wand, and the condiments and dinnerware on the table stacked themselves into a barrier between him and the tofu arachnid. Petra summoned a large jar of mustard from the bottom of the barrier and opened it, innocent humor twinkling in her eyes behind her chunky purple glasses. As she applied the mustard to a brioche bun, the spider shot through the space and leapt onto Andrew, face-hugger style.

"Uncle!" he shouted. "I cry, 'Uncle!'"

Norah sighed and twitched her wand across the enchantment. One by one, the tofu sausages detached from Andrew's face and stacked neatly on the top plate of his dishware-and-condiment barrier. Norah's dad Lincoln chuckled. He was a large, barrel-chested man with silvery tufts of hair sticking out of the deep V of his organic linen shirt.

"Dad's afraid of spiders!" Leaf chanted in a singsong voice. Andrew glared at Norah and speared a sausage.

"I can't understand why you, a grown man, have the palate of a six-year-old. Don't we have the same taste buds?" This came from Andrew's identical twin Quint. Growing up, they'd traded places without Norah knowing. Andrew was covered in too much ink now to pull that off. It was a hazard of the trade; Andrew ran a tattoo parlor in the warehouse district of downtown Los Angeles. It shared a huge space with a fine art gallery, and they called themselves Skin & Wall, advertising as the best places to put expensive art.

Andrew, his wife Jackie, and Leaf lived in a chaotic industrial loft a few blocks from his business, and he had walked home on a Friday afternoon for family lunch. Petra and Norah's dad Lincoln were visiting from Berkeley and were on cloud nine amid the boisterous tomfoolery.

Quint nibbled his sausage, wrinkled his nose, and slathered it with the ginger-tomato jam he'd brought from one of his cafes. He offered the jar to the others but had no takers.

"I give people the best, and they beg me for Heinz," he complained, a wan expression on his face. The upscale condiments he had stocked at his coffee-and-sandwich joints had yet to be a success.

Norah pulled Leaf into her lap and whispered in the six-year-old's ear, "Do you know how to use your wand as a squirt gun?"

Leaf giggled and pulled out his wand, a slim slip of bamboo. The material surprised Norah. Bamboo wands were Ferrari-fast. You didn't usually put a six-year-old behind the wheel of a Ferrari.

Leaf had impressive motor skills, and Norah watched as he summoned a glowing image from the air. It was a fluffy rabbit, detailed for his age, and it went to Lincoln in a series of light hops.

Lincoln, who had had rabbit familiars over the years, smiled and patted the childlike apparition. As his fingers made contact, the rabbit sprayed a huge stream of water into his face. Lincoln sputtered, then redirected the jet to his water glass. After wiping his face, he fixed Leaf with a mock-stern gaze. "Thank you, Leaf. I was quite thirsty."

Everyone at the table laughed, and Lincoln broke into a huge smile. Leaf would have to work *much* harder than that to do any wrong in his grandparents' eyes.

"You're going to have to teach me that one, bud," Norah told her nephew. As he gave his parents the side-eye, Leaf stood on her lap and whispered instructions into her ear. It was a simple but clever spell. She'd have to use it against her brothers sometime.

"How's the business, Norah?" Lincoln took a pointed sip of water. "Met anyone interesting?"

Norah thought about Vince and the rope of fire that had followed her through LACMA. "I signed a new actor. A light elf." Her parents had enough to worry about between their grandbaby and the organic farm. If anyone threatened them, she would take care of it.

"Forget about work. How about your personal life? Have you *met* anyone interesting?" The mermaid tattooed on Andrew's bicep wiggled her eyebrows and made an obscene gesture.

"I don't have time to date." Norah stuck her tongue out at the tattoo.

"You make time for what you love." Quint had a far-off look in his eyes.

"Oh, please. You spend so much time wooing the fairer sex that I'm surprised your cafes are still in business."

"It's not my fault women love a man with access to free coffee. You know we're opening a fourth location in Echo Park."

Norah snatched the tomato jam from him and applied it to her hot dog. It was, she was forced to admit, delicious. Quint looked smug as she went for a second spoonful.

"We brought gifts!" Petra announced. Her mother had given up on bothering Norah about her love life years ago. Norah couldn't decide if that made her Atacama desert of a dry spell better or worse.

Petra placed CD-sized wheels of cheese in front of Andrew and Quint. Norah knew the pale-yellow crust hid delicious streaks of blue mold and herbs.

"Where's mine?" She pouted.

"Shush. I brought *you* something special." Petra reached into a bag she'd hand-quilted from scraps of Oriceran fabric she'd picked up over the years. It was quirky, and its interior was deceptively large.

Petra fished out an old 1930s wooden tube radio a foot and a half wide and ten inches tall. As Norah ran her hand over it, it crackled with magic. The antique was very well-preserved. Its glossy walnut exterior arced across the speakers in undulating lines. The dial in the middle looked like it belonged to an old rotary phone, with labels for local stations.

Norah picked it up. It was heavy. She put on her best 1930s radio announcer voice and used her wand to make it come out of the radio's speakers.

"It was a cold night, and the rain came down like cats and dogs and birds and lizards and hedgehogs. Much more rain, and Norah Wintery, private eye, would have to build a brand-new zoo. That's when a stranger knocked on her door."

Andrew snorted. "I'm sorry, but I can't respect the era that invented podcasting instead of rock and roll."

Norah saw that the simple spell she'd used to throw her voice had sparked against a magical field clinging to the old radio.

"It's enchanted." She looked at her mother.

"That's right." Petra nodded. " It's a very old enchantment, much older than the radio. From what I know, the power in that radio has been transferred from object to object as technology changed. Mostly objects related to music or entertainment.

"According to my records, the enchantment was housed in a seventeenth-century harp before it was transferred to the radio. Before that, it was in a copy of the *Canterbury Tales* handwritten by Chaucer."

Leaf reached to touch the radio, and his mother Jackie

reflexively pulled him onto her lap, whispering a warning in his ear. Leaf frowned but folded his hands in his lap.

"What is it, a spooky amp?" Quint asked. Norah sent a tentative thread of magic to the radio. When it neared one of the buttons, the magic disappeared. The enchantment had swallowed the spell whole. A short burst of static that sounded like a burp came from the speakers.

"You'll need a lot more firepower to affect that radio," her mother announced. "Transferring the enchantment reportedly took fifty wizards standing directly on top of one of the energy vortexes in Ojai."

"When was that?" Norah asked.

"In the late 1930s."

Careful not to emit unwanted magic, Norah fiddled with the buttons and dials.

"In addition to its powerful magical properties, it picks up NPR," Lincoln added. Norah quirked an eyebrow at her mother.

"About those powerful magical properties..."

Petra's eyes gleamed. "Once you tune it to your frequency, it will give you the temporary ability to see and feel people's true intentions."

Norah ran her hand over the polished walnut.

"It's an electric knife for carving through Hollywood horseshit." Lincoln laughed. Leaf gasped at the swear word, and Andrew shot his father a dirty look.

"I mean Hollywood lies," Lincoln amended.

"What's horseshit?" Leaf asked, eyes twinkling as his parents cringed.

"It's what comes out of the mouths of everyone who works in television," Lincoln explained.

Petra rolled her eyes. "Your father insists entertainment should have stopped at cave paintings of antelope herds."

"I like a nice cave painting," Lincoln protested.

"Gramps isn't wrong," Norah told Leaf. "LA can be a tricky place to live."

She pointed her wand at Andrew. "If you try to turn him into a child star, I will frame you for murder and have you sent to Trevilsom."

"I would never in a million years. His classmate is on a Disney show, and she's a little piece of sh—"

"Shenanigans!" Jackie substituted. Norah laughed and directed her attention back to the antique. When she turned the radio's tuning button, an odd sensation swept over her. It was like pushing the wrong sides of two magnets together.

She retracted her hand and sipped her iced tea instead. Tuning could wait. She stared at her mother, who looked very satisfied. Petra wasn't vain, but she used magic to keep the gray out of her thick, nearly black curls. The radio was an impressive gift, but something was eating at her.

"Should we have this?" she asked. "What if someone steals it?"

"The vault is gone," Petra told them matter-of-factly. "It's as safe with you and Madge as it would be with anyone."

"Maybe don't broadcast that you just acquired a powerful magical artifact," Lincoln suggested.

"With your talent for magic, it might come in handy in a tough spot. I saw something on my Facebook the other day—a viral video of a dancing studio executive. I wondered if you had anything to do with it."

Norah frowned. Harry Bing had gone viral, but not in the way she wanted. Somehow, his publicist had twisted what should have been an embarrassing encounter into *Agent treats diners to playful tabletop jig.* He would be on at least one late-night show the next week. How had her mother known? The woman was psychic.

"I'm not a superhero. I'm just making movies about them," Norah countered, trying to change the subject.

"Hm. We'll see," her mother replied. Norah looked at her feet. She had gone on a few Silver Griffin adventures as a teen and missed the thrill of the chase.

Before she could argue about the best place to keep the radio, her brother butted in. "Hey, where's *my* powerful ancient artifact?" Quint asked. "How come I don't get a direct line into other people's brains?"

"If you want to know what people think about your sandwiches, read your Yelp reviews," Petra shot back. "Why did Marilyn P. give you one star?"

"Er, I may have ghosted her," Quint replied. Petra looked at him disapprovingly.

"Be grateful for your cheese, son," Lincoln offered.

Norah chuckled as she ran her hands over the radio's beautiful, polished wood. The enchantment crackled under her fingers.

CHAPTER FIVE

Fred Astaire danced nimbly in black and white across Norah's TV. He had always mesmerized her. Not literally, though. She loved to watch him dance, and knowing he was a light elf made things even better.

Roberta was one of Norah's favorite movies, but despite the compelling back-and-forth between Astaire and Rogers, she was distracted by the 1930s radio that was sitting on a white wicker plant stand in the corner of her living room.

A voice from the coffee table interrupted her contemplation of the antique. "Hey, missy. Are you replacing me with a new box? If you're kicking me out, you have to give me thirty days' notice. I heard it on a legal podcast."

Norah turned to her roommate Cleo, who sat on the low glass coffee table in front of the television.

Cleo wasn't a traditional roommate. For one thing, she didn't pay rent, though Norah couldn't blame her for that. It was hard to find work when you were in a two-foot by two-foot wooden crate.

Cleo had been a pixie for several hundred years. In 1912, she'd watched a cursed silent movie and been sucked into the crate she'd been standing on. The curse had burned complex magical runes into the crate's wood, including two enormous spirals bound by ovals that looked like dazed eyes. Norah knew that technically, Cleo didn't have eyes. She could "see" out of all six sides of her cube, but anthropomorphizing gave her somewhere to focus.

"You should have told them about that deranged elemental at LACMA." Cleo shifted in her crate.

Norah shook her head. "I've never seen them happier. I can't ruin that! Have you tasted their blueberry chevre? It's like lying in a berry patch while someone milks a goat into your mouth."

"I haven't tasted anything in a hundred years."

Not that they hadn't tried. A year ago, Norah had poured half a bottle of triple sec over the wooden box on a rowdy night. Cleo had been unaffected, but the resulting ant infestation had nearly gotten her evicted. Now, she mostly ate in the kitchen.

"As much as I'd love to watch Fred Astaire wear holes in a dozen more pairs of soft shoes, you should consider getting out of the house," Cleo suggested.

The credits played when the movie ended, and Norah let another Astaire/Rogers dance confection auto-play. "I've got everything I need right here."

"Aren't you sad that your best friend is a talking box?"

"You're not a box. You're a temporarily cubic pixie. Besides, I have things to take care of."

Norah stood, and her eyes darted around the room for

something to take care of. A blue glow between two wide-leafed plants caught her eye.

"Wake up, Vesta," Norah announced. Vesta was a virtual home assistant Norah had hacked with magic. Voiding the warranty? Worth it. The eight-inch-high onyx cylinder trilled and floated into the air, disturbing the leaves of a plant that looked like a fiddle leaf fern but was an Oriceran hybrid. Veins of light shot through the rustling leaves.

Vesta floated to Norah. Her cylindrical speakers pulsed blue as she "spoke." "What's up, boss?" the virtual assistant asked.

"Summon rainclouds," Norah commanded. There was a pleasant chime, and miniature rainclouds materialized in the apartment over the forty or so houseplants Norah tended in her spare time. The clouds darkened, churned, and rained softly into the waiting terracotta pots.

Norah started humming *Singing in the Rain*, and the hybrids swayed and lit up. Photoluminescence sparkled through the veins and along the edges of the leaves. The runes on Cleo's box glowed in time with the plants. It was ten times better than a laser light show. This was why Norah loved magic.

The simple chore of watering plants filled a well that had been empty since the night at LACMA. Norah grabbed a wicker basket from a nearby alcove, then announced she would pick some lemons out in their garden.

There was enough daylight left for citrus harvesting. It was high summer, and the white blossoms on the trees had largely disappeared. When Norah crushed a green leaf between her fingers, it smelled like zesty sunshine.

A lesser fruit-picker would harvest from the bottom of

the tree, looking for the low-hanging fruit. Norah had never liked to take the easy road. Instead, she grabbed a ten-foot ladder from the side of the complex and spent the next few minutes inside a veil of greenery, inhaling lemon oil and selecting bright yellow fruit. After a while, she heard footsteps and a voice from below.

"That better be you, Norah, and not a fruit pirate. Or an overstuffed squirrel."

She smiled at Stan's voice and clambered down the ladder. An errant lemon tumbled out of her overflowing basket as she descended, and when she reached the bottom, she saw that Stan had caught it. As she set down her basket, the elf bit through the rind of the yellow fruit. He chewed and swallowed, then grinned at Norah's expression of disgust.

"Elf taste buds." She wrinkled her nose. They spent a few minutes joking about Stan's young friend Frondle, who her neighbor said had a good head on his shoulders even if he was a bit bright-eyed.

Norah had often wondered if Stan would return to Oriceran now that his career as a stuntman was over. The elf was a true cinephile, and as he had once told Norah, "There's no popcorn in the Dark Forest." Shudder.

When Stan was halfway through his second lemon, they were joined by another neighbor, Billy Warble.

"Lemon?" Stan offered. Norah objected on the grounds that the lemons were hers, and she didn't think she could stand to see a human being eat one whole.

"I'm all right." Billy laughed. The wizard was normally a cheerful person, but today he looked exhausted. A thin trail of sweat trickled across his forehead.

"You take up running as I suggested, Billy? I swear, it's the best." Norah peered at his sweaty face. Billy wiped it, then scratched a rash on one of his wrists. There were dark crescents of blood under his fingernails.

"Hm? Oh. No. I've been renewing the ward on my place."

"Against burglars?" Norah asked.

"I'm not sure. I found eight dead ladybugs on my doormat this morning, among other ill omens." Billy described the dread he'd felt for the past few days. He saw the same faces everywhere he went. Maybe it was paranoia.

"On top of everything else," the wizard finished, "I think I'm allergic to my sage." As he raked his forearms with his fingernails, his sleeve rode up. Norah's mouth dropped at the faded tattoo underneath: two letters in a looping scroll, SG.

She'd known Billy was a wizard. They'd even celebrated a few full moons together. A former Silver Griffin agent? News to her.

`When he caught Norah staring, Billy pushed his sleeve back over the tat. "Whoops. I'm getting careless in my old age."

Norah lowered her voice. "Andrew knows some good tattoo removal people."

"Isn't that like a doctor knowing a good mortician? Thanks, but I can't bear the thought of erasing the last remnant of that life."

Norah did talk him into letting her use the blue gum eucalyptus wand on his rash.

"We'll keep an eye on your place," Norah offered. Stan

raised an eyebrow. "Eat my lemons, pay the price," she told him sternly.

"Thanks." Billy still looked worried. First Vince, now this. Something was up.

CHAPTER SIX

Garton Saxon sat on a hand-carved wooden throne. Harry Bing had to admit the man belonged there. Behind the gilded lion and dragon atop the elaborate seat, gold drapes caught the overhead lights. Behind the drapes was twenty thousand square feet of empty Silver Lion backlot and a terrified art department assistant. The lanyard around her neck identified her as Kaylyn, and she was paler than Saxon's crisp white shirt. Its thread count was an infinity sign.

"Isn't this fantastic?" Saxon asked, rapping the throne's carved armrest. Kaylyn shuddered.

"Did you declare independence from California?" Harry Bing asked. He hoped Saxon would get to the point soon. The man was like a tectonic plate; he went where he wanted at his chosen speed. As Harry waited, his eye was drawn to a tiny gilded cage resting a few feet away on the concrete floor of the lot. Two white mice huddled inside.

"I'm rebooting Henry the Eighth with a supernatural twist. Reimagining the king as a misunderstood hero trying to save his kingdom from the demons who possess his horrible wives."

Saxon had just gotten a divorce. He'd been widowed for a few days before the paperwork was signed. No one had looked closely at the death.

Bing eyed the white mice. "Did Good King Henry have animal sidekicks?"

Saxon stared at him until Bing broke eye contact and wiggled in the chair. It creaked, and Kaylyn's eye twitched uncontrollably. Harry knew the studio head was drawing energy from the assistant's terror.

"Let's go to my office." Saxon hopped off the throne. Harry reminded himself to find Kaylyn later if she needed someone to comfort her.

Garton Saxon's office was a luxury 1891 Pullman railcar, refurbished and parked in the middle of the Silver Lion lots. The office was a china shop full of spindle-legged furniture, antique ceramics, and hand-blown lightbulbs, and Saxon was the bull. An old light elf, Saxon had revealed his true identity as a magical a few years ago by plastering one wall of his office with memorabilia from his past lives. He'd worked in motion pictures since Edison had electrocuted an elephant on camera. Some people said he'd given Edison the suggestion.

After a brief stint constructing sets for George Melies, Saxon had started acting in silent films, always as the villain. He'd worked as a producer in the studio system in the thirties and forties, then reinvented himself in the 1960s as the king of TV infomercials. He never aged, but Los Angeles had a short memory and an appetite for new talent, so he always made his way back. Now he owned a studio outright.

Saxon threw himself into a carved wooden chair cushioned with pale green acetate. Bing thought he heard the wood crack. If Saxon offered him a chair, he'd be afraid to sit down. Saxon might feel free to smash his antiques, but Harry doubted he extended the courtesy to his guests. Not that the elf had ever offered him a chair.

Saxon hung the mouse cage on a fine filigree hook dangling ominously over his desk. He tented his fingers and leaned close to Harry.

"They got it right in the thirties with the old studio system." Saxon was staring at a photo of himself with a gleaming blonde starlet, his hand unabashedly planted on her ass.

"The lines were clear. If you wanted to work, you worked within the system. Now, everything's fractured. Chop off the head of Netflix or Hulu and some other streaming nobody rises to replace it. Production companies are vomiting content without any control."

As Saxon spoke, he waved his hand, and the cage containing the pair of white mice disappeared. They tumbled two feet to the desk, squeaking in pain as their bodies hit the mahogany. Saxon continued to move his hands methodically, tracing lines and shapes. The mice elongated into furry snakes, then more frightening creatures. Harry shuddered at the stretching skin and cracking bone. His feet were itching to run out of the railcar, but he didn't dare.

Now the white creatures were over six feet tall, their elongated jaws ending in fanged overbites. They flanked

Saxon's delicate secretary's desk, muscles coiled. The one on Saxon's left shoulder, who had a vicious scar over its right eye, moved toward Bing in an unmouselike way. Saxon stopped him with a gesture, then trailed a long finger over a large beacon lantern on his desk.

The beacon was a cubic brass box with a handle on top and an amber-tinted diotropic bullseye lens on one side. Currently unlit, it was the only sturdy thing in the room other than Saxon. As the elf brushed the bronze with his fingers, Harry thought he saw the lens glow faintly.

"Most people are very stupid." Saxon's finger still touched the beacon. "They want to be told what to think. I'm here to help. I want to consolidate Hollywood into a single operation with enough power to control public opinion about magicals. When magicals understand that their reputations live or die by my flashbulb, they'll all get in line. I am going to execute this vision, Bing. There's no place in it for has-beens who can't close a deal with a measly little witch."

Saxon wasn't blinking, and neither were the mice shifters. Perched on his tiny chair, the studio head took his hand off the beacon and stretched his fingers to the nearest white beast. The creature's jaw quivered as he did, and a large glob of saliva fell onto the floor. Saxon looked at the wet spot with distaste, then dropped his hand and vanished the saliva with a few finger signs. "Don't let anyone get the drop on you again. Understand?"

Harry left the studio so quickly that he wondered if his feet had been enchanted again. He was halfway back to Beverly Hills before he stopped sweating.

CHAPTER SEVEN

The office complex where the auditions were being held was soulless, but the atmosphere was lively. Romaz, an upstart organic ketchup company, had approached Norah with a request for magical talent. Hollywood still cast most magicals in human-passing roles, so this was a unique opportunity to start a national conversation.

She normally wouldn't go on an audition with a client, but because Romaz had asked for magicals, she had been curious. She had decided to accompany a twenty-two-year-old wizard named Duncan "The Dunker" Monroe. The kid had gotten D-list famous from funny videos, first on YouTube and now TikTok. At twenty-eight, Norah felt too old to understand TikTok, but The Dunker's following grew like an overfertilized weed.

The audition was held in a huge mirrored dance studio with a wooden floor. Norah sat, crossed her legs, and leaned back against the mirror. She could look at the competing talent from every angle, dividing her attention between the auditionee and the magicals waiting in the wings. Some were openly anxious, and some were faking nonchalance. Some were genuinely checked out, numbed by years of taking their fifteen-second shot in rooms full of people who looked just like them.

Right now, the witch in the center of the room was using her wand to levitate loose ketchup, manipulating it into the shape of a goopy red human hand. After walking around a folding table on its fingers, the hand flew through the air and fed the witch a French fry. She swallowed it whole, along with the ketchup fingers. Impressive magic, but the overall effect was cannibalistic, and the Romaz executive's lips quirked in distaste. The casting director dismissed the witch with a few curt words, and she headed out the door with a look of pained familiarity on her face.

Madge, hovering near the ceiling, dropped onto the barre near Norah's face.

"That witch was wearing a wand holster." Norah scoffed. She found the plastic holsters some witches and wizards wore on their belts uncool.

"What a loser," Madge agreed.

"If you ever see me wearing one of those, hit me with a vaporizing spell." Norah laughed.

Next was a vampire doing a bit about how Romaz was almost as good as blood. Cute, but nothing you couldn't do with a human actor and novelty plastic fangs. The Transylvanian accent? So last century.

"Slim pickings today," the pixie muttered. Norah wasn't as sure. A lot was going on in the room.

Over the next forty-five minutes, witches changed tomatoes into ketchup and back into tomatoes. Elves stacked tomatoes like snowmen and made their vegetable puppets banter about what they wanted to be when they grew up. *Marinara! No, salsa! No, ketchup!*

The Romaz executives' eyes drooped as time dragged on, and the casting director looked worried. She was gazing past the dark elf in front of her at the vampire who had auditioned earlier. Slurping from a blood box, the vamp was waiting patiently for the bear shifter he'd carpooled with.

The casting director had placed a protective hand around her neck. Norah frowned. Human prejudices were hard to shake.

The bear shifter was the best of the bunch. He controlled his shift with laser precision, sprouting fur all over his body while barely changing shape, his face stuck halfway between man and bear. The actors who hadn't left laughed jealously as he performed a character called "the tomato monster," spewing red spit and pieces of trash as he gobbled raw vegetables, foil condiment packets, and full glass bottles of ketchup. It was slightly disgusting and extremely funny.

Finally, they called Duncan's name. He sprang up and walked confidently to the center of the room, announced himself, and flicked his wand. He grabbed six glass ketchup bottles from a side table, placed them around him in a circle, and began conducting a magical symphony. Ketchup danced from one bottle to the next, and the red goop gave small whoops. Over the next ten seconds, the pace picked up, and the sounds became a catchy tune. The Dunker was a showman. Norah decided she wanted to produce his album.

Near the end of his audition, rivulets of ketchup flew everywhere. They snaked around one another, twisting whirls, braiding, and splitting. Then, suddenly, the streams pointed directly at Duncan, hurtling toward him at lightning speed. He looked like he was about to have a major *Carrie* moment, except the second before the streams of ketchup hit his shirt, they stopped dead. Norah couldn't hear a pin drop, but she listened to a cell phone beep. After a tense pause, the ketchup flowed above Duncan's head and formed a bottle shape.

The casting director smiled and asked Duncan a question, which was a good sign. They went back and forth for a few minutes, and the executives grinned and nodded. One of them shook Duncan's hand so Norah was sure he'd booked it. So was the next auditionee, another young wizard who trudged into the center of the room with hopeless resignation.

They weren't even in the car when Norah got the call offering Duncan the role. The young influencer whooped at the prospect of national residuals.

The second Norah walked out of the studio, a light elf in the corner followed her. She didn't look out of place in matching floral separates, but she also hadn't auditioned. She strode to the nearest bathroom, locked the door, and pulled out a cell phone with ten normal buttons and one enormous embedded diamond the size of a robin's egg.

The elf pressed the jewel and held the phone to her face. "Yeah. Wintery nailed that Romaz audition. They're still going through the list, but it's over."

The light elf listened as a flood of expletives hit her ear, then a dial tone cut them off.

CHAPTER EIGHT

Norah lay on the cool red tile of her Spanish colonial apartment, enjoying the show Vesta was putting on for her. The virtual assistant was projecting a real-time image of galaxy cluster SMACS 0723 into the space below the ceiling.

It was like looking into the center of black opal. Each spiral and dot of light was a single galaxy; this was only a tiny sliver of the universe. Norah wondered if Oriceran was out there or if it was somewhere else entirely below an equally infinite sky.

The main downside of being a witch in Los Angeles was the smog, which made it almost impossible to see the stars. Evan's lunar magic was muted here, and she couldn't draw power from Vesta's virtual projection, but Norah enjoyed a return to her astral roots.

After a few cosmic minutes, her tea kettle whistled. On her way to the kitchen, Norah picked a sprig from the plant under her brightest window, an Oriceran mint hybrid in a vivid blue pot. On one of Stan's trips home to the magical planet, he had smuggled her a plant that was supposed to have emotional and physical cooling properties.

Norah tossed the slip of greenery into a metal strainer in a First Arret mug, along with a small copper scoop of her herbal blend, which she kept in a cookie jar shaped like a jaguar. She pulled open the sliding glass door to her balcony while her tea steeped. She'd only taken a few sips before realizing that Stan had gathered a dozen people there, including Billy and Frondle. He waved her down.

She serenely descended the red tile steps, relishing their cool texture under her bare feet. Slipping into the circle of visitors, she let her eyes unfocus slightly.

"Are you high?" someone enthusiastic asked. Frondle approached her skittishly. He was a hundred years old and still acted like a kid on his first visit to the grownups' table.

"I'm not high." Norah smiled slowly. "If anything, I'm low."

"Oh, wow. You're on sp—"

"Quiet, Frondle," Stan warned him good-naturedly. The younger elf's mouth snapped shut at light-speed.

The herbal experiments Stan abetted weren't strictly legal by Oriceran standards. She didn't think California had gotten around to banning magical herbs. Stan introduced Norah to the circle, which had gathered around a large bowl of guacamole resting on a small tiled table. A few faces were familiar: Stan, Frondle, Billy, and Stellan, the prop fabricator. A few were new, including Gwen, a dryad who lived in Griffith Park, and Cinnamon, a half-human, half-siren who was an exotic dancer at Jumbo's Clown Room.

"Cinnamon just moved into the building," Stan announced. As the young half-siren took Norah's hand, a current of energy like a deep and quiet river flowed up the veins of her arm, into her spine, then dropped through the soles of her feet into the earth.

That tea was stronger than I thought.

Ten seconds later, Cinnamon gently extracted her hand, which Norah hadn't realized she was still holding. She coughed. "You're not looking for representation, are you?"

Cinnamon laughed. "Honey, I work three days a week and make mid-six figures. I'm not giving ten percent of that to *anyone.*"

"I must be in the wrong business. You work with many magicals?" Norah asked. The sunlight caught Cinnamon's strawberry-blonde hair from behind, making it look like the sun's surface. Norah stared.

"Not many. Lot of turnover at clubs. Not great for staying under the radar. Plus, I'll probably get murdered by my human coworkers when they find out I'll look twenty-three for decades."

Cinnamon's skin looked very soft, like velvet, and it took all Norah's strength not to reach out and stroke it.

No more tea before parties, missy.

Stan sidled over and waggled his eyebrows at Norah's dilated eyes. "Enjoying the fruits of Oriceran, I see."

Norah pulled her gaze away from a hummingbird dipping its beak into a hibiscus flower at the other end of the courtyard. "You should have warned me." She was incapable of sounding stern.

"Where's the fun in that? Are you enjoying my little circle? I thought it was high time–no pun intended–I finally had everyone over. In the daylight and everything. Sad that Millie had to miss it, but she won't begrudge me a little vitamin D."

Millie was Stan's on-again, off-again girlfriend who, as a vampire, would not have appreciated the sunlight.

Stan explained that the group of magicals had been meeting for decades in one form or another. Until recently, they'd had to disguise their true purpose. "We tried to pose as an AA group, but word got out, and down-on-their-luck humans kept showing up at our meetings. Plus, one dingo shifter kept eating heroin addicts. He got clean a few years ago, though. Moved to Encino with his new family.

"Then, in the sixties, we tried being a new-age religion, but people kept hearing about us and attending meetings. Angelenos love a cult. It took us until the mid-nineties to disappear."

"What did you do?" Norah asked.

"We pretended to be an improv troupe. Better than a gas leak at keeping people out."

Norah laughed. Quite a few of her clients were in improv troupes, and she was constantly inventing new excuses for avoiding their shows.

"What was your fake troupe's name?" she asked.

"The Secret Society of Magical Elves."

"Hah. It must have been hard to stay underground."

"Truthfully, what you're doing now is harder. Showing your face to the world, advertising your strange new talents. Ah, well, bravery is for the young."

Norah grabbed her wand from her pocket; her fingers were sensitive to the smooth grain of the wood. Then, she floated a tortilla chip over to the guacamole bowl and plunged it in with a spurt of green magic. Fully loaded with guac, the chip flew across the courtyard straight into her mouth. The crunch sent a shiver up her tea-addled spine.

Norah had the gene that made cilantro taste like soap, so she often found Mexican food difficult to eat. This stuff was delicious, although the garlic flavor was intense.

"I hope you're not kissing Millie with that mouth," Norah said, watching Stan shovel a heavily laden chip into his mouth. He shook his head as he chewed.

"Nah. She's working on the rough cut of a new film. She'll be holed up in the tombs for a week."

"The tombs" was what Stan called the underground offices in Burbank, where Millie worked as one of the most coveted editors in the industry. The vampire had also owned a sizable crypt in Hollywood forever. Stan had taken her to a few midnight cocktail parties when she first got to town. She'd met her first client there.

Norah levitated another chip to herself, not noticing the small ball of fur zooming across the lawn. As the chip floated across the sidewalk, the fur ball leapt into the air and grabbed it.

"Hey! That was my guac!"

The tiny Pomeranian, chin stained green, stared at her with smug disinterest. Norah bent and scratched it behind the ears, which it grudgingly permitted. She had to admit she agreed with the dog. The guacamole was addicting. Suspiciously addicting.

She pointed her wand at Stan. "This doesn't have drugs in it, does it?"

He shook his head. "No. I might have used a little magic

to make the cilantro taste good to people who hate cilantro."

Norah ate another chip. There it was, an unfamiliar herbal note, and her eyes widened.

"You're a genius, Stan. You're going to make a billion dollars on this."

The people around her laughed and talked. Gwen, the dryad, appeared deep in conversation with Norah's lemon tree. She hoped it wasn't saying anything too mean about her. It was hard to imagine returning to the days when they had to keep everything secret.

"Next time we meet with the crew, I'll invite you. We might go to a restaurant instead of a church basement."

Norah filled her mouth with more of Stan's excellent guacamole.

"Ith a deal," she replied with a green-toothed grin.

CHAPTER NINE

The next day, Wednesday, found Norah wishing her office was bigger than a waiting room. So many people were there when she arrived at 9:30 that she had to push through to see what was happening. They were all gathered around a fire-engine-red crockpot on a tray table, plugged into the wall with an orange cord. Several spider plants were arrayed around the appliance.

Norah's first thought was that Madge was serving party meatballs. Then she got closer and realized the crockpot was full of water. It must have been turned on the lowest setting so as to keep things warm rather than cook them because Madge was splashing around in a high-waisted red and white polka dot bikini. When the pixie saw Norah, she clambered out and shook her wings, spraying water all over a dark elf.

"Who doesn't like a hot tub!" Pride spilled out of Madge's voice.

Norah wrinkled her nose. If she curled her toes and

covered herself in baby oil, she might be able to get one foot into the crockpot.

Madge was hosting a wide range of magicals, including Frondle, who wore a gold Speedo that might have looked expensive if it had been made from more than two square inches of fabric. He was also wearing pool floaties and drinking something from a two-quart mason jar topped with a tiny umbrella.

It took quite a bit of alcohol to get light elves tipsy, and Madge had bravely accepted the challenge.

"Norah! It's me! Frondle!"

He attempted to fold her into a hug, but Norah kept her feet planted and her body firmly away from the young elf's Speedo area.

"Glad to see you're putting yourself out there, Frondle. Getting face time with everyone."

She was tempted to snatch Madge from the air and give her a good talking-to about boundaries, but the pixie's extroversion was a big asset to the business. A deep breath calmed her enough to greet everyone else at the pool party.

As it turned out, Madge wasn't alone in the hot tub. Two faeries were with her, models from New York who were in town for LA's Fashion Week. They chatted about the Balenciaga show, which had taken place four hundred feet above the Pacific Ocean, filmed by drones and livecast to a human audience on the beach in Malibu.

One of the faeries, a pale woman with enormous Atlas Moth wings, shook off droplets of water and hovered in front of Norah's face.

"Without magic, humans had to develop ingenuity. There's a lot of interest in magical textiles in the couture space. Combining new materials and innovative designs will produce breathtaking work this year."

"I want someone to make Spanx that don't take an hour to put on," Madge shouted. The party-goers laughed.

"I know you'd rather fly into a woodchipper than put on shapewear," Norah shot back. She felt the same way.

As she chatted with Madge's guests, two dwarves she didn't know played with the magical dominoes in the corner of the room. Madge must have invited them. The game would eventually take over the room if she kept supplying tiles. For now, it was quite pretty. The organic white-and-black shapes were striking.

"Can I talk to you for a sec?" Norah turned to Madge, keeping her voice cheerful. She pushed into a corner of the room and held her wand above her head, drawing a slow spiral around herself.

As the eucalyptus swirled, blue sparks glowed in the air, and the lively conversation in the room faded into silence. She found cone-of-silence spells like being dead, but sometimes there was no choice. Although she trusted Madge's taste in friends, she barely knew half the people in the room. Besides, Madge's hovering wings created a comforting rustle of white noise. Norah inhaled deeply.

"You're not going to chew me out, boss?" Madge asked. She didn't sound worried.

"Crack-of-dawn hot tub parties aren't my thing, but no," Norah replied.

"Okay, good. Because one of those fairies is dating the director of the movie we're sending Frondle out for next week. It's a big scene, and I'd rather not piss her off."

Beyond the blue glow of the spell, the fairy with moth

wings playfully scooped a thimbleful of pina colada out of Frondle's cup and drank it. Her tiny face came alive with laughter.

"Tell him to wait until after he wraps to steal the director's girlfriend," Norah suggested, trying not to wonder what a three-inch tall fairy and a human man could get up to together.

"He's young, but he's not stupid," Madge told her. "Good work signing him. What do you need?"

"I wanted to ask if you know about Harry Bing."

"The agent? Huh. Google could probably tell you everything I know, including that he's an asshole."

"He went viral last week." Norah's voice dripped irritation.

"I saw that on my Insta reels. Hilarious."

"Ugh." Norah had been too disgusted to tell Madge about Alcove.

"Anything I should know? I can ask around."

"You're the best." Norah tapped the glowing spiral surrounding her. The spell burst into shining dust that hung in the air for a few seconds before dwindling into nothing.

Riotous Calypso music slammed into Norah's eardrums. She could not work in the middle of this. Sighing, she took her laptop and slipped out the door.

The pizza place was quiet in the mornings, and Norah didn't think they'd mind her taking up a table for an hour or so. Ji-woo brought her the usual slice, but she was so engrossed in her work that she let it get cold.

"Something wrong with the pizza?" Ji-woo asked, refilling her iced coffee.

Norah looked at the paltry bite she'd taken. She hadn't even taken the lid off the kimchi ranch.

"You know I would swim in this stuff if I could," Norah told him, tapping the tiny plastic container. "I needed to escape the office for a bit. Madge is having a hot tub party in our new crockpot."

Ji-woo laughed so loudly that Norah almost knocked over her laptop.

"This place is yours for whatever you need. Whether you order food or not." Ji-woo smiled. "Seriously. Just don't tell anyone I said that. I don't need tech bros here for six hours a day, screaming about stocks and eating the disgusting keto cauliflower crust Dad insists we keep in stock."

"My lips are sealed," Norah assured him. She stared at an email for a few minutes before tapping the laptop with her wand. A two-foot-wide magical screen blazed to life above the laptop. Norah typed in a complicated password and entered the magical side of Discord. She sometimes came here to chill and chat, but today she kept her earbuds out and headed to the forums.

Scanning the casting thread, she took note of new roles, including a Cyrano de Bergerac reboot with a Kilomea as Cyrano. She didn't have any Kilomeas on her client list. For pragmatic reasons, the large creatures were the least likely to have visited Earth. Two of the members of GWAR had made it work, though.

Norah jotted mental notes and sent a quick email to Madge, then stretched her fingers and headed into the #Hollywood-gossip channel.

Does anyone know Harry Bing?

The message appeared with a beep, and Norah sat back to wait. Discord was useful, although it was difficult to convince new people to join. Only some casting agents there had revealed their magical natures. Many spent more time looking at threads like "good haircuts for hiding pointy ears" than working in solidarity with other magicals. Some feared casting too many magicals would push them out of the closet.

We're building a foundation. The payoff comes later.

Killing time, Norah checked out the #seeking-representation thread. It was often a total shitshow, and it was prime hunting grounds for a game Norah and Madge called Find-the-Worst-Headshot.

There were a few good ones today, her favorite being a tiny pixie in a US Marines uniform who was stuffed into a bullet bandolier. The pixie, who had a round, almost-chubby face, was dwarfed by her pith helmet. Madge would get a kick out of it.

She was about to take a screenshot when another post caught her eye.

Hey casting crew. I'm connected with former Silver Griffin agents looking for a new gig. HMU if you're looking to add a few righteous names to your list.

Norah clicked on the name of the person who had made the post. Unlike many social networks, the magical Discord forum didn't allow anonymous posts.

Lauren Bouchard. Huh. Norah had never heard of her.

She wrote the name in a small notebook covered with a jungle leaf print. Then she typed a quick DM.

Hey Lauren, I'd love to discuss the SG agents. Happy hour?

As she hit send, a tremendous crash came from upstairs, followed by a loud thump and a piercing bell.

Norah hit the stairs running and shouted to Ji-woo to put the pizza on her tab. When she threw open the door, the ringing bell hit her eardrums, although the waiting room was empty.

As Norah burst into the main office, covering her ears, she identified the source of the noise. A large and powerful offensive spell glowed in the air above Duncan, the wizard client who had landed the ketchup gig. She hadn't realized he packed so much magic. The bright orange funnel was a glowing, vibrating mandala. It blasted a warning about the even more formidable spell growing in its depths.

A sturdy silver-haired shifter of moderate height who was flushed with anger had faced off against the scrawny wizard. He wasn't one of Norah's clients, and she struggled to retrieve his name from her ever-expanding mental Rolodex. *Lorenzo.*

Norah generally didn't mind when magicals shifted in her office, except Lorenzo's alternate form was a rhinoceros, and the transformation might punch out the walls. Unfortunately, being able to shift into endangered species had given Lorenzo a massive ego, which had bumped into The Dunker's influencer confidence.

Lorenzo's skin rippled, and Norah cringed. Pulling out her wand, she moved between them.

"*Fight Club* is a movie, not a fun activity for eleven in the morning." She pointed her wand at Duncan. "I don't care how much money you make me in national ketchup residuals. If you wreck my business, I will drop you from my list."

She looked at Lorenzo, desperately trying to think of what she could use as leverage. If he turned into a rhino, there might not be a big enough lever in the world. "I happen to know of a large American zoo that's quietly looking for a new spokes shifter. Leave my office peacefully, and I will get you a meeting. It's a lot of money for minimum work."

The small waves rippling across Lorenzo's skin slowed and then dissipated. "After you," he growled at Duncan. Norah glared as they trudged out of her office past the two dwarves playing dominoes. The dwarves were so engrossed in the ever-expanding game that they barely looked up. Then again, dwarves were accustomed to ruckus.

The hot tub continued to steam on the side table. She waited until Madge's head sheepishly emerged from where she'd been hiding underwater. Looking at Norah's face, Madge sighed.

"Party's over, people. You don't have to go home, but you can't stay here."

Frondle swayed happily to a tune that only he could hear, and Norah decided the party was over.

"Where are your clothes?"

Frondle looked at his Speedo, which he considered

appropriate everyday wear. Sighing, she pulled out her wand and cast a temporary glamour of jeans shorts and a tank top. As she walked him to the door, she hoped it wouldn't fade in the middle of his Uber home.

"Get something to eat. Try the kimchi ranch downstairs." She pushed him out of the office, set her laptop on the table, and slumped into her chair. Norah watched the remaining magicals filter out of the office with a sour expression on her face.

As soon as everyone was gone, Madge flew over and dropped a glossy pamphlet in her lap. Norah picked it up and read the title. *Crockpot Cooking for One.*

"Very funny. I hope there's a recipe in here for misbehaving pixies," she said, flapping the pamphlet to blow Madge several yards away.

"Oh, please. If you wanted a boring life, you would have started an accounting firm, not a Hollywood agency."

There was some truth to that. Norah's ex-boyfriend was an accountant. It hadn't worked out.

"Do you want to get brunch?" Madge asked. "I could use some food."

Norah looked at a test tube rack full of tiny tropical drinks, then at Madge, who flew in wild, tipsy loops near the floor. She sighed.

"Fine. You're buying."

CHAPTER TEN

Norah was so tired when she got home that evening that the knock on her door surprised her. She tapped the identification rune on her door. *STAN* glittered in the air, and she opened the door in her pajamas and robe.

"You forgot we were going out." Stan raised a brow.

Shit. Stan had promised to take her to a jazz club in Burbank tonight. Because it wasn't work, it hadn't made it onto her calendar.

"We can reschedule."

"No. I was looking forward to this. Give me five minutes." Norah slid in socked feet across the tile to her bedroom, where she threw on black cigarette pants, a black sequin crop top, and an oversized black blazer. She traced the lines of a small spell etched into her mirror, then closed her eyes and waited as her makeup levitated from her bathroom sink and applied itself to her face.

She'd spent so long tinkering with the spell that it might have been quicker to learn how to do perfect cat-eye liner, but on days like today, it was worth it. After twisting her hair into a messy bun and donning her Hermes sneakers, she ran back to the front door.

"That was seven minutes." Stan looked up from his watch. Taking in her transformation, he whistled. "Worth it, though. Let's roll."

Stan drove a sherbet-orange Ford Thunderbird with a hula girl bobbing on the dashboard. Norah would have found it unbearably ostentatious except that Stan had been lovingly maintaining it since the day when he'd driven it new off the lot in 1957. Drivers on the 101 shot them glances oscillating between appreciative and envious.

They found street parking almost immediately in Burbank, and Norah stared suspiciously at the dashboard hula girl, touching it with the tip of one finger. A surge of powerful magic flowed through her, and she yelped.

"Don't tell parking enforcement." Stan winked.

"I won't if you make me one," Norah tapped the statue with her wand. Powerful light elf luck magic was at work inside the plastic, engineered into brilliant folds and glistening flourishes. Norah knew people in LA who would kill to find reliable street parking. She had contemplated murder when circling a particularly busy block.

Stan hustled her out of the car and led her to the Baked Potato. The club's facade was nothing special, red with gray Tudor beams and covered in bright yellow signage. The jazz club's mascot was a lumpy brown potato with a bright smile, thick eyebrows, and pointy shoes. In its stick-figure hands, it held music notes.

According to the lemon-yellow marquee, a band called Toto and the Gumballs was playing tonight. The doorman, a huge bearded man directly out of Central Casting, nodded at Stan as they walked in the door.

"This is one of the oldest magical clubs in Hollywood, and it's protected by strong magic," Stan remarked. "Anytime a human walks by, they keep walking. They get hungry, tired, or decide they hate jazz. An old, old spell."

Norah had never seen so many magicals in one room. The bartender, a red-headed witch whose curly hair stuck out from her head in a magnificent static frizz, used her wand to pour six drinks at once at the packed bar.

On the low rectangular stage, a light elf adjusted the knobs on an amplifier glowing with magic. Tucked into a corner, an A-list actress in a shiny purple jumpsuit nursed a small pink cocktail. Not A-list, but A+++ list. Even Norah, whose work brought her into regular contact with celebrities, stared. Her clients got jobs, but none of them were household names. Norah's eyes glittered. This place might be poorly lit and minimally vacuumed, but it was a potential goldmine.

"This is amazing," she whispered to Stan.

"I should have carted you here sooner." He ordered them whiskeys from the bar, handing Norah's over with a warning. "This tantalizing firewater is made with Oriceran-grown barley and distilled by dwarves, so take it easy."

Her small sip felt like pouring molten gold down her throat, and she settled into a chair to watch the end of the band's set. Toto was a small dark elf with a mohawk, and the Gumballs were a motley crew, its most notable members being a dwarf barely taller than his clarinet and a Kilomea playing the loudest trumpet Norah had ever heard. She wasn't much of a jazz nerd, but she thought she recognized a few riffs from Oriceran melodies.

"You should come back and see their full set sometime," Stan suggested quietly. "Very groovy."

Norah grinned.

"As much as I love to hear music played professionally, I believe you promised me a loud Britney Spears-heavy karaoke set."

Despite his warnings, Stan threw his Oriceran whiskey down his throat, grimaced, and ordered another.

"Take it easy," Norah cautioned. "You're driving."

"The pixie who lives in my trunk can drive us home," Stan retorted. Norah couldn't tell if he was joking. Before she could ask, a friend pulled him away, and Norah went back to people-watching. *Okay, fine. People-eavesdropping.* Two people behind her had an animated conversation.

"Honestly, I'm glad I can wear a ponytail now, but I might get a pixie cut."

"Your hairdresser is a pixie?"

"No, I mean, I might cut my hair short. Really short. Do you think I would look good bald?"

"Aren't you afraid of being discriminated against?"

"For being bald?"

"For being an elf."

"Nah, man. I'm keeping it pointy."

Norah heard a sigh.

"Things are easier, I grant you, but I miss the old cloak-and-dagger days. Illicit portals, secret handshakes. Subtle nods to other magicals across the room."

"Hello, fine folk," Stan greeted. Norah turned as he walked up to the light elves she'd been listening to.

The one who missed the good old days had a narrow face and green eyes. The other was shorter, with black hair slicked back in a severe ponytail and onyx studs glittering in the points of her ears.

"Norah, meet Sylomere and Jethra."

"Call us Syl and Jet," Jet suggested, sticking out a hand. Norah shook it.

"You must be Norah, the agent for magicals?" Syl asked.

"That's me," Norah agreed, hoping she wasn't about to be dogpiled with questions about getting into acting. Or worse, standup comedy.

"Can I see your wand?"

"Jet, don't be rude!"

"I'd show her mine if I had one."

Norah chuckled but cast a glance at Stan, who nodded. Wands were intimate tools, and handing them to another person was like allowing them to inspect your foot from close up. It was beautiful work, and she was happy to share it.

She pulled out the blue gum eucalyptus and held it out in an open palm.

Jet ran a single pale finger down the length, and Norah shivered as the magic crackled. The wand thought these elves were friends. That was a relief.

"Stan carved this for you?" Jet asked.

Norah nodded. "In addition to turning my home into a wooden menagerie with his tiny statues."

Stan huffed. "Complainers don't get new birds."

"You know I love your work, but it's wasted on me. It should be in a gallery. You should talk to Andrew's business partner about doing a show downtown."

"I'd rather pull down my pants on that stage than watch strangers paw at my babies. How vulgar. Although I suppose it makes sense in the context of fleeting human lives. If you live as long as an elf, you can afford to make art for one person at a time."

It was an interesting way of looking at the situation.

Syl's eyes were wide and remote, and Norah realized she was looking through rather than at her. "You resisted using the blue gum eucalyptus." Singsong undertones rippled through her voice. Oh, shit. Prophecy voice.

Norah nodded cautiously. "I wasn't happy at first. The wood is weak on offense. I was worried about getting into tight spots with nothing in the tank."

"Hmm." The drawn-out syllable rose and fell like a melody. Then the pale elf's eyes focused, and a serene smile appeared on her lips.

"Stan is wise. That's the wand of your heart."

Norah slipped it back into her pocket, squeezing it appreciatively. She could feel in her bones that it was true.

"Syl is psychic," Jet announced. Then, her eyes widened, and she leapt from her chair. "There's the list!"

The room exploded into a racket that drowned out Toto and most of the Gumballs. Magicals running at top speed to a point in the back of the room flashed past her eyes.

"What's going on?" she asked Stan, wrapping her fingers around her wand.

"Something extremely hazardous. A powerful and dangerous force beyond human ken."

Norah's brows knit together. "What?"

"Karaoke," Stan answered. Norah loosened her grip on

her wand. Then she tightened it as she remembered what happened when former theater kids competed for attention. "Don't worry, I already signed us up," Stan said. Norah considered casting a defensive spell.

"Us? No. No way. I came here to watch *you* cover *Hit Me Baby One More Time*. If this crowd hears me sing, they'll have you sent to Trevilsom for violating their magical rights," she warned.

Stan's eyes glittered. "I'll take my chances." He went to get another drink. Norah looked at the stage, which was high and very lonely. She trudged after Stan.

One and a half whiskeys later, after Jet brought the house down with a soulful Alanis Morrisette cover, the dwarf running the list, Nugget, called Norah's name. There were a few appreciative whoops from the audience. *Oh shit. Some of my clients are here.* She looked at her Hermes sneakers. They glowed as she stared longingly at the exit, then indicated she would sing *Into the Breach*.

Nugget forced a wireless microphone into her hand as she made the long climb to the stage. Eyes in the audience bored into her soul for an eternity before the music started. At the last minute, three words from an old Fred Astaire movie glowed in her mind.

"Wait! I want to change my song." She pushed through the crowd and whispered something into Nugget's grime-covered ear before going back up front. Gripping the mic with her left hand, she pulled out her wand with her right to supportive murmurs. *You're in Hollywood, Norah. Give them a show.*

Music flowed out of the big speakers in the corner. As Stan gave her a low thumbs-up, she opened her mouth. As her thin, reedy voice fizzled out in the enormous room, she waved her wand subtly. Behind her, in the back corner, an ominous three-foot-wide raincloud formed. With a boom of thunder it floated forward, letting out a deluge that magically disappeared before it hit the floor. Considering how sticky the floor was, Norah wondered if she should let it touch down.

When she felt the first raindrop brush her hair, Norah turned, plastered a shocked expression onto her face, and sprinted away. That got a big laugh from the crowd.

Norah continued the cat-and-mouse chase with the raincloud throughout her set, using chairs, tables, and even a cymbal from the drum set as umbrellas as the raincloud backed her against the wall.

As the song reached a climax, her sneakers glowed, and Norah leapt off a chair, hitting the raincloud with a flying Chuck Norris roundhouse kick. The cloud rammed into the nearest wall. Falling in a graceful arc, Norah pushed off the corner of the bar to land squarely on top of the cloud, where she stomped it with her feet until it was smushed into the floor.

The Baked Potato erupted with laughter, and Norah grinned. Adrenaline pumping, she headed to the bar for a celebratory drink. As she did, a small man on a stool sitting at the bar spun around. An impish smile quirked upward below his broad forehead and bright eyes.

Norah's jaw dropped so far that she swore she could feel her chin get sticky. Her feet were made of concrete.

The bartender pointed at a hand-blown glass bottle on the top shelf with her wand, and an elegant spout of whiskey filled Norah's glass.

"Nice number. This one's on the house. Have you met Fred?" the witch asked.

With great effort, Norah closed her mouth and stuck out a hand. Her arm was shaking so badly that it took the elf in front of her a few seconds to grasp it.

I did karaoke in front of Fred Astaire.

"I'm so sorry!" she shouted louder than she meant to.

The light elf laughed.

"I don't know if I would recommend you for the Broadway revival, but as I famously said, make 'em laugh."

"That's what I thought!" *Get yourself together, Wintery.* "I should have brought my talking box!" Norah shouted again, and Fred Astaire patted her hand.

"Next time. Lovely to meet you, miss," He gently excused himself, leaving Norah staring at the bar stool he'd hopped off. She clambered onto the black vinyl.

"I'm sitting on Fred Astaire's stool!" she shouted to the bartender, who fortunately ignored her.

Norah stopped shaking halfway through the Very Famous Actress' rendition of Black Sabbath's *War Pigs*. She conjured surprisingly gritty darkness for someone who made seven figures a year. That was why they called it acting.

Stan sidled up next to her. "Fred said there was a woman at the bar acting strangely. You haven't seen her, have you?" He grinned.

"Why does everyone but me know Fred Astaire?" she shouted.

"I know everyone." Stan smirked primly. "Fred retired to Oriceran long ago, but he comes back every few years to see old friends."

Norah imagined how many tickets she'd be able to sell to a Fred Astaire revival tour.

"Do you think he'd be interested in a live performance?" she asked.

"Stop working," Stan scolded. "Enjoy the music."

An eardrum-rattling scream of metal lyrics hit her ears, and Norah suddenly felt unsteady on her stool. She spun to ask the bartender for water.

This witch probably knows more magicals in Hollywood than I do. An idea accompanied the thought.

"Hey, do you know Harry Bing?" she shouted as the witch approached. Her voice didn't come close to cutting through the heavy metal, and Norah laughed as they whipped out their wands in unison to cast cones of silence. Norah put hers away, figuring the bartender had magical audio engineering down to muscle memory. The bar's roar faded as a faintly glowing cone surrounded them. Norah rubbed her ears.

"Do you know Harry Bing?" she repeated. Halfway through, she realized she was still yelling and lowered her voice.

The bartender's heavily lined eyebrows shot up. "From that viral dance video? I'm Rosemary, by the way."

"Norah. Yeah, that's the guy."

"I've only heard rumors." The bartender ran a hand through her tangle of red hair, uneasy.

Norah's eyes darted across the packed bar. "I bet you hear a lot of rumors."

"I do, yeah. However, people don't tip snitches."

Norah sighed. "Witch to witch?" She tried to look pathetic. The bartender winced.

"Fine. Solidarity. Whatever. Ugh. Harry Bing is famous for getting his way, even with the deck stacked against him. When people cross him, things go wrong. Weird shit. He had a client in a horror movie a few years ago who got lowballed by the studio. Harry found out the co-star was making twice as much money. On Day Six of the shoot, the animatronic swamp monster puppet came to life and bit the director's hand off."

"That's more than a little weird," Norah agreed.

"Yeah. More recent productions, ones openly using magic, have found that crossing Bing creates problems. Protective spells fade quicker than they should. Magical stunts go wrong."

"Sounds dangerous."

"Give Bing what he wants, and it's smooth sailing. Or so I've heard."

Norah nodded, thanked the bartender, and slid a twenty-dollar bill across the bar.

"I hope I see you back here," Rosemary commented. The tip folded into an origami crane and flew in a wide spiral around the room before nesting in the bartender's red hair.

As Norah made her way to the restrooms, she bumped into someone. Apologizing, she saw one of the Gumballs. The wizard zipped his keyboard into a hand-quilted case, and he smiled when he saw who it was.

"Hey there! You're Stan's friend, right?"

"Is there anyone in this town Stan doesn't know?" Norah asked.

"Unlikely. You know he helped actors unionize in 1933? Saved more than a few lives on the picket lines, too."

"Nothing about Stan surprises me anymore," Norah

deadpanned.

"He looks out for everyone, especially magicals. Helped a lot of us out at one point or another."

Norah looked inside the quilted case, where a small carved wooden bird was nestled in brightly printed cotton. *Maybe Stan doesn't give me carvings because he likes me. Maybe I'm the only one in town whose house isn't full of them.*

"My cousin was killed a few years ago, and Stan pulled me through."

"I'm so sorry," Norah replied. The musician shrugged.

"He knew what he was signing up for when he joined the Silver Griffins."

She snapped to attention. "Is that why he was killed?"

"Yeah. Someone hunted him down. Everyone said it was a deranged loner, but it was too clean for that. Someone had a plan and a lot of help."

He pulled out a photo of a thirty-something wizard with dark brown skin and a cheerful smile. Norah brushed her fingers against it, furious at whoever had taken the young man's life.

"You're the agent? The one who specializes in magicals?"

"That's me."

"I've heard of you." Norah almost smiled, but the man's expression was stormy. "Which means that other people have, too. You watch yourself. The antimagical set is more organized than people realize."

Norah thanked him for the information and went to find Stan. She'd hoped Vince was acting alone, but now she wasn't so sure. Like a pixie in a crockpot, she might be in hot water.

CHAPTER ELEVEN

The air conditioning at Skin & Wall soothed Norah's nerves, which were frayed from rush hour on the 101. Stop-and-go traffic nauseated her, so she closed her eyes and let the cold air whoosh across her skin.

When she opened them, she found Clive, her brother's business partner, staring at her. He waved and turned his attention to an installation of a titanic oil painting. The ten-foot square depicted interlocking abstract shapes stacked in a tower and floating in an ocean. As Norah stared at it, she felt uneasy. There was something profane about the painting. It carried a distinct but undefinable atmosphere of sorrow.

If she stared at it too long, someone might expect her to have art opinions, so she hightailed it to Andrew's half of the warehouse.

The tattoo studio was airy and well-lit, with sketches and photos of body art hanging from the ceiling by monofilament wire. Taken together, they looked like snow or hail. She shivered, although the room was warm. It was no fun tattooing goosebumps.

Andrew was bent over a tall elf, pressing the undulating black shape of a tattoo gun against his head. His eyes darted to her as she touched a sketch above her head and sent it spinning. It depicted a bright green train running on tracks through a dark forest.

Andrew exchanged a hushed word with the elf and stood. As Norah walked over, she saw a lace-like pattern in emerald green tucked into the triangular point of the elf's ear.

The elf's face was red, and he was sweating. Elves were normally unflappable, sometimes irritatingly so, but she knew their ears were sensitive. Getting them tattooed had to hurt like hell.

"Gimme another twenty minutes?" Andrew quirked a brow. Norah nodded and headed to one of the puffy white chairs in Andrew's waiting room, where she fell fast asleep. After a few minutes, she was woken by a high-pitched noise, like a Pomeranian's bark interpreted on a kazoo. She had her wand in her hand before she processed the noise. The elf in Andrew's chair squealed.

Elves were elegant. Elves were powerful. Elves were not supposed to whine like toddlers in tutus. A snort escaped Norah's nose, and her eyes met Clive's across the room. He listened with equal delight.

Norah decided to risk Art Talk.

"How's business?"

Clive was a big man who had reminded her more of a lumberjack than an artist. His work was sculptural and sturdy. "We hardly sold anything in the last show, but I have high hopes for this one. Critics might call it gimmicky, but I believe in the work. The painter was part of an Earth–Oriceran cultural exchange organized by UCLA last year."

Norah looked at the tower on the wall that had alarmed her when she walked in. Its familiarity clicked into place.

"That's Trevilsom, the magical prison."

Clive looked at the explanatory plaque he was installing.

"I guess so. You recognize it? With this Oriceran-influenced stuff, I never know if the artist is being impressionistic or working from deeply bizarre subject matter. Sometimes it's both."

Norah wandered the gallery. One painting, massive in scope, showed nothing but sky and clouds.

"What's this one called?" she asked.

Clive thumbed through the plaques. "Palace of the Elf King. I guess it's not literal? Pretty, though."

Norah wondered whether painting an invisible palace was easier or harder than painting a visible one.

A much smaller portrait at the end of the hallway stopped her in her tracks. This one was unambiguously realistic, with rich colors and dark shadows reminiscent of Caravaggio. In the painting, a young witch stared at a fist-sized hole in her chest. Blood soaked her yellow sundress, and her dropped wand was frozen in the air below her fingertips.

Norah felt like someone had offered her a bite of her intestines. Tears welled in her eyes. Violence against witches and wizards had been a constant threat during her childhood. Until recently, she'd thought she'd left it in the past.

Clive joined her and stared at the painting. "Andrew and I talked about this one. I thought it might be a bit literal."

Norah shook her head. "It's beautiful. It also makes me want to puke."

"Capital-T truth is a bitch. I should have warned you."

The high-pitched squealing died after another few minutes. The tall elf limped out the door, shadowed by Andrew. He walked over to Norah and Clive and stared at a spot on the white wall above the painting of the dying witch.

"It's good art, but I can't stand looking at it. In the past few weeks, I've gotten half a dozen urgent requests to cover Silver Griffin tats. I hate it, but I might have to start charging. I can't keep my shop open, do pro bono work, *and* help Jackie with Leaf. Not unless someone has invented a magical replacement for sleep."

"How is the world's greatest nephew?" Norah asked. Maybe after she was done here, she would pop over to the loft and say hello.

"He's six, so he's a beautiful, perpetual crisis."

"You know I'm always happy to babysit."

Andrew's face perked up at the offer. "Thanks for coming. I've been meaning to talk to you." He pulled Norah away from the oil painting to his small office. Unlike the antiseptic studio, the room was a mess. A paper landslide had assaulted Andrew's laptop. He unceremoniously swept the documents to the floor, and Norah sat on a metal folding chair behind his desk.

As Andrew tapped his computer with his wand, an enormous magical screen appeared in the air. Norah watched with interest as her brother navigated to a well-designed but benign-looking website about Gothic architecture. He typed in a complicated string of letters and numbers, then double-clicked inside the mouth of a gargoyle guarding a buttress.

The screen disappeared and then exploded into a cube. Letters and numbers flew through the digital space, stacking into towers and creating currents of information in white, neon, and black.

"What is this?" Norah asked.

"The magical dark web." Andrew pressed his lips together. "It's the nastiest place I've ever been." Andrew had spent his twenties going to underground raves in Berlin, so Norah took this pronouncement seriously.

"Will you beef me up with protective spells before I dive into the muck?" he asked Norah. Touched, she got to work with her eucalyptus wand, tracing electric blue runes over the permanent ink on the backs of Andrew's hands. The mermaid on his bicep looked afraid.

After finishing a rune with a flourish, Norah inspected her work. Andrew's hands were encased in magical sky-blue gloves. "That's the best I can do on short notice," she told him. As he gripped his wand, the mermaid tattoo covered her eyes with her hands.

Andrew reached into the three-dimensional space with his wand and cast several small spells related to metal and electricity. Finally, the letters and numbers he touched glowed and shifted, swirling into a portal. The perspective shifted, and Norah's stomach jolted as the open hole zoomed into them. They tumbled in and fell until a three-by-three grid of transparent heads popped up. The heads were three-dimensional but still like death masks, and as Andrew rotated the grid, Norah gasped.

"What?" Andrew asked.

"That wizard on the lower left. I recognize him."

It was the young wizard from the photo the keyboardist had shown her last night. The former Silver Griffin agent. His head wasn't still. Every few seconds, a red starburst inside his skull exploded outward. The graphics were unsettling, reminiscent of blood spatter.

"Did you know him?" Andrew asked.

"No. He was a friend of a friend. What is this?"

"It's a site called Dark Hound. It's a magical web sleuthing collective dedicated to tracking down and killing Silver Griffin agents."

"The red starbursts… They're witches and wizards who have been killed?" Norah watched one pulse through the head of a young witch with sandy blonde hair. Andrew swallowed.

"Yeah. They're all ex-Griffin." He rotated the grid, and Norah's stomach sank as she recognized a second face. Billy Warble.

Acid pushed through her esophagus, and beads of sweat dampened her forehead.

"That's my neighbor," she blurted.

"Really?" Andrew's expression switched from angry to frightened.

Norah's blood boiled. "We have to shut this down! Magicals might not be popular, but killing them is not legal."

"One of my hacker friends is working on it, but the main server is heavily protected. There's a machine learning algorithm running underneath everything else. It looks at data from known Silver Griffin agents to create a most-likely-suspects list. Then the algorithm gathers massive amounts of information from around the web to identify patterns. The system prioritizes photos, names, and locations input by users, but it doesn't need them. Whoever is running this has a ton of digital firepower."

"So, it's not some college kid on a laptop?" Norah asked.

"Not unless that kid invented quantum computing without anyone knowing."

Norah thought about Vince and fire ropes. She sighed.

"I have to tell you something. Do you remember when LACMA got shut down a couple of weeks ago?"

Andrew swiveled his chair to stare at her. His brow furrowed as she told her story. As she described her meetup with Vince, a vein in his neck started to twitch. When she finished her story, he pressed his lips together.

Norah had expected him to be angry. She hadn't expected his anger to be directed at her. "Jesus, Norah, you can't run into an explosion without backup."

The hair on the back of her neck stood up. Andrew and Quint had never been able to shake the habit of treating her like her kid sister. "Last time I checked, I wasn't a defenseless little mouse."

"Ugh. I don't think you are."

"Yes, you do. You still think of me as a useless kid who has to be protected while you go out and do the fun stuff with Mom and Dad. I'm not seven anymore."

"I know. That doesn't mean you have to do everything alone."

"I'm trying to protect our family," Norah growled.

"So am I. I didn't tell you this, but I covered Mom and Dad's tattoos while they were down here."

Norah's breath caught in her throat. Her mother had once told her that the day she was inducted into the Griffins had been the third-best day of her life. It came after the births of her children but before her wedding. Even when it became dangerous, she'd refused to cover her tattoo.

"We have to find the source of the leak," Norah declared. "Before a lot more people get hurt."

Andrew glanced at the three-dimensional grid of wizards and witches. The ones who weren't dead were in serious danger.

"If that's your neighbor, you might not be safe," Andrew continued. "Maybe you should come to stay with Jackie and me, at least for a little bit.

"No. I refuse to abandon my home and friends to murderous internet killers. We have to find the person leaking the names of Silver Griffin agents, and we have to stop them.

"I agree, but no more secret midnight rendezvous. No more destroying public art!"

"I almost died. Sure, worry about the installation."

Andrew smiled, his good humor resurfacing. "If you had to pick something to destroy, at least you picked kitschy populist garbage."

"Hey! I like the lampposts."

"I rest my case. Go make a Michael Bay movie, philistine."

"I am, actually." Norah's expression was smug.

"Wait. Really?" Was that jealousy on Andrew's face? Norah's effort to lean back nonchalantly was undercut when she tipped her metal chair over.

Andrew pulled her to her feet, laughing, and started interrogating her about the new project. Norah exhaled, relieved, as the conversation returned to normal. Well, almost normal. In the background, cherry red starbursts continued to pulse.

CHAPTER TWELVE

The long glass window along the south side of the living room gave Garton Saxon an excellent view of Los Angeles. It was also soundproof, which was important on days like today.

Garton spent most of his time in a restored mansion in West Adams, whose architecture was an eclectic grab bag of Moorish colonnades and Victorian turrets. He despised this Hollywood Hills house, a blocky concrete number with a ghastly infinity pool.

Still, he needed a place to do dirty work, and earthquake risks in Los Angeles made it difficult to construct reasonably sized underground lairs. This bourgeois gray cube in Beverly Hills would have to do. At least it had a carriage house for his assistant Heberd.

Heberd, short even by dwarf standards, had done an admirable job getting Saxon's guests settled. All three were tied to the room's tall concrete supports. Because of the soundproofing, they were not gagged, although none were screaming, which was good. Saxon hated it when his guests burned through their vocal cords before the party started.

The room was so quiet that Saxon heard squeaking from the lavish multi-level Victorian birdcage in the corner of the room. White fur shimmered in the gaps between the carved wooden bars. The cage was a miniature replica of his West Adams mansion. Nice to have a touch of home in all this concrete.

Saxon's eyes moved from the mouse cage to his trio of tied-up guests. The thrill he always felt at such times raced up his spine. There was no sense rushing the moment.

He assessed the contents of an antique copper bar cart parked near the kitchen, poured light elf cognac, whiskey, and sweet vermouth into an etched glass cocktail shaker, then added a spoonful of Benedictine and three generous sloshes of bitters. After a vigorous shake, the mixture went into a hand-blown Venetian tumbler.

As he sipped, he moved to the nearest concrete pillar and stared at the quivering silver mustache of the middle-aged wizard attached to it.

"I was gonna tie 'em to chairs, but all your chairs are made of fucking gilded toothpicks and shit. You gotta get some real furniture, man." Looking down at Heberd strained Garton's neck, and the dwarf was so ugly he tried not to do it often. The undersized dwarf was desperate for anything or anyone who could give him stature, a quality that made him useful in circumstances like this.

"I shouldn't have to live in squalor because people are brutes," Saxon reported. Last year, a struggling dark elf had splintered Saxon's favorite chaise lounge—an original from Versailles. Of course, she'd been appropriately reprimanded. He inspected the jute rope that secured the wizard to the pillar, tapping it with one finger. The strings glowed briefly and contracted, digging into the man's skin. A soft noise of pain barely reached his ears.

Saxon sipped his cocktail and frowned. "Have you ever tried a Vieux Carré?" he asked. Sweat dripped down the wizard's pale forehead, and he didn't answer. "It's a delicious drink. Very complicated. I had my first one in New Orleans a hundred years ago. This one is adequate, but it's unfinished. It's incomplete. I ran out of Luxardo cherries yesterday, and it's not the same. I'm a solution-oriented man, so I suppose I can find a substitute."

Placing his drink on a small end table that had once belonged to Katherine Hepburn, Garton flexed his fingers, then drew a complicated series of shapes around the man's right eye. Thin tendrils of light surrounded it.

As he moved back, a thread of light unspooled from his work and connected to his finger.

Garton tugged on the thread.

The man screamed as his eye bulged out of his head like an apple caught in a radiant white net. Somewhere near Saxon's feet, Heberd trembled with excitement. Gently and slowly, Saxon pulled until he felt the eyeball stretch to its maximum limit. He would feel that final, satisfying pop if he twitched his finger.

Saxon released the glowing thread, and the eyeball snapped back into its socket. The screaming wizard blinked furiously. He stared desperately at various objects to confirm that he could still see.

"You're lucky I don't want to eat an eyeball," Saxon muttered.

His three unlucky guests were professional rivals. They all owned companies that supplied production assistants to understaffed shoots around town. The other commonality was that they had all refused to sell him their businesses.

"No one ever screws me over twice." He rolled sweet botanical cognac around in his mouth. Should he try a citrus twist? Grapefruit? He could try lime if he subbed a high-quality tequila for the whiskey. "You know why? Because you have to be alive to screw someone over."

"I got swindled by a ghost once," Heberd interjected from below his eye line. Saxon shot him a dark look, and the dwarf shut his mouth.

The witch tied to the far pillar wore a sheer silk blouse whose collar was already stained yellow with tears. Garton rifled through his mental Rolodex. Jasmine. Her name was Jasmine.

"Please," she begged. "I'll sell you the company."

Garton entwined his fingers into a blossoming flower shape and shot a magic stream at the witch's head. As if touched by static electricity, every one of her platinum-blonde hairs stood on end. Her head looked like a dandelion puff.

When Garton twitched his pinkie, he yanked out a one-inch by one-inch patch of hair at Jasmine's temple. She screamed, but not in time to cover the ripping sound. Pinprick-sized drops of blood welled in the bald patch.

Saxon twisted the hair into a looping flower using crisscrossing beams of light. Victorian hair art was a difficult craft to master, especially with magic, and he admired the results of his efforts. He'd gotten better at this in the past fifty years. At a nod, Heberd shuffled to the eastern wall and removed an enormous oil painting of a nude figure ripping out a man's throat.

"Careful!" The Bouguereau portrait was the only thing in the house Saxon loved. Heberd climbed off the stepstool and leaned the painting against a nearby wall, revealing a glass case in a hidden recessed alcove. Soft lighting illuminated black velvet covered in hundreds of twining pieces of hair. Complicated auburn knots. Twining brunette vines. All of them were happy memories.

Saxon's guests started screaming. Saxon floated the new blonde flower over to Heberd on a pillow of light, and the dwarf pinned it to the board.

"Please don't. It's that new agent's fault!" the witch tied to the far pole screamed.

Saxon's head whipped around. He didn't like being reminded about problems he still needed to solve.

He waved away the spell on the witch's hair, and it fell around her shoulders in a limp lump.

"What's that?" He forced his face into a pleasant expression. The witch's lips quivered.

"She said it was important for magicals to stay independent and retain our ability to work together. She's putting together packages to help magicals start their careers."

Heberd sat on the stepstool. "Indie competition would not be good for business, boss," he shouted.

The dwarf was right. Saxon had big plans and wanted a wide, clear, obstacle-free path ahead of him. He tossed his empty glass into a corner of the room. A pleasant chill shot up his spine as the glass shattered. Then, he strode up the short steps to the entryway of his home and hauled his large brass beacon off a hook.

After marching back to the living room, he placed it near the window. He tapped it with one finger, and the glass surrounding the central light flickered to life with intricate waves of magical symbols. Saxon placed his fingers in a careful orientation on the glass and inhaled.

"*Lux intellecto bellica*," he murmured. Three beams of light shot into the people's skulls tied to his pillars, blowing them back. Light from inside their skulls escaped from their nostrils and eye sockets, and the fluid-filled sacs of their eyeballs glowed as the bright beams bleached out their irises and pupils. The witch's body distended. The air smelled like ozone, and the overhead track lighting briefly cut out.

Saxon waited a few moments, then removed his hands from the beacon. Light drained out of his victims like water from a pitcher, and they slumped in their ropes. He approached the witch whose hair he'd ripped out. She was pale but breathing. Shallowly, but still. Garton nodded.

"Send them to my office when they wake up. We've got a lot of work to do."

"Yes, boss." Heberd replaced the oil painting on Saxon's wall.

CHAPTER THIRTEEN

Norah scrolled through the news story on her phone, her eyes darting from the Perez Hilton headline *Emerald Shitty* to the photo of a straining Saxon holding the green glass chandelier inches from a starlet's terrified face. Near his left elbow was a woman with a wand, shapewear noticeable under her ripped dress. No face was visible.

"At least I made the news. Well, my body made the news," Norah muttered.

Saxon looked effortlessly muscled. TikTok had already started calling him "Elf Daddy." She shuddered. His eyes had slid over her body like Vaseline, and she wasn't looking forward to an encore.

No one had died, and the crash had generated a tornado of free publicity. Had Saxon sabotaged the chandelier as a publicity stunt? Maybe, but she suspected darker motives. Norah sighed and climbed into her Prius. The creep could wait. For now, she had secret agenting to do.

There was a saying she'd heard on repeat when she first

moved to town. "Everything in LA takes twenty minutes to get to." Twenty minutes later, Norah turned onto a side street near the Fremont Branch Public Library. After parking down the block, Norah dropped oversized sunglasses over her face and headed toward it.

The Los Angeles Public Library website proudly listed the Mediterranean revival building's status as a historical and cultural monument. That was true but incomplete. The library had been constructed by Silver Griffin agents living on Melrose in the 1920s. The agents had ceded control to the extremely competent city librarians, although the building was still used as a Silver Griffin dead drop.

Norah's father had suggested these locations as the perfect place to set a trap. If a dispatcher had gone rotten, they might be looking for victims in these old haunts. She suspected Lincoln had ulterior motives. In addition to a secret mission, he had sent her a sizable list of books to pick up for him, mostly contemporary science fiction with a few old Agatha Christies for good measure. Norah smiled at the security guard near the library's entrance and headed to a back room that had been added in the late 1990s.

She closed her eyes and reached for her wand. When it was in hand, she sent exploratory magic threads into the air. One of them caught and returned a crackle of silver magic through her arm, jostling her shoulder.

"Ow!" She rubbed it and reached for the spell that hung invisibly in the air. When her wand touched it, a rectangle outlined with magical writing glowed. Magic sizzled as the rectangle stretched until it touched the floor. The edges grew brighter, and two dimensions became three. When the portal had grown, Norah ventured into the compact space beyond. A shift in air pressure unbalanced her as her inner ear argued with her rational brain about whether the floor beneath her feet existed.

The transparent walls of the reading room looked into the library, although the room's bending qualities distorted the space beyond. Norah had entered her first grimoire cache when she was twelve, a slip of a closet under the peaked wooden roof of the Mill Valley Public Library in Marin County. Staring out of the room, she'd asked her mother if M.C. Escher was secretly a wizard.

This cache was well-illuminated because its five bookshelves were constructed from light beams. The shelves floated at eye level; they must have been built in collaboration with light elves.

Witches and wizards kept caches throughout the human world. This one was well-stocked. Norah ran her hand along the spines on one shelf, pausing as she brushed a book covered in luxurious platinum-blonde hair. Curious, she opened it and admired how the hair tossed itself out of the way of the front cover. *From Not to Hot: Glamours for Every Occasion.*

Great. Even the LA Public Library wanted to give her a makeover.

She slammed the book shut, giving the platinum-blonde mane an aggrieved tousle as she shoved it back into its gap. She noticed a small terra cotta pot one shelf below, peered inside, and found a delicate book growing there, its pages open like a flower.

Norah gently compressed the petal pages together to

read the cover. *Trees of Forbidden Knowledge: Graft to Harvest.* The table of contents looked interesting, and she had to resist a strong urge to plunk herself on the floor and spend several hours improving her knowledge of horticultural magic. She pulled a small water bottle from her purse, sipped it, and then tipped a little into the book's pot. "Don't go anywhere," she told it and, with a sigh, got down to business.

According to her parents, Silver Griffin agents had passed messages to one another via an old rune dictionary on a bottom shelf. After a minute of hunting, she found a stately black tome covered in eye-catching geometric silver embossing.

"*Sixteenth-Century Indo-European Runes and Their Etymancical Origins.* Huh. No wonder you're so dusty."

Leaving obvious fingerprints in the thick dust on the spine, Norah flipped the book to Page Thirty-three, scribbled a latitude and longitude on a small slip of paper, and left it inside. After she replaced the book, she moved back into conventional space. Her ears popped as the room's fluorescent lighting turned the world a sickly yellow.

Norah tapped the glowing spell circumscribing the portal, and the magic contracted into an invisible rectangle like swallowed bubblegum. Norah shook her head as the room's air currents returned to normal.

The latitude and longitude she'd left in the book were for a safe house in Topanga Canyon—the cheese in her family's little mousetrap. *I hope this works.*

She looked at her watch. Not the way she'd wanted to spend a lazy Sunday, especially after the disastrous premiere. Still, this was a top priority. One down, five to go.

Sighing, she waved to the security guard and steeled herself for a long day.

CHAPTER FOURTEEN

When Norah reluctantly answered Andrew's summons to a family meeting that weekend, she didn't expect to be greeted by a goat.

It was a silky black, with white tufts behind its legs and two prominent white lines running down its face. When Norah scratched it between the ears, it stomped a front hoof in pleasure.

"Pepe usually bites strangers." Norah's father sauntered over from the other side of the downtown loft and enfolded her in a hug. As he pulled away, he shot a warning look at the goat, then slipped a gray velvet lead around its neck.

"Why did you bring a goat?" Norah asked.

"He was sick last week, and your mother wanted to keep an eye on him. I'm starting to think he faked it because he wanted to take a road trip."

Pepe bleated in an offended tone and planted his hooves. The goat slid across the smooth concrete as

Lincoln tugged on the lead. "Okay, okay, I'm sorry for impugning your character. *Mea maxima culpa.*"

Pepe nodded, and his wiry chin whiskers shook. He trotted primly down the hallway after them.

As she emerged from a side room, Jackie put a finger to her lips. "Leaf went down for a nap. The goat got him very excited."

Norah nodded, then, as an afterthought, pulled out her wand and traced crosshatches in the air. When she tapped the overlapping threads with her wand, they expanded into a noise-dampening net that covered the hallway. Pepe trotted over, attempted to eat one of the magical blue threads, and glared at Norah when his face went through the spell.

"What have you been feeding him?" she asked her father.

"Mostly hay," her father replied with a note of hesitation in his voice.

"Mostly."

He sighed. "Don't tell your mother, but I gave him some cuttings from our Oriceran juniper tree last month. Now when he burps, he smells like a gin and tonic. Also, he's getting smarter."

Norah shook her head. "Remind me to loan you my copy of *Animal Farm.*" Pepe quirked an eyebrow. " Don't let the goat read it."

After she stepped into the high-ceilinged living room, Norah applied protective spells around the doors and windows. Lincoln gave up on trying to restrain the goat and it followed her around, taking optimistic nibbles of every spell as the twirling runes embedded themselves into the floor.

She fished a net bag full of bright yellow lemons from her courtyard tree out of her purse and fished for the ugliest one. The goat's teeth were covered in green slime, and she cringed as she held the citrus fruit in her palm. Pepe took it with a grateful grunt and transported it to the far corner of the room, where he ate it in small bites with incredible gusto.

"You should meet my friend Stan," she muttered. "Trade disgusting culinary tips."

"Are you giving that goat my lemons?" Quint was behind her, giving Pepe the stink-eye.

"Don't be greedy." She shoved the net bag into his chest. As he grabbed it, another lemon spilled onto the floor. It tumbled over the concrete before rolling to a stop halfway between Quint and Pepe. They both went for it, and the goat won. Quint frowned.

"I'm halfway through confecting new citrus curds for my signature scones. Don't make me find a new lemon guy."

"Keep me flush with free scones, and you can have all the lemons my tree can produce." Pepe gave her a wide-eyed, tragic stare. "Well, almost all the lemons."

Andrew and Petra emerged from the kitchen with trays of cucumber sandwiches and several large pots of tea. Her brother had broken out his wedding china, which he only did when he needed something from his mother.

She settled on an antique emerald-green loveseat, then stuffed several tiny sandwiches into her mouth. That gave her another minute before she had to tell her family about the threat to the former Silver Griffins.

"I'd like to thank Mom and Dad for making the trip down south so soon again and bringing us new friends," Andrew began. This last bit he directed at Pepe, who sidled to the coffee table. His slit-pupiled eyes went for an innocent expression.

Jackie shook her head. "Leaf is going to beg me for a pet goat for months. Years, maybe."

"Talk to us during lambing season, and we'll find you a nice runt!" Petra told her cheerfully. Jackie rubbed her temples forcefully with her hands, attempting to erase the possibility from her brain.

"You can always visit the farm," Lincoln added brightly. Pepe stomped his foot cheerfully.

Norah swallowed. The English Breakfast tea was tempered with sugar and cream, but it was still bitter in her throat. "Please don't be mad," she started.

Quint grinned.

"This should be good." Lincoln leaned forward, interested.

The rundown of events, starting at LACMA, took fifteen minutes, but it felt like an eternity. Quint's expression moved from delighted at not being the screw-up for once to alarm. Norah thought her mother might be angry that she'd been keeping secrets, but Petra was just intent.

When she finished, Andrew retrieved his laptop and showed the family Dark Hound. Norah's stomach flipped when the grid of witches and wizards showed one redder starburst than before. Norah pointed out Billy and relayed the strange occurrences peppering his life, including his suspicion that he was being followed. The room fell silent. Finally, her mother slurped her tea and forcefully replaced the cup on the coffee table. China clattered.

"Tea's not gonna cut it." Petra reached into her bag up to her elbow. Objects thumped and clattered as she rifled through them. Finally, she pulled out a hand-blown glass bottle, its surface covered in thin blue stripes. The stopper in the bottle's narrow neck was carved from smoky quartz and had neat rows of magical symbols spiraling around it.

Petra smiled darkly. "Oriceran sunfruit brandy. Drain your teacups and steel your skulls."

Norah drained her teacup and cautiously held it out. As Petra opened the brandy bottle, a sound like a windchime falling off a roof escaped. Then the music mellowed, and the bright splashing of the liquid on the thin ceramic wove it into a pleasant melody.

The sound intensified as Norah swirled the cup in a small rhythmic circle. The drops of magically imbued liquid cast prismatic rainbows on the white ceramic. After receiving his cup, Quint matched her motion, and the musical threads blended together.

"This isn't going to make me duel my inner child or something, is it?" Quint asked.

"It's like tequila, only it makes you smarter rather than stupider," Petra declared.

"Even tequila would struggle to make Quint stupider," Andrew joked. Petra shot him a piercing look. He coughed in embarrassment, then dutifully held out his teacup, which she ignored.

"Jackie?" Petra asked. The younger woman and Andrew exchanged fraught looks.

"Oh, shit," Quint whispered.

"We were going to wait to tell you..." Jackie's voice trailed off as cautiously hopeful expressions crept onto their parents' faces.

"We're due for kiddo *numero dos* next January," Andrew announced. He looked guiltily at Norah. "I didn't mean to steal your thunder. I didn't realize Mom was going to dip into the stuff on the top shelf. Er, top purse pocket. Whatever."

Norah set down her teacup, raced over, and nearly toppled Andrew with a hug. She repeated the gesture with Jackie, albeit more gently.

"We haven't told Leaf yet, so keep your traps zipped until we do."

"This deserves a toast!" Petra grinned.

Andrew raised an eyebrow at his wife, who said, "Ugh. Go on, drink your magic booze. There's no reason we both have to be boring."

Petra finally filled Andrew's teacup and raised her own. "To the newest Wintery!"

"Hear, hear!"

Music echoed through the teacup as it neared Norah's lips. The brandy danced down her throat like a distilled solar flare, tasting of fresh clover and warm hay. She felt as if some large and cheerful person had placed her brain on a pile of fresh flowers in a beam of dusty afternoon light.

Norah touched the wave of afternoon sunshine flowing into the loft from the large western windows. It sparkled on her fingerprints.

Her family's eyes were wide. Their pupils stretched to the edges of their irises.

"Now that everyone's fully illuminated, let's try to solve this Griffin problem." Petra's eyes widened, and she climbed onto the back of Andrew's sectional sofa, ignoring Jackie's worried looks at the cleanliness of her farm boots. She looked comfortable, so Norah climbed onto her own sofa. Her mother was onto something. It was nice here. Easier to see the full outline of the room.

In moments, the entire family stood on the furniture. Norah's dad balanced on the back of a wooden rocking chair like a grizzled sea captain swaying in rough seas.

"I'm going to check on Leaf," Jackie muttered. Pepe sat back on his haunches and eyed the sunfruit-addled family with healthy skepticism.

"How are so many former agents being exposed?" Lincoln mulled. The rocking chair creaked below him.

"I hate to say it, but I think it must be someone on the inside," Norah answered. The creaking stopped. Petra's face grew very serious.

"A few of our friends in the Bay Area have had problems. At first, I thought they were bored, so desperate for the old sense of danger that they were finding ways to spook themselves. I think you're right though, Norah. I'm sorry to say it."

Her mother's hazel eyes were watering. New lines had etched into her skin, and not from smiling. "You would have made a tremendous agent, Norah," Petra whispered. The lines deepened.

"I am an agent, Mom."

"You know what I mean. You're a born defender, built to use that blue gum eucalyptus as a diamond-clad shield around everyone you love."

Warmth rushed into Norah's chest. How much of it was from the brandy?

"I want to get a tattoo of the sun!" Quint blurted.

Lincoln's head turned very slowly to his eldest. He blinked and held up a finger to halt any protest. "You're a genius, Quint! Let's all get tattoos of the sun."

"Who will tattoo the tattooer?" Andrew asked, his voice mystical.

"No tattoos until the brandy wears off." Petra's voice was loud and firm. "Now, who would know agent names from multiple Silver Griffin cells?"

Norah's eyes darted around the circle. An idea, like a pinprick of light, increased in size until it was a ferocious blaze.

"A dispatcher." Her family's dilated eyes darted at her. Her mother nodded.

"That makes sense. A dispatcher would hear everything. They'd know our hobbies. Our haunts. Our favorite colors."

"Chartreuse," Quint whispered. Petra ignored him.

"They might not know where we've gone since the Silver Griffins disbanded, but they'd know where to start looking."

Lincoln climbed off his rocking chair and descended onto the floor, shifting until he was lying on the cool concrete. Dappled light played across the ceiling.

"Who could betray so many of us?" he asked sadly. Pepe trotted over, sniffed Lincoln's boot, and stuck out his tongue to take a tentative taste. Lincoln shooed the black-and-white goat away.

SIGN YOUR FEARS AWAY

Andrew climbed off his chair and sat crossed-legged on the floor, patting his father's knee.

"We need to smoke the traitor out."

"How?" Quint asked, happy to remain balanced atop a midcentury acrylic sideboard.

"I have an idea." Lincoln twined his fingers and rested them on his round belly. He held up his teacup for a refill. After Petra obliged, he sketched the outline of a plan.

Three hours later, Norah strolled out of the building. Her hand itched to rub the clear film clinging to her left wrist, but she resisted.

"I can't believe I let Quint talk me into getting a tattoo," she muttered. The family that inks together...doesn't get jinxed together? Even Jackie had gotten one, although she and Andrew had drawn the line at tattooing their six-year-old son. However, Andrew had been able to whip up and print out an impressive temporary tattoo, which had nipped a brewing tantrum in the bud.

"Norah?" someone behind her called. Petra had followed her out of the studio. Petroleum jelly seeped from below the matching bandage on her mother's wrist.

"I'm glad we have you in our corner." Petra patted her arm. "To be honest, I'm excited to see where you go with that blue gum eucalyptus. I've never seen someone weave defensive magic like you do."

Norah sighed. "Of course, Mom. Just until we get this Silver Griffin situation sorted out, okay?"

"A temporary solution." Petra nodded, although the

twinkle in her eye suggested she was lying. "Have you got anything in that wand for a bad itch? Fresh ink was a lot easier in my twenties." She pulled her hand away from the bandage, sighing.

"Sure, Mom." The eucalyptus wood was cool and steady in her hand. Norah sent a wash of cooling blue light over her mother's wrist and, after a moment, her own.

"Come on. I'll walk you to your car."

CHAPTER FIFTEEN

Norah stared at the item draped over Cleo's carved wooden corners. "It's dark magic, I'm sure of it."

Cleo snorted. "I'm ninety-percent cursed. I'd be able to tell."

"I swear, the man who invented the thumbscrews had nothing on whoever made these."

The control-top shapewear rustled in the condo's A/C. Norah poked it with her wand, distaste curling her lips.

"You don't have to wear it," Cleo told her.

Norah grimaced. Under normal circumstances, she wouldn't. Two days ago, Stan had presented her with a vintage beaded dress that the silent film actress Clara Bow had worn in *Kiss Me Again*. He claimed he had found it at the back of his closet.

The neckline was high, but the dress clung and dropped low in the back. The paisley beadwork was impeccable, and the clean lines had enchanted Norah, even if she had to turn to the dark side of undergarments to zip it.

She picked up the tan nylon/spandex blend and slunk

to her bedroom. "If I don't make it out, I want you to have the condo," she shouted to Cleo.

"Once more into the briefs, dear friend, once more!" Cleo shouted after her.

She didn't fidget once in the limo. She couldn't. There was no room in the tight cylinder of the dress. She might have made a mistake. There was a strong chance that human women had grown extra organs since the 1920s. At some point, she might have to breathe.

As she rode west, the dark shapes of palm trees stood out against the pink and orange sky. Smog may be bad, but it made for great sunsets.

"We've come a long way, kid! Our first Hollywood premiere!" Madge buzzed around the inside of the limo. A ruffled yellow bodysuit had transformed the pixie into the spitting image of an expensive cupcake with wings. "You look like a million bucks, although I'm not sure our friendship will survive your offensive use of shapewear."

"It was the only way into this dress. Now I'm a sausage in a casing," Norah muttered.

The limo pulled up in front of Mann's Chinese theater, and Madge's wings flapped harder in excitement. "Put your game face on, Nor."

As Norah clambered effortlessly out of the limo, the falling faces of the photographers behind the velvet ropes amused her. A few snapped disinterested shots, and a man in a black-and-white baseball cap whispered, "Who is that?" to his colleague.

The woman next to him muttered, "Some nobody. Great dress, though."

Norah sighed. Maybe next year, her clients would climb

the list from D to C or B. She beamed at the cameras as she went by, recalling with effort the advice she'd gleaned from a TikTok video about posing. One foot forward, hand on the hip.

The paparazzi were much more interested in Madge. One asked the pixie to stick around while he swapped to a telephoto lens.

"I'll see you inside." Norah nodded at her partner. The photographer asked Madge if she'd ever considered studio modeling as Norah walked away. He wanted to work on shooting small. Had some miniature set ideas. She lost their voices amid an animated discussion about photography and scale, reminding herself to look up the guy's name later. He could be a potential ally. Maybe the next time she signed a faerie or a pixie, she'd ask him to do headshots.

The building's focal point was two large red pillars with decorative finials beneath a peaked gold roof. An enormous promotional poster hung between the pillars.

The Wonderful Wizard was an ambitious project, a movie that hewed closely to L. Frank Baum's *The Wonderful Wizard of Oz*. A real wizard had been cast in the title role, with dwarves as the Munchkins and a cowardly lion shifter. All the magic in the movie was real, captured on thirty-five-millimeter film. Special effects had only been used for touch-ups. It was a chance for everyday people to see magic in action, especially in parts of the country where few magicals had chosen to live.

The traditional red carpet had been swapped out for a low pile version printed with large yellow bricks. Norah appreciated the sentiment, but it would look garish in photos. Not that anyone would be putting *her* in a fashion roundup the next day.

"Norah!" someone called. She spun, and a beaming Frondle burst forth in a skin-tight tuxedo.

"What are you doing here?" Norah exclaimed. He was new in town to have been invited to a blockbuster premiere. Frondle took the question's rudeness in stride.

"Agnes invited me." He pointed across the carpet at a glamorous silver-haired woman in her late fifties or early sixties who was immersed in an animated discussion with the film's producers. Norah's eyebrows shot up.

"Are you two..."

Frondle pulled his collar down to scratch his neck. "I know it's a Hollywood cliché to date a woman forty years younger than me, but I can't help myself. She's an old soul."

The glamorous producer turned and smiled at the young elf with a vaguely predatory expression on her face. "Well, have fun. Try not to get in over your head," Norah advised.

"Frondle!" the woman called and the elf trotted back to her, eyes puppy-dog wide. Norah hoped he would fare better than some of the ingenues she'd known.

Norah accepted a champagne flute from a roving server. She let the bubbles tickle her nose as she made the rounds greeting clients and acquaintances. One of her clients had played the chieftainess of the munchkins, and a bird shifter named Carlisle had played a talking stork.

She walked inside with Carlisle, complimenting on his stunning eggplant-velvet tuxedo. The dark walls of the rectangular room were bathed in emerald light. Norah looked at the source of the illumination and gasped.

A scale model of the Emerald City hovered near the ceiling. Transparent glass, spires, and towers plunged downward to look like a chandelier. Norah traced the serpentine path of one road through verdant orchards and lemon-lime outbuildings into the rich jewel-toned heart of the city. Delicate blown bridges arced over streams frozen in silica. According to a small bronze plaque, the piece was studded with ten thousand Oriceran emeralds, a gift from the Crystal People.

The miniature Emerald City was not attached to the ceiling by any visible means. It floated twenty feet in the air. Surreptitiously unzipping the golden fan of her clutch, Norah grazed her wand and pulled a small amount of power through her body and into her eyes. She looked again.

Aha. Thick magical ropes held the city aloft, tended by four magicals standing in the room's corners—two witches and two wizards.

A flurry of activity near the witch in the far northwestern corner caught her eye. A tall wispy man in a blinding white tuxedo had approached, asking questions and gesturing wildly with a champagne glass that discharged its contents onto the ballroom floor.

Norah's eyes furrowed as she noticed the chandelier tender in the northeastern corner drain a full glass of champagne and trade it for two new flutes. He swayed back and forth, alternating sips between his left and right hands. Oh, well. She was here to make connections, not judge other people's work ethics.

A small figure pushed past her, and she winced as the beads on her hip caught. The person was slightly shorter than her, so she was surprised when he turned to reveal pointy ears. Most light elves were taller. Much taller. He wore a very interesting outfit, a cross between traditional light elf robes and modern menswear embroidered in delicate monochromatic stitching. When the elf murmured an apology, her breath caught in her throat.

"Garton Saxon!" she exclaimed. The out-and-proud light elf and legendary producer was at the top of her list of people to meet and greet tonight. *No time like the present.* "I'm Norah Wintery."

Recognition flashed in his eyes. "It's very nice to meet you, Norah. Please excuse me." After a curt nod, he resumed his beeline across the room. Norah sighed. So much for her big meeting.

Saxon bumped and jostled several more people as he barreled forward, but his victims sucked in their complaints when they realized who he was. Was he doing it on purpose?

Saxon's warpath ended near one of the maintenance witches. Maybe he was involved with the chandelier somehow. He said a few angry words, and Nora realized she recognized the woman. What was her name? Copper. No. Penny? *Penelope. That's it.* The witch ran a company that supplied production assistants, and she had given Norah her first job when she'd shown up in LA five years ago with no connections. Odd for her to be doing grunt work. Hollywood was easier to fall than rise in. She would say hello when Garton was done.

As Norah walked over, however, Penelope headed down the hallway. Norah picked up her pace, then screeched to a halt as a rip near her knees sent a single tube bead clattering to the floor. Shit.

"Penny!" Norah shouted. The witch didn't turn. Norah walked as fast as she could, keeping her stride short.

"Penny," she called louder and touched the witch's arm when she caught up. The woman turned with a blank expression on her face. At first, Norah thought it was a classic case of "Have-we-met" Hollywood rudeness. "Hey. It's me, Norah."

Nothing. Penelope's face stayed as blank as raw pulp, her eyes shifting in and out of focus. She turned her head very slowly as if it were submerged in viscous pitch.

"Pleased to meet you. I have to get back to work." Penelope continued down the hallway, her feet slapping the tile like sandbags. Something was off.

Someone shouted in the ballroom behind her. Norah turned, and a second yell joined the first, then low-grade panicked chatter rose from the ballroom. Norah started to run, ignoring the pop-pop-pop as her dress bled its embellishment. Shit. She was sure Stan had meant it as a loaner.

The hall opened into the ballroom, where the crowd was backing away from a human-sized white rat facing off against the fourth maintenance wizard. The rat's mouth and jagged incisors dripped with blood, and the wizard's wand trembled in his white-knuckled grip.

The magical energy in the room shifted so suddenly that Norah grabbed the nearest wall to balance. She closed her eyes. Someone worked light magic at the top of the room. She rushed to unzip her clutch, impeded by the emerald acrylics she'd grudgingly decided to wear. Her fumbling fingers swiped air as the clutch dropped to the floor.

When she sank to her knees to pick it up, her skirt split from knee to hip. She was past caring about flashing her Spanx to the glitterati. Another rip echoed. Norah checked the structural integrity of her dress, which was more of a distressed tube top at this point, then heard a crescendo from the top of the ballroom.

There was a deafening crack and the air pressure dropped. Norah's stomach dropped too as the floating Emerald City shuddered and descended half an inch, straining against the last threads of magic keeping it aloft. She grabbed her purse and took a deep breath to steady her fingers as she plucked at the tiny enamel zipper.

From now on, dresses with pockets only. Her shaking fingers gripped the pull with a *zzzzzip*, and the wand was in her hand.

It was too late. Norah's eyes glowed with magical sight in time to see the last threads of magic snap. The green glass city plummeted, met by the terrified cries of the hundreds of well-heeled people on the ballroom floor. An actress in flowing silver tripped on her gown as she ran, the fall barely saving her from being shish-kebabbed on an emerald spire. Glass shattered.

The Emerald City was on the floor. Except…that wasn't right. It hadn't fallen all the way. Instead, it had been caught about five feet off the ground. Screams and protests rose from the writhing pile of celebrities underneath. They eventually got to their feet and began to stream out, revealing a single straining figure. Garton Saxon.

The light elf was in the dead center of the falling chandelier. Symbols glowed on his bulging muscles as he held the scale model aloft with branching beams of magical light.

Norah shot blue magic out of her wand to help him. Other witches and wizards who weren't in the drop zone joined her, pulling wands out of purses and breast pockets. Even Madge had flown to the edge of the chandelier, little wings working overtime as she helped hold the disk up. A steady stream of people crawled to safety, shedding stilettos, sequins, ostrich feathers, and Swarovski crystals in the fray.

Norah kept the magic flowing, straining against the heavy glass for several minutes until the marble floor beneath the chandelier was clear of people.

Clear except for Saxon, that is, who hadn't twitched from his strongman stance.

Norah cleared her throat. "We need to keep this thing floating while Garton Saxon gets out. Everyone who can grab hold, do so." She diverted a magical aid into her vocal cords for amplification. An elf to her left bent light, and a wizard laid the foundations of a support spell.

Even a few tux and gown-clad humans moved forward, holding the glass up with simple muscle. The money these people had spent on personal trainers was finally paying off.

It was enough. It would have to be enough. Norah nodded at Saxon. "*Go!*"

The beams of light streaming from his fingers fell in waves as he released them. The Emerald City sagged, fractures deep inside the glass structure crackling like calving glaciers. Magic and teamwork barely edged out gravity.

Norah strained, pouring everything in her wand and all of her resources into the stream of blue light holding up the glass. A final seam near her right boob popped.

Saxon slipped out from beneath the edge of the glass disk as the front of her dress flapped around her ankles, a lolling tongue of destroyed silk and beads.

A starlet in pink yelped in alarm at the sight of Norah's sweat-drenched taupe bra.

Norah rolled her eyes. Hollywood. "Let's lower the glass to the floor." She inched the magic lower, easing the emerald glass onto the tile. The taller spires disintegrated as they settled, and the sounds of glass cracking filled the room for another minute.

Finally, it was over.

Norah's wand clattered to the floor. She left it there, nestled in a drift of crushed green glass, and doubled over with effort. When she stood, she almost tripped on the loop of fabric pooled at her ankles, the last remnants of her dress. Stepping out of it, she shivered in her underwear as a room full of the most powerful people in Hollywood looked at her in disgust and admiration.

Garton Saxon was terminally unreadable. His measuring gaze consumed her control-top compressive corset shapewear as he appeared at her side.

"What's a girl like you doing in a grandma getup? I pictured you in red lace."

Norah was too tired to be disgusted. "It's not my fault Clara Bow was the size of an underfed sparrow," she muttered. She grabbed Saxon's shoulder.

"What did you do to that maintenance witch?" she whispered. Surprise barely registered on his face.

"You must be exhausted." He removed his flowing charcoal velvet robe and placed it around her shoulders. "I'll try to keep the panty pics off TMZ."

Norah buttoned the robe without taking her eyes off the elf.

"You and I ought to have lunch," he added. "Seeing how we're both magicals taking this town by storm."

Norah's eyes became slits. "I would love to dig deep and discover everything you've done." She spoke lightly. "You know, across your long career. Sounds fun."

Saxon chuckled. "In that case, it's a date."

CHAPTER SIXTEEN

Norah's phone burned a rectangular hole in her skull. She stared at it, yelled at herself to stop staring at it, put it in her pocket, took it out to make sure the ringer was on, turned the ringer off and on again to double-check that it was on, and then nearly jumped out of her seat when it buzzed in her pocket. She scrambled to retrieve it, disappointed to discover it was another telemarketer.

"Remind me to devise some evil anti-telemarketer curses. I want to go full hellfire," she told Madge. The pixie was busy typing an email on her phone, a task she usually completed with her feet. Given that she was about the same size as the phone, she often looked like she was playing a game of *Dance Dance Revolution*. It was entertaining and very distracting.

"One second," Madge wrapped up her secretarial jig. "Who are we cursing?"

"Telemarketers."

Madge's flapping wings grew loud in the silence.

"You need to stop staring at your phone."

"If the trap springs, I don't want to miss it. Timing is everything." Norah resisted the urge to stare at the black rectangle. Then gave up and glanced at it. No new messages.

Madge snorted derisively. Norah was amazed that such a small, deep noise could come from such a small being.

Her phone dinged, and Norah's adrenaline fired. It was Andrew. She opened the message with shaking fingers. It was a photo of Leaf riding Pepe around the apartment.

Cute, but not what she was waiting for. Still, she showed Madge, who cooed dutifully. Norah put the phone on the table, which continued to draw her eyes.

"Have you considered distracting yourself with work?" Madge asked pointedly. "We gotta keep the coffers full, babe. I don't want to end up on the streets, sharing a birdhouse with some derelict sapsucker."

"Technically, you'd be above the streets." Norah laughed.

"We all gotta land sometime. What time's your lunch with that USC producer?"

"Noon."

"Why don't you head over early? Drink a latte. Take a walk. Whatever."

It was either that or labor beneath Madge's judgmental glares for the rest of the morning. Norah grabbed her purse.

"Fine. No hot tub parties while I'm gone."

"No promises!" Madge shouted after her.

Norah shook her head and checked her phone for the millionth time.

Her air conditioning barely kept out the midday heat

on her drive downtown, and she was relieved when she made it into the Natural History Museum's parking structure. Even that was hot, though, and she relaxed when she slipped through the museum doors, the cold air a welcome slap in the face. After buying a ticket, she took the stairs up to the third floor and fell into the chessboard dark-and-bright space of the gem and mineral hall.

As a kid, the animals had pulled her in. Particularly the whale skeleton in the pavilion downstairs. As an adult, though, the model seemed sad, like it had taken a wrong turn into the inland air.

Now, she loved the rocks. Inside the Halls of Gems and Minerals, cubical displays of tourmaline and amber marched in clean rows. There were echoes in the orderly collections of the glowing shelves of the grimoire cache. Or maybe she was obsessive.

Norah wandered the calming labyrinth, her instinctual magical senses pulsing softly around her. Here and there, energy swelled and bloomed. Contortions in the natural vitality of the universe were associated with these crystals.

As always, Norah's feet pulled her to the Canyon Diablo Meteorite. Many hands had smoothed out the pockmarks on the polished black stone. A gift from the stars. She placed both hands on the rock, one of the few things in the museum visitors were allowed to touch. Then she let waves of pulsing silver flow through her fingers, then out of the top of her head and through her feet, looping into the black rock in cool arcs. She let it run a few cycles on her, and her steady fingertips pulsed with colorless light when she pulled her hands away.

Rocks were great. They couldn't ask you questions or

demand you get them lucrative sponsorship deals, or cry in your office.

The museum had a new display, a head-high block with jutting clusters of pale pink crystals that tapered into nasty spikes. This new display was not in a glass case. It wasn't even on a podium. A curator had plunked it in the middle of the floor. Maybe that was the point—to impress without artifice. The hall was empty, so Norah tapped the tip of a pink spike with a finger. She was rewarded with a drop of blood, a welling red sphere she put in her mouth.

"Ow." She sucked on it, annoyed that so little care would be taken with visitor safety, when the rock moved.

Norah darted away from the slicing points of the rotating crystal and scrambled for her wand in her purse.

"Can I help you find something, miss?" the rock asked.

Norah yelped, then caught herself. The crystal was not an undifferentiated massif. Instead, it was split into four limbs and an inhuman but unmistakable head. It was a crystal woman, rose quartz. Norah had read about them in a children's book about Oricerans.

Crystal people, calcified,
Gems and minerals with eyes
Rocky knees and craggy feet
Crunching up and down the street.

She'd never seen one in person.

"It's rude to touch strangers without permission," the crystal woman scolded haughtily.

"I'm, um, very sorry. You're right. I thought you were an exhibit," Norah stammered.

"I am an exhibit. That's no excuse. Next, you'll tell me

you'd feel comfortable cavorting around the Louvre, poking the Mona Lisa in the eye?"

"I'm terribly sorry," Norah rambled. "I'm Norah. Norah Wintery."

"Hmph. Technically I'm a curator. They get very fussy about me calling myself an exhibit. I'm no block of ignorite. The name's Lustre. It's a pleasure to meet you." This last bit was a transparent lie. "Would you like to read my interpretive sign?"

Lustre puffed up to display a metal plaque drilled into her chest. Norah hesitated. She wouldn't want people reading her boobs all day, but it felt rude to decline. Perhaps crystal people felt differently.

Lustre is a rose quartz crystal person and Oriceran native at the forefront of living natural history. She is graciously working with the Natural History Museum's gem and mineral department to further human understanding of geology and geomancy.

As Norah leaned in to read the small text, a magical current like the natural auras emitted by conventional Earth minerals tickled her nose. This was deeper and more vivid, however. Older, too.

Norah drew back. Lustre's gaze was even more piercing, thanks to the thin crystal spikes lining her eyes like lashes.

"You're a witch," Lustre observed. Norah nodded.

"What did you say your name was?"

"Norah. Norah Wintery."

"How do I....hmmm, Wintery. Ooh, now I remember! You're the Hollywood agent, right?"

"That's me."

Rock scraped on rock as Lustre perked up. The floor

shivered as the crystal woman moved closer to Norah. "You know, I've been thinking about getting out of museum curation and into show business. I've got this idea for a reimagined version of *127 Hours* where I play the boulder Aron Ralston's arm gets trapped under."

Norah moved back and bumped into a display case. A shrill alarm sounded.

"It's very erotic," Lustre whispered. The alarm blared again.

"Please step away from the exhibits," a piped-in voice instructed.

"Sorry," Norah whispered, half to Lustre and half to the room.

"Here, take a headshot." Lustre shifted a cluster of crystals near her shoulder to reveal a small cave-like compartment from which she retrieved a rolled-up glossy sheet.

"Thanks for the informative rock curation." Norah glanced at the headshot. It was divided into four different upsettingly familiar looks. Lustre in a cowboy hat. Lustre in a toga. Lustre in a lab coat. Lustre in a bathing suit.

Who was taking these headshots? Props weren't cheap, but using the Village People photography school was not a winning move. Still, she slipped the photograph into her purse and escaped into the sunlight outside the museum.

After waving down a rainbow-painted hand cart circling the green lawn outside, Norah blew a few bucks on an iced tea and a plastic cup of tajin-seasoned mango. She shoveled the dripping fruit into her mouth as she meandered through the rose bushes of Exposition Park and stuck her nose in one especially large orange-and-yellow flower. She sang it a quick greeting.

The flower didn't move. *Right. Earth flowers.* Nearby, a mother pushing a double-wide stroller edged away from her. Sighing, Norah found a shady tree to sit under while she waited for her meeting.

Her contact was a film producer who taught a few classes a year at USC. An angular man with dark hair, David Malcolm was direct to the point of rudeness. Still, he was extremely insightful and good at drawing out his students' best ideas.

At noon, Norah found him sitting on the shady half of the Natural History Museum's wide marble steps, accompanied by a cheerful college-aged witch. There was a third young person as well, whom Norah assumed was a student. They were buried so deep in an oversized hoodie that she couldn't tell if they were human.

David shook her hand and introduced her. "Katie is a witch. She enchanted the conference room where we run screenwriting workshops to drop green goo on anyone who fails the Bechdel test." He sighed. "We lost a lot of guest lecturers last year."

Norah snorted, and iced tea exfoliated her nostrils.

Katie grinned sheepishly. "My team just premiered a horror short about a cannibalistic tree."

"So, it eats other trees?" Norah asked.

"That's right. We cast a dryad as the monster, and I helped with magical effects. We put it together for about a thousand bucks."

"It looks great," Malcolm added. A flush of pride crept up Katie's neck. "Katie's the department's best-producing student. She's too savvy to ask you, but I wondered if your agency might have any summer internships."

"Hm. We're a green agency. Let me get back to you on that." Norah made a mental note. Katie's face fell. "If things don't work out at First Arret, I can pass your name to like-minded people."

The grin returned.

Malcolm gestured at the black hoodie. "This is Brym. I barely managed to wrestle him away from the campus' dark room."

A pale hand emerged from the shadowy depths. When Norah shook it, the fingers were cold.

"I take it you're a photographer?" Norah asked. After a muffled mumble, her phone beeped. Brym had airdropped her a magical portfolio. She pulled out her wand and tapped the link. The icon, a small scroll, zipped off the phone and fluttered in the air, where it unfurled in three dimensions into a slithering ribbon.

As the ribbon grew in width and length, perforations appeared along the sides and resolved into a film strip, or the magical equivalent. The celluloid danced in the air, moving faster as sunlight flashed through the frames. The speed of the scrolling strip increased, breathing life into the images.

The film clips showed young people and intimate scenes of campus life. One was an overhead shot of students in hammocks, passing snacks and books between them. One showed an open door at the end of a brutalist dormitory hallway. The lit room beyond looked inviting, full of music and laughter, but as the camera approached, the door shut, the warmth and camaraderie beyond the photographer's grasp.

Finally, there was a self-portrait of Brym. This time, the

voluminous hoodie enveloping his face was dark gray rather than black. The images were well-composed and evocative. Norah let the whole strip run, and it attracted the attention of a few people chatting on the museum steps.

"Brings new meaning to 'moving pictures.'" Norah smiled.

Brym coughed. "I'm interested in silent folk films of the 1910s." His voice was muffled.

"I have a box you should meet." Her sarcasm made the comment sound dirty.

"You said she wasn't a creep," Katie whispered to Malcolm, who rolled his eyes.

Norah coughed. "My pixie friend Cleo. She was turned into an enchanted crate by a cursed silent film. It's a whole thing. Sorry."

"It's cool." Brym waved her off.

As the four of them chatted, Norah felt a growing sense of excitement and the satisfying click of pieces snapping into place. She wasn't sure what the big picture would look like, but she was glad to have the outline. Talent to mix and match in infinite iterations.

Madge had been right. Norah left the meeting with a buzz of enthusiasm that reminded her why she'd started an agency.

The Frolic Room reminded Madge of a hollowed-out tree. Dim lighting. No frills.

It had its charms. Even in the middle of the afternoon,

with the sun the same color as the neon yellow sign identifying the bar, it was dark. The room was long and narrow, with a bar along one wall and a counter on the other. Behind the counter was a 1963 mural in which caricatures of Hollywood royalty cavorted under a Grecian colonnade.

A large martini sat on the counter in front of Marilyn Monroe's right boob. Madge sat on the glass rim, splashing her bare feet in the bone-dry gin. She normally would have gotten disgusted looks for doing that. People were ridiculous. If you could fly, your feet were as clean as your hands. She ripped off a chunk of olive, sloshed it around in the gin, and shoved it into her mouth.

"Ah, the taste of history."

No one at the bar looked at her because they were all fixated on her drinking companion, a willen. It was larger than most, the size of a Great Dane. The deep crevices between its fleshy wrinkles held onto light like black holes.

The willen had divided its front and back legs between two bar stools. When it stuck its tongue into its vodka soda, it had a thick coating of white fungus. Madge politely tried not to look.

"I don't think you can smoke in here," the willen squeaked.

Madge stared at her cigarette, which was the size of a splinter.

"I won't tell if you won't." A miniature cigarette produced less lung irritation than twenty minutes in traffic, or that was what the gnome who sold them to her always said. She took a drag. "You're barking up the wrong tree, or should I say squeaking down the wrong hole? Anyway, I'm out of the advice business."

"Don't you work at a Hollywood agency?" The willen eyed her skeptically.

"Yeah, but I make deals. Not small talk."

The willen's skin rolls rippled as it sighed, emitting a faint musk. A woman at the bar murmured something to the bartender, who shrugged and poured her a shot.

"On the house." The bartender winked.

The Frolic Room had quenched Hollywood's thirst for the hard stuff since 1934. It had almost certainly operated during Prohibition, so the matchbox of a bar had seen weirder shit than the wheelings and dealings of a pixie, guaranteed. No matter how bizarre her associates were.

As it removed its face from its beverage, the willen reached into a skin fold on its chest. Metal objects rattled like coins in a rubber sack until it pulled out a tiny shining antique eyeglass chain in perfect condition.

"It's an original. Authentic. Made for a Victorian doll."

"Haunted?" Madge asked, wings fluttering with excitement.

"If that's important to you. An eyeglass chain from a haunted doll with haunted eyes."

An almost-inaudible squeal escaped Madge's throat. "Now you're just being rude. Willens never give up their treasures." She splashed him with a kick of gin to underscore her point.

"Normally, you'd be right. I was going to make an exception today. If you're not in the advice business…" The willen's voice trailed off, its skin drooping as it moved a sad paw back to its neck.

"What do you want?" Madge asked. The paw paused,

hovering where the chain best caught the light. The infinitesimal links swayed enticingly. Madge salivated.

It usually took an emergency to part a willen from anything that reflected light. She'd seen one of the creatures cross the 101 during rush hour to pick up a crumpled ball of aluminum foil.

On the TV screen behind the bar loomed Dracula, his shadow crossing the face of a white-gowned woman lying in a bed. Madge shifted. Maybe this was an emergency. She leaned forward, ignoring the rancid breath as the willen lapped its drink.

"A handful of my ruffian cousins have fallen out of touch. Mice shifters. Rare. Stopped talking to their parents. Stopped going to the warren moots. Weird. They're not nice boys, but they're social creatures. You know?"

"Sure." Everyone except for film editors and standup comedians was a social creature. She didn't say that, though.

"So I hear from this gnome—not out of the kindness of his heart, mind you. I had to give up an antique cocktail ring covered in freshwater pearls for the pleasure of his information—that some devilish trap has snapped shut on them. Someone's using them to make moves, like they're puppets. Crazy shit."

"What do you want me to do about it?" Madge's gravelly voice dropped an octave as she blew out a long trail of smoke.

The willen leaned in, breath thick, gesturing with a yellowing claw for Madge to come closer. Wings whipping, she flew to him and shook droplets of gin onto the counter below.

"I want you to break into the Silver Lion offices," the willen whispered.

"I think you're mistaken about the nature of my skills," Madge replied.

"Hmmm. It's not just about getting onto the studio lot or any…human impediments. I got more keys tucked away than a janitor in a lock factory. The offices are protected with a magical ward. Sturdy shit. Serious voodoo."

"The bigger the treasure, the thicker the door," Madge mused.

"Exactly. You're a gal about town, so I wanted to know if you had any advice about who to talk to about my little problem."

"A locksmith. Of a sort."

"Uh-huh."

Madge's wings blew the willen's breath back into its face, and it winced. Served the thing right. Maybe it could steal a fancy gold toothbrush next. She sighed. "You'll want to talk to a wizard known as the Mechanic. Spends all his time at the Hollywood Smog Garage."

The willen grinned. A rope of spittle flecked with bits of moss connected its top lip to its bottom. Madge shuddered. There was a plink and a splash, then the eyeglasses chain lay coiled in a sparkling pile at the bottom of her martini glass. Through the gin, she saw the willen tucking a few stray spoons from the bar into its stomach folds.

"Thanks—" she started.

The willen was gone. All that was left was a lingering musk and the uncomfortable stares of six bar patrons. Madge flipped them the bird in quick succession. The woman at the bar squinted, too far away to see what

Madge was doing. Sometimes she regretted living large. Human eyesight was too miserable to appreciate obscene pixie gestures, a waste of her extensive knowledge.

Pleasant fumes wafted to her, the liquor in the almost-full martini cool and inviting.

"What am I gonna do with all that gin between me and my new bling?" she muttered. Then, laughing maniacally, she raised her big arms into a graceful point and dove in.

The storm drains beneath the Smog Garage were rarely used, and clots of dust and urban excretions collected around their dark rectangular openings.

Everyone called the wizard who ran the place the Mechanic. He slid out from under a Prius, wiping grease infused with magic off his hands. He'd never had an affinity for wood and twirled the combination wrench he used as a wand around his finger.

The actress-slash-barista who owned the Prius had begged him for something that would stop her catalytic converter from being stolen. Six times was enough. After debate, the Mechanic applied a glamour that made her car look like the converter had already been stolen. To amuse himself, he'd added a bonus backup curse that would make every song the thief listened to for a month sound like a Gregorian chant.

The Mechanic had just put away his tools when long, flesh-colored shapes oozed from the storm drains. Frowning at the click of their nails on the concrete floor, he crossed his arms. He had a soft spot for the big hairless rats, but some of his most expensive tools were also his shiniest, and he had to pay rent like everyone else.

"Hey, folks." He slipped a titanium diagnostic probe into a pocket and zipped it shut.

The greased golden ring on his index finger slipped off easily, and he prepared to throw it on the floor as a distraction from the more expensive items.

There were four willens, the most the Mechanic had seen together. They paced in agitated circles around the silver Prius. He put two fingers on his wand. Maybe he could make the garage look like it had been robbed.

The Mechanic sighed. It had been a long day. He pulled a metal chair out of a corner and waited. The largest willen broke off from the crowd. As he sidled over to the Mechanic's chair, precious jewels appeared in his paws, and he fondled them before they disappeared back into pale pink skin folds. There was a long flash of a golden crown studded with some precious Oriceran gemstone whose colors shifted from blue to maroon.

Shit. This wasn't some lackey. The Mechanic was sure the big rat was letting him know he was the reigning king.

"I'm Ryland." The approaching willen smiled.

The Mechanic nodded, suppressing a perverse impulse to bow. "Are you here to deliver good news or bad news?"

"All news is delicious." The willen smacked his lips.

"Not to me." The Mechanic leaned back and waited.

"We need a lock picked. Big beast of a thing with all the magical bells and whistles."

A willen at the periphery of the Mechanic's vision plucked four shiny gold screws out of a plastic tray resting on a wooden bench. "Your information might be outdated.

I'm walking on the bright side of the security business at the moment."

Near the Prius' front tire, a paw inched toward a silver hex wrench that nicely caught the late evening light. "Hey!" The Mechanic turned. "That's my lucky hex wrench."

Ryland hissed at his companion, and the paw retreated.

"The job might not be right with the law, but it's right with justice," Ryland told him. The Mechanic leaned forward as the creature spun a tale about his cousins and weird rumors that had started circling in Oriceran and Earth. The Mechanic had to admit something was up. Even his human mechanics had started talking.

"I might be persuaded to take the job," the Mechanic admitted.

"We have shinies. Sparklies, too." Ryland laughed, and small gold trinkets glittered in the dark creases of his throat.

"I'll call you with an estimate if you meet my first demand."

"What's that?" the willen asked.

"I want my diagnostic scanner back."

The willens sighed in unison, their loose skin pulsing. The scanner dropped to the floor with an alarming crunch.

The Mechanic loosened his grip on his wrench wand. "Don't let the garage door hit you in the tail." Before he finished the sentence, they disappeared into the dark rectangle of the storm drain.

CHAPTER SEVENTEEN

Norah put the sapphire-blue walkie-talkie up to her mouth. "Bubblegum for Big Faun." She stared at the small device, then, cursing, took her finger off the button—a step she had repeatedly forgotten.

The receiver crackled to life, the static laced with traces of green magic. "Gofer Big Faun. What can I do for you, Bubblegum?" Amusement laced her father's voice.

"You're supposed to say over. Over."

"Copy that. Over, over."

"You only have to say it once. Over."

"Over."

Silence. Norah sighed and opened the door to the next room, where her father was collapsed in a beanbag chair, scratching Pepe behind the ears.

"I still can't believe you brought the goat," Norah stated. Pepe trotted over, snorted, picked up his tiny hoof, and stomped on her toe.

"Fuuuuuuuuuuu………rrrry monster." Swearing around her parents still felt wrong, even though both Lincoln and

Petra cursed judiciously. Sometimes in the Oriceran languages.

"He's fine. I deputized him." Lincoln patted the goat's head when he trotted back over.

"We have cell phones," Norah complained, staring at the blue receiver. "I'm not sure enchanting walkie-talkies to cover miles of territory was the simplest solution."

"Cell phones offer limited opportunities for cool nicknames." Lincoln stared at Norah like she was still five years old.

She sighed. Yesterday, the coordinates she'd tucked into every dead drop location in LA had disappeared. Each set of coordinates pointed at a different safe house location. All of them missing at once had thrown a huge wand into her family's hex. Norah had suggested they divide and conquer, but her stomach churned when her father loaded Pepe into his Subaru.

She waved. Pepe stuck out his tongue. "That goat is going to steal my birthright."

"Settle down, Esau." Madge's deep voice crackled. The pixie was sandwiched between the pages of a large encyclopedia—an entry on owls. She claimed that the weight of the book was soothing. As far as Norah could tell, Madge had avoided her proscription on crockpot parties, but the pixie was flying slowly today. She'd arrived licking an aspirin like a lollypop, her face concealed behind a dark-tinted monocle she'd affixed to her face with a hair tie.

Norah peered through the blinds.

"Stop peeking. They'll make us." Madge's voice barely filtered through the pages.

"I'm not peeking," Norah protested.

"Yes, you are." The pixie emitted a low moan.

"Are you okay? Did something happen?" Norah asked, peeking between the pages of the book. The tiny eye that met her gaze was bloodshot.

"Yeah, something happened. It's called gin. Now go away."

Norah left the pixie to drool on a barn owl photo and paced the room. Ten steps across. Ten steps back. The safe house was a one-bedroom cottage perched on top of a hillside halfway up Topanga Canyon, on one side of a triangular plot bordered by two roads. Sagebrush and honeysuckle sloped down under the broad shade of California live oaks. There were hot green hills in the distance, and a dappled mare occasionally trotted over to the corner of a pasture to consume great tufts of clover. Norah couldn't see any of it because Madge wouldn't let her look out the window.

After a half-hour, Norah had paced a dirty path into the hardwood floor. When her walkie-talkie crackled to life, she yanked it to her ear.

"Big Faun for Bubblegum, over," her father began.

"Gofer Bubblegum, over."

"I am in position at location four, over."

"Copy that, Big Faun. We are holding steady here at two, over."

"Copy that. Talk soon—"

Before he could finish, a small statue of a rearing stag near the doorway shrieked so loudly that the windows rattled. Something had tripped their perimeter alarm spells.

Madge was instantly in the air. The encyclopedia

slammed shut behind her. No more waiting; it was time. A blue mist flowed from the stag statue's mouth, forming a fist of light. Its fingers unfurled as it pointed down the hillside. As Norah thrust open the blinds, a horse whinnied in the distance.

The desiccated sagebrush along the hillside shook. Norah's knuckles were white on her wand.

A coyote trotted out from behind a low bush.

Norah slumped. After a glance over Norah's shoulder, Madge flung herself face-first onto a yellow velvet pillow.

"I'll go reset the perimeter," Norah told her. By the time she left the house, the coyote was gone. She made her way through a clump of dried grass, counting the protective crystal talismans woven into the fence's barbed wire. All accounted for. Her Hermes sneakers were covered in mud, and she wondered if luxury magical shoe repair was available in Hollywood yet.

She tapped her wand where the coyote had broken the perimeter. It was cooler here but not that cool, and beads of sweat dropped from Norah's forehead, sizzling against her wand's blue flow of magic.

Before she finished, Norah sent a bullet of blue gum magic racing along the perimeter they'd established around the safehouse, across the hillside, through the garden, and over a little stream that flowed into an overgrown drainage ditch across the access road. The bullet made two full circuits and zipped back into her wand with a satisfying pop. Pleased, Norah shoved her wand back into her pocket and wiped her hands on her black yoga pants.

When she looked up, she nearly dropped her wand. She

was face to face with the biggest wizard she'd ever seen. Well, not face to face. More like face to pecs.

How had someone so big gone through so much dry vegetation in silence? Norah stumbled, and a misplaced tree root under her left heel dumped her on her butt.

The echo of the alarm from the house reached her, but she heard no shouts of warning or support. *Shit*.

The hand she'd put out to break her fall scraped the edge of a paving stone, and she reached for her wand with a palm slick with blood. The blue gum eucalyptus absorbed the blood, returning healing magic that temporarily clotted the wounds.

Where was Madge? She must have thought the coyote had returned, or that Norah had tripped the alarm herself during repairs.

As she opened her mouth to shout, the enormous wizard extended a muscled arm to her. He wore a device on his wrist like something from a nineteenth-century medical manual. An articulated glove like an exoskeleton, carved from wood and polished to a gleam. Long wooden cylinders were screwed into the wood above his first, second, and third fingers.

Three wands. Triple shit.

Norah had never seen anyone use three wands before. It was lunacy, like using a flamethrower as a pointer.

He was twice her size and had three times the firepower.

Norah opened her mouth to warn Madge about the intruder when the wizard pointed at her. Ropes of magic shot from his first two wands, one deep indigo and one blazing orange. They twined together like friendship bracelets. The instant before the blast hit her throat, it was almost pretty.

With a crash, the twining magic pinned her to the ground, half-choking her as it pressed her windpipe into the soil. She tasted iron as her tongue scraped across her teeth.

I'm being choked to death by a blueberry vanilla swirl.

She could barely move her wand hand. Flexing her fingers, she traced a minute circle off the ground, cross-hatching it with rays extending outward like a child's drawing of a sun. She twisted her wrist awkwardly and sent the spell to her head. As magic slammed into magic, it cracked. Her spell stretched into a protective hoop around her neck, tearing through the constricting purple and white noose in its path.

Whomever this wizard was, he was very powerful...and batshit-crazy. She had dual-wielded wands on exactly two occasions, and she had only performed well-known spells she had practiced for months.

This guy was winging it.

Her protective spell worked, and Norah felt a pinprick of pride as the pressure on her windpipe eased enough for her to breathe. She had developed this spell after a conversation with one of her parents' hacker friends about parallel programming. If you unraveled an opponent's magic in twenty different places, it was hard for them to keep up repairs.

The magic around her neck weakened in six locations. Norah thrust her wand up, reinforcing the weakest with a glowing blue stab, then gasped as the loop popped open. She barely rolled away in time to avoid a lilac fireball. She covered her face as an army of burrs poked through the thin black fabric of her pants.

"Fly, my pretties," she croaked. Her sneakers glowed as she leapt to her feet and jumped backward in a soaring arc that took her the eight feet to the house.

The wizard barreled forward. Where his huge boots stepped, dry blades of grass crackled and smoked. Small orange flames licked at his heels.

Shit. He was pulling power from the life energy around him. It was an easy way to amplify your power. It was also dangerous and illegal.

The wizard pointed all three wands, and power flowed into him from the nearby forest. Thin rays of sunshine hit the man's face as the leaves of the towering live oak above him died on the branch and burst into dust. Seconds later, color flowed out of the great trunk, and the wood blackened and split. With a crack, it burst into flame and fell backward, lighting the forest beyond.

The heat of flames reddened Norah's face. Shit. If she didn't take this guy down in the next sixty seconds, the fire might swallow her.

The wizard activated his third wand, and pulsing crimson magic joined the purple and white.

Great. A strawberry swirl.

Topanga Canyon was a witchy place, and the Silver Griffin agents who had built this safehouse had chosen a plot of land atop a small ley node. Norah reached into this energy source and pulled its magic into her, letting it move in a great flowing circle between her and the earth. She drew a spiral in the air in front of her and a churning cone sprang forth, ten feet high, drilling toward Edward Wandhands.

She called this spell "I'm-rubber-and-you're-glue." It was designed to turn a spell back on its casters and had been beta-tested by more than a decade spent in a house filled with prankster older brothers. Very effective against practical jokes, although Norah hadn't tested it against war magic.

The deflection spell picked up steam as it crossed the ground to the mountainous wizard. Then the stream of red magic twisted into a vortex, and Norah's heart sank.

A magical well was the first spell she'd learned to cast. It was a tiny hole you could pour magic into. A well would snuff it if a spell got out of hand. The magic was useful defensively, too. Usually, it stopped a magical squabble dead. However, a wizard generally didn't have two more wands churning spells behind it.

Norah slowed her deflection drill, steadying her hand against panic. Behind the crimson well, the purple and white magic streams had splintered into tiny shards, brutally pointed and fletched with light: arrows of magic, suspended and waiting. When the well sucked up her drill, the war wizard would release them. Norah would be lucky if she could stop half of them.

A smoking orange fire roared behind the enormous man's black silhouette, and a second tree dropped. Norah blinked, and the ash on her eyelashes fluttered to the ground. A speck of charcoal broke off a nearby tree and flew to the wizard. Fire-altered air currents? No, the trajectory was familiar.

It was Madge. Dodging cinders and risking her paper-thin wings against errant sparks, the pixie flew her butt off toward the wizard. If he saw her, it would be over in seconds. A scrap of his enormous power could rip her guts out easier than swatting a mosquito.

Norah couldn't let him see her. She coaxed power from her drill into the shape of an enormous rabbit the size of the mare in the nearby pasture. The wizard looked at it, confused.

"Fuzzy bunnies? That's the best you've got, you pathetic little witch?" His deep baritone boomed above the roaring fire at his back. Norah cringed. There was no emotion there. It was like being insulted by a volcano.

The wizard sent a tendril of purple magic toward the bunny. When it made contact, the magic collapsed and blew a stream of water toward the wizard. Against the glowing flames, it was steam before it hit his face.

She didn't think it was the heat turning him red. Fury rising, the wizard's hand moved, and the magic-sucking crimson well moved to Norah's deflecting drill. Ten feet. Five feet.

Then the wizard's finger plunged to the earth, driving the crimson magic into the ground, where it dissipated in the bedrock.

Now.

Norah threw her full force at her reflecting drill, and it surged forward. Where the blue magic touched the ground, fires fizzled out. Norah squinted, barely able to pick out shapes in the smoke. *There.* Madge rode the wizard's wand finger like a bucking bull, tearing at the skin of the knuckle with her pointy acrylic nails.

Bless the dwarves for inventing everlasting glue.

The wizard reached over to slap Madge with his free hand, but it was too late. The drill hit the wall of hovering purple arrows, and they spun back to their source. It was like watching a dandelion puff suck its seeds out of the air and back into its head.

The wizard screamed, and Norah leapt as high as she could. When her magical sneakers kicked in, she soared through the air. Below her, the enormous wizard was pincushioned by pale violet darts, a bleeding human porcupine.

A wounded animal could still be dangerous, and Norah positioned herself in the air so she landed on his wrist below the apparatus that held his three wands. These she sawed off with magical disks and encased them in a blue orb that would absorb any residual magic. She started to pull at the wooden glove of the wizard's hand, then stopped and swallowed bile when she realized the thin spindles of wood were screwed into his hand bones.

"*Madge!*" Norah shouted.

The pixie crawled out from below the wizard's wand arm.

"Hey, boss. I think it's time we talked about a raise," Madge replied, coughing.

"You're smoking," Norah replied.

"Don't I wish."

Norah sent out a small blue thread of magic to put out the tiny fire on the point of Madge's right wing. As the pixie looked over, another coughing fit wracked her small body.

"Thanks, boss," The pixie flew unsteadily to Norah's shoulder. Norah winced as her acrylics dug into her neck for support but kept her mouth shut. The pixie deserved a thousand crockpot parties.

A groan at her feet announced that the wizard was still alive. The purple and white magic spears had gone, and he leaked blood like a sieve. The battle might be over, but the war was just beginning.

Dissolving her reflective spell, she sent two bursts of magic into the wizard's torso. The first stabilized him and began knitting up his wounds. The second spell made copies of his red blood cells, which would keep him alive—a course of action Norah was not at all sure about.

As she leaned over the man's enormous chest, Madge's nails dug deeper. Norah's eyes widened in horror. The wizard was still conscious. *Shit.*

Never look a gift horse in a thousand seeping puncture wounds. "Who are you?"

The answering wet rasp was barely audible. Norah touched the wizard's throat, which had been punched by a magical arrow. Blue magic coursed around the hole until the gurgling stopped.

"Who are you?" she repeated.

Crackling fire drowned out the man's heavy breathing. "Gus," he finally whispered. "Hired muscle."

"Hired by who?" Norah asked. She tapped him on the chest, ignoring his screams as her fingernail touched raw flesh. Moving her wand in an intricate pattern, she paused the healing spells working in his body. He would stay stable, but his wounds would only knit together at the snail's pace of normal human healing.

Color seeped out of the wizard's face, and cold beads of

sweat dotted his forehead, although they were quickly evaporated by the nearby fire.

A crack startled her, and she barely had time to yank her wand up to stop a burning branch from using her as kindling.

The rectangle of the walkie-talkie dug insistently into her hip. Norah sighed and picked it up.

"Bubblegum to Big Faun."

Her father picked up instantly, voice anxious.

"Gofer Big Faun. Over."

"How many water elementals do you know? Over."

"Maybe a dozen? Over."

Norah sighed and told him to send them all over. She wove a heat shield around herself, Madge, and the fire wizard, then tried to push the fire back on itself. It wouldn't last.

The wizard's glassy eyes lost focus. He was slipping away.

"Oh no, you don't." Anger and firelight flickering across Norah's face, she dug an index finger into a weeping hole below the rib cage. The pain brought him around.

"Who hired you?" she asked. The wizard whimpered and pressed his mouth shut.

She was running out of time. "Tell me who sent you, and I will take you to an air-conditioned room and stuff you with painkillers."

She pushed the tip of her finger in another quarter of an inch, wondering if there would be enough soap in LA to wash her hands when she was done.

Another whimper.

"Play a dangerous game and win a dangerous prize. I'm

counting to ten, and then I'm going inside. You can stay here in a nice little oxygen bubble and heat shield. I'll leave you some water. I'll keep the temperature at a nice comfortable one hundred and thirty, maybe one hundred and forty degrees. I'm sure you'll live a long time. Hours, at least."

Something viscous poured under her nail as she pushed her finger in further. "One," she said. She hoped her threat to sous vide the guy would be enough.

An orange-red plant in Norah's peripheral vision caught her eye. It was a pencil cactus, knobby red stems baking in the heat. The plant reminded her of the red sunbursts on the Dark Hound website, the ones identifying murdered Silver Griffin agents. "Two. Three. Four."

The wizard's breathing rate increased. Good. He was afraid.

"Five."

"I'll tell you everything! Please, take me inside."

Norah eased off the pressure on the wizard's abdominal wound. "Name now. Air conditioning later."

"How do I know you won't just kill me?"

"If I wanted to indiscriminately murder people, I'd be working for the assholes who hired you. Six."

More panicked breathing. Then: "Her name is Wendy. She's an old Silver Griffin dispatcher. Messed-up hands."

Relief ballooned around her. After pulling her finger out of the mercenary wizard's stomach, she scrambled to her feet and released a protective net of magic that would hold the fire off for a few minutes.

With Madge clinging to her shoulder, she trudged to the house, pulling the wizard behind her with antigravity magic. Changing the laws of physics took energy, and she was exhausted when she shut the door. Layers of protective magic surrounded the safe house. It wouldn't have lasted against the triple-wielding wizard, but it could hold off a wildfire for another half-hour.

The other houses in the canyon wouldn't be so lucky, though. A panicked equine scream cut through the flames, jolting her out of her exhaustion. *The horses. Whoever's looking after them...*

Norah knocked the wizard out with a powerful stunning spell and, after taking a deep breath, left the protection of the safe house. Shoes glowing, she crouched and made a massive leap onto the roof.

The fire hadn't crossed the roads at the bottom of the hill. That was good.

After she rubbed her stinging eyes, Norah looked at the live oaks engulfed in flames. Fires were energy. If she could deplete that energy, she could stop the spreading blaze. Her nerves jangled at the thought. Filled with that much raw power, she'd be a minor god—or she'd be burned into witch jerky.

Another terrified whinny rose over the smoke. The fire was rapidly approaching the edge of the dappled mare's favorite clover patch.

Norah made a choice. She moved back two paces, her sneakers scraping the high-friction roof tile. Wand in hand, she filled her body with blue light, ran, and jumped.

She had never flown so high or so far. As she landed in a triangle between three burning oak trees, flames licked the blue light pulsing under her skin. Heat burned the soles of her feet even through her shielding magic. Anything but the enchanted sneakers would have melted.

She couldn't suck the energy from the fire into herself. She'd explode. No, she needed to channel it into a spell. Something bigger than anything she'd ever done.

Norah looked at her feet and began tracing powerful runes on the tips of the Hermes sneakers. Her wand wanted to draw on power from her body or the comforting pulse of the ley node at her feet, but she blocked those avenues, forcing the spell to draw energy from its surroundings. She sketched an outline of a wing. As it filled with dancing lines of blue, the fire in the trees around her snuffed out.

She drew another wing, and the extinguishing circle grew wider. The spell feasted on the fire's energy as the lines at her feet twisted and deepened.

By the time she finished the fourth wing, the fire had shrunk to a few orange patches, hot spots at the edge of a chilly, lifeless circle. Norah closed a final line with her wand, and four magical wings fluttered to life at her feet. They flapped chaotically as they lifted her two feet off the ground in uncomfortable jolts. She had made herself a pair of flying shoes, and they were trying to take off.

"Stop that." The wings folded reluctantly, and she dropped onto the smoking earth.

Her body still felt overstuffed with magic, and flares of energy jerked her limbs at odd moments. She sent this last reserve into the ley node at her feet, where the earth swallowed it with a slight vibration.

As she turned back to go inside, someone shouted at her from toe-level. "What exactly did you do?"

Madge had walked out to find her. The pixie was a huge opponent of bipedal movement. She'd taken to the ground with her wing wrapped in a Kleenex and hopped over pebbles and cobblestones.

Norah looked at the glowing wings on her shoes, which rustled eagerly at her glance.

"I just acquired an extremely expensive pair of shoes."

Stan found Norah in their complex's small pool, a turquoise puddle tucked into the leafy garden between the two condo buildings. Two stars were visible in the blue-gray smog overhead. She slipped under the surface for a few seconds, surprised that her feverish body wasn't boiling the pool water into steam.

Twelve hours ago, she'd left the safe house in the capable hands of half a dozen water elementals, who had been more than up to managing what little fire she'd left them. They had arrived ready to flex and had seemed disappointed by the reduced scale of the problem.

Water streamed off her face as she reemerged. Stan stood patiently under an avocado tree, munching on a lemon.

"How did things go with Gus?" she asked.

"Oh, he's safely tucked into some uncomfortable Oriceran lodgings."

"What's going to happen to him?"

Stan shrugged. "Justice, I guess. Maybe Trevilsom. He forged his cauldron, and now it's time to drink the soup."

"Quite a trick with the three wands," Norah ventured.

"Easy enough as long as you don't mind leaving chaotic destruction in your wake."

Norah dunked her head again. She'd spent the last two hours lathering herself in Oriceran aloe. She was pleasantly soporific but still the color of a tomato.

"Are your parents going to be okay on that air mattress?" Stan asked.

Considering that it had reality-bending properties and produced a memory foam mattress the size of a studio apartment, Norah thought they'd survive. "Yeah. Thanks." After a heated debate made hotter by the smoldering ashes of the safe house, Norah and her family had decided to wait until the next morning to go after Wendy.

"If you need anything else, I'm around the corner," Stan told her. Leaning over, he placed a small wooden statue on the pool's edge. As Norah swam over, water sloshed around the polished wood. It was another small carving of a bird.

She looked at the wings in the rippling turquoise light. They had been captured in an instant before flight. They looked like the ones she'd just enchanted onto her sneakers.

The dawn light was still thin and cold when Norah's mother pressed a cup of coffee into her hands. Her nose wrinkled at the first sip.

"What's in this?"

"Goat milk."

Norah sipped her drink. The milk had acidic grassy undertones. Not bad, but it was weird.

Petra looked at the fine white heat blisters on Norah's collarbone.

"You don't have to come today. Your father and I are, after all, professionals. Haven't entirely lost our touch."

"Are you kidding? I'm not gonna miss the big takedown."

A loud thump from the closet sent ripples across Norah's coffee cup. Without asking for permission, her mother flung open the doors. Inside, the Hermes sneakers flapped wildly, barely restrained by a net laundry bag. As Petra poked the bag, the right shoe slammed into the left and got tangled in the drawstring.

"You should buy them a proper cage." Petra tutted. "What are you feeding them?"

"They're shoes." Norah looked at her mother blankly. "So, sweat, I guess? Maybe a little toe fungus?"

"You've got to look after your feet, especially as you get older. I put a fresh bottle of goat's milk lotion in your bathroom."

"Hmm." Norah sighed. She hoped they would be able to track down Wendy today. One more night in her apartment, and her mother might reorganize her life beyond recognition.

"If you're coming, you'd better get dressed. Your father has breakfast ready in the kitchen."

"What percentage of that breakfast is goat-based?"

Petra's nose twitched as she churned through the mental arithmetic. "Forty?"

Norah sighed and hauled herself to the kitchen. "Fine. I'm wearing my new shoes!"

Wendy worked downtown at a diner identical to one you might find in small-town Ohio or Iowa. That meticulous verisimilitude was presumably why they charged eighteen dollars for waffles.

Norah and her parents found street parking around the corner and split into two teams. Petra watched the front, and Norah and Lincoln slipped down a narrow alley into a parking lot in the back. The asphalt was dirty, and it smelled like a dumpster. More than that, it was occupied by a black-clad teenager with green hair and a pirate's bounty of metal in her face.

The young woman was applying spray paint to a gray-painted wall bordering the lot. The emerging shapes were organic, vivid fungal whorls that marched up the wall in drooping arcs. It was an interesting mural. Lincoln cleared his throat.

"What are you doing here?" He put on his best Dad voice.

"Who's asking?" the teen retorted.

"I own this parking lot!" Lincoln stated.

"The diner owner is a thirty-something vegan with an undercut. You don't look like a thirty-something vegan with an undercut."

"I don't own the diner. I own the parking lot behind the diner. Scram!"

"Scram? What are you going to do, flash a switchblade and try to dance-fight me?"

Lincoln sighed. "How about twenty bucks to take a two-hour break?"

"Promise you won't paint over it?"

Lincoln looked at the young woman dimly. "I pinkie-swear."

The spray paint disappeared into a ratty backpack, and before Lincoln could blink, the girl had grasped his pinkie with hers. After plucking a twenty from his pocket, she absconded with it across a chain-link fence.

"I like your grasp of color theory!" Lincoln shouted. He and Norah settled behind one of the dumpsters to wait. She debated casting a sanitation spell on the sticky curb but decided not to waste the energy. An hour later, as the dawn light gained power, a beat-up sedan rolled into the parking lot, and Wendy got out.

Her hair was the color of leftover gravy, and as she lit a cigarette, Norah saw something was wrong with her hands. They caught her tying her apron strings as she walked across the parking lot.

Sensing something wrong, Wendy fled down the alley at Norah's approach, only to find a wand-ready Petra. She forced Wendy back into the parking lot.

"Hello, Wendy," her mother greeted. Wendy had dispatched calls to Norah's mother on dozen of occasions, and while they'd never been more than acquaintances, the betrayal had cut Petra surprisingly deep. The women faced off across a ten-foot stretch of dirty asphalt.

Wendy molded her alarm into a flytrap-sugar smile.

"Petra! Oh, my God! It's been years. I thought you might have hopped a portal to Oriceran."

Tossing her cigarette carelessly behind her, Wendy advanced on Petra, her arms open in a wide embrace. When they were almost touching, Wendy dove for her wand, plunging a twisted hand into her apron.

Norah was faster. A lasso of blue light constricted around the older witch's hand and yanked it skyward. The fireball spell discharged harmlessly into the air.

"*Calcifico*!" Petra shouted. Thick, slow-moving energy crept up Wendy's body, paralyzing her.

Norah and Lincoln flanked Petra. "You've just been petrified," Norah announced.

Petra smirked. "It's my specialty. Very useful when I had twin toddlers."

If Wendy had a comment about her new condition, it didn't make it past her frozen vocal cords. Petra removed the woman's wand, frowning at the twisted curl of her hands.

"Nice work, Mom. Let's get her to the car." Norah hoisted the frozen witch into the air with a small disk of electric blue magic.

Lincoln, who had always been adept at trickery and disguises, cast a roughshod glamour over Wendy to make her look less like a floating ice statue and more like an ordinary woman strolling beside them. Norah brought up the rear as they moved through the alley, poking Wendy's body with jolts of magic. As they rounded the corner, Norah's parents stopped dead.

"Shit," Lincoln cursed. Norah peered around his silvery head.

Her parent's minivan had been loaded onto a yellow tow truck.

Petra's mother inched forward, but Lincoln restrained her.

"Wendy's glamour won't hold up to municipal scrutiny."

"I told you it was a street-sweeping day," Petra muttered.

"The sign said alternating Wednesdays except in holiday weeks."

"It's not a holiday week," Petra observed.

"So, it shouldn't be alternating," Lincoln agreed. Norah shook her head. She had been towed within forty-eight hours of arriving in LA.

"The city has baptized you. Congrats," Norah stated.

After a quick family squabble, they determined that calling a rideshare was too risky. Andrew wasn't picking up, and it would take Quint too long to drive in from Venice. Their voices were so loud that they almost didn't hear the person trying to catch their attention.

"*Pssst*. Hey!"

It took Norah a minute to track down the voice. It was the green-haired teenager.

"Well, well, well, if it isn't Banksy herself." Lincoln sighed.

The young woman scratched her septum piercing. "I find Banksy's work corporate and uninspiring."

"He didn't mean it," Norah apologized.

"If you don't want my help, I can go," the teen mumbled. Her black clothing was thrifted, threadbare but carefully mended. A rip in her black jeans drew Norah's eye. There, stitching together the tear, were several silver-embroidered magical runes for protection from disease and passing silently through shadows. Several stick-and-poke tattoos traced out well-known simple spells on her arms. She eyed Petra's wand with interest.

Could it be a trap? Only one way to find out. "Please. We would love your help. I'm Norah."

The girl sniffed. "Name's Nostril."

"Pleasure to meet you...Nostril," Petra replied. The girl stared blankly for another moment before spinning and announcing, "Elevator's this way."

Nostril led them behind the Hall of Records' unmemorable massif to a set of rickety silver elevators under a blocky awning. They clambered inside, and Nostril pressed the number two with a greasy finger painted with glow-in-the-dark polish.

The machinery groaned to life. Lincoln's eyes darted to Norah. Should they be trusting a goth teenager?

"Did your parents name you Nostril?" Petra asked cheerfully. Lincoln rolled his eyes.

"They call me Nostril because it's my favorite place to put stuff. Or it was before Shay helped me get clean."

The elevator door opened into an abandoned hallway with sickly overhead lighting. Nostril led them through a set of swinging doors to an escalator, then into a wide gray tunnel.

"Welcome to the LA underworld," Nostril muttered. Norah had heard about this place. Miles of underground tunnels beneath the city. When they weren't being used for dystopian film shoots, they were abandoned. Nostril grinned. "Miles and miles of poorly lit concrete culverts stretch before you. Try not to get lost."

A slanting shadow cut a triangle across the concrete where a culvert fed into the tunnel. The shadow twitched and then dissolved into a human figure. She moved out, ankle-high boots splashing in a trickle of murky water.

Norah had met a lot of beautiful people, but the woman in front of her was on another level. She shone in the shitty light, even in a long-sleeve navy jumpsuit. A mechanism clicked into place between Norah's ears.

"You're Shay," she stated. "The Tomb Raider."

Shay Brownstone smiled, and Norah's heart fluttered. "Yeah, but don't spread it around. I'm doing a little work in these tunnels, following rumors about a case of pre-Prohibition magical moonshine. I see you've met my intern."

Nostril slouched more than someone with bones should be able to.

"This is my territory. You're welcome as my guests," Shay continued. "I have just the place for you. Nostril, lead these nice people to the old jail."

Nostril nodded and shot down a wide circular tunnel. After dropping the glamour, Lincoln helped Norah keep Wendy floating through the cramped spaces. They wove in and out of a series of concrete boxes, maintenance accesses, and dimly lit rectangular corridors until finally, Shay opened a door behind a dripping pipe.

There was a small jail cell inside: bars, narrow bed, the whole nine yards.

"Back in the good old days, the city used these tunnels for prisoner transport. Now it's all self-described 'urban explorers' making TikTok videos," Nostril grumbled.

"You'd better wait a few years before complaining about the good old days, young lady." Lincoln scoffed. "Otherwise, you'll have nothing left to enjoy when you're my age." He cheerfully shoved Wendy into the jail cell. Norah tapped the door with her wand and thick magical chains clanged against the metal, securing it.

Petra closed her eyes and pointed her wand. A fine cloud of transparent green magic washed over the frozen witch, gently erasing the spell that kept her locked inside her body. In under a minute, Wendy kicked the door hard and repeatedly with her worn-out white sneakers.

They let her wear herself out. Leather scuffed against the rusted bars until a loud crack bounced around the bare walls. The furious witch had broken a toe. Refusing to acknowledge the pain, Wendy curled up on the cell's narrow bench, drawing her feet up and wrapping her arms around her knees.

"Would you like me to heal that?" Norah asked.

"Fuck you!" Wendy spat.

"Suit yourself." Norah shrugged.

"What's your problem, Wendy?" Petra asked. "Is it money? Is that why you're doing this?"

Wendy snorted.

"You sent some brazen muscle after me," Norah said. "Almost burned down half the Santa Monica forest."

"Good," Wendy snapped. "Whatever it takes for them to understand what they did to me."

She massaged her right hand with her left. Knotted scars covered the woman's hands, curled into permanent talon-like arcs. The shiny keloidal skin climbed up under her long sleeves.

"When the Silver Griffins collapsed, nobody warned me. One day, I was in my treehouse doing my job, then all the communication lines went dead. The people who found me weren't very nice, and the Silver Griffins didn't do shit. Have you tried fixing two smashed hands with a splintered wand and no help?"

Petra moved forward and placed a hand on the bars.

"Wendy. I didn't know."

The imprisoned witch struck like a viper, bursting off the bench. Her talon hands raked toward Petra's face. Norah's mother moved away from the fury, catching only a thin scratch on her forearm. Seeing the blood well, she reached for her wand, then hesitated and pushed her thick hand-knitted sweater back over her arms.

"Years of my life, and not a single person came for me. Not until now." Wendy looked at Petra.

She spat through the bars, and it landed short. Norah poked the viscous globule with the toe of her sneakers.

"We can help you. There are spells for setting the bones in your hands. Healing your skin."

Wendy laughed, a shaking sound that retreated inside her body as she curled back on the bench. "It's too late for you and me. I'm not the only one crippled by resentment, among other things. Oriceran's gates have been thrown open, and chaos hurtles Earthward. The time for healing is over. The time for burning has just begun. Magic always rises to the top!"

The words knocked the breath out of Norah's chest. Her skin crawled as she walked to the laughing witch.

"Where did you learn that phrase?"

Wendy met her gaze and smiled, the cold in her eyes leaching the warmth out of Norah's face. She shivered.

"The world has abandoned us, but we have each other.

You'll see the pattern as soon as the fringes knit together. The spider's web will cover you all, now that we have our spider."

She said this as if she were talking about a god.

"Who is it? The spider? Your new leader?"

Wendy's eyes bored into her through the bars, shadowed by a shift in the light. Except…

It wasn't a change in light; it was a change in her eyes. The whites darkened and grayed and then…dissolved.

Acid thundered into Norah's esophagus as ash puffed from the now-empty eye sockets. She grabbed her wand and threw a spell toward the older witch, a generic healing wash. Nothing happened, or less than nothing. The woman's body sucked up the magic and sent it into the ground.

Had Wendy performed some primal, wandless magic? Norah filled her eyes with power and gasped when she saw the spell. Someone had cast an antimagic well using Wendy's life force as the power source. Any counter spell she sent to it would disappear.

The rot spread from Wendy's eyes across her face and raced down her neck. Her skin and organs turned to ash, and she looked like a skeleton uncovered at an archaeological dig. Then the angles of the bones collapsed inward until her body fell to dust. A single point of light winked out and died with Wendy.

A soft cry of dismay echoed off the concrete. After a moment, Norah realized it had come from her mouth. What had just happened? Who had cast the spell? Was someone watching them?

"What was that?" she asked. Lincoln was silent.

"I don't know," Petra whispered.

If she didn't know why, at least she could find out who. Norah gripped her wand and sent out a soft pulse of magical energy, checking for a trail. There!

A soft line of dripping acid-green magic ran from the dust pile that had been Wendy into a large pipe hanging from the ceiling. Tracking its trajectory, Norah kicked the cell's door open and ran into the tunnels. After it exited the small room, the pipe cut across the tunnel and rose into an access shaft twenty feet away. Norah craned her neck, trying to follow the magic. She was too far away.

She looked sternly at her feet. "We're going to take a quick trip." Glowing wings fluttered. "No funny business, and no stopping along the way. Got it?" The wings shivered. There would never be a better time to test this hazardous experimental magic.

After raising one foot, Norah flew.

The old spell on Norah's shoes had worked with her muscle energy and strength. It had been like jumping on a trampoline. Different, but not so different.

These refurbished Hermes sneakers were on another level. Using them was like riding a flying yoga ball, and despite every effort from the small muscles that stabilized her legs, she tipped backward. The shoes surged up and she fell for real, screaming.

Her feet caught her, turning her upside-down. She dangled, maintaining a death grip on her wand. It wasn't comfortable, but it would do for now. The shoes, flapping mightily, hauled her up the shaft as blood pooled in her face.

At least she was where she needed to be. Getting her

bearings, Norah touched her wand to the magic trailing up the shaft. It should have been thick so close to such a powerful spell. Instead, the traces were faint, and the magic disappeared as the shoes pulled her up.

"Take me back down!" Norah ordered. "Gently."

A faint leathery grumble echoed in the shaft, but the wings slowed their flapping and lowered her onto the concrete. The second she put a hand on the ground, the shoes dropped her, and she rolled across the floor. When she scrambled to her feet, her mother's eyebrows practically touched her hairline.

"They're new shoes. They need breaking in," Norah grumbled peevishly.

"What did you find?" Lincoln asked, eyes creased with worry.

"More questions," Norah replied. "The trail disappeared." Water dripping from an overhead pipe echoed off the walls.

"What wizard would have that kind of power?" Petra asked. Her question weighed down the cold, damp air.

CHAPTER EIGHTEEN

Norah tapped the magical whiteboard covering one wall of her apartment and a sketch of Wendy sprang to life, pushing scraps of magic out of its way. The image of the dead woman sent a chill up Norah's spine.

The board was covered with information. There were clusters around Vince, Wendy, and Garton Saxon. What was the link?

"Vesta, look for patterns."

Her magical home assistant floated over. "My crime-solving capacity is limited," the cylinder chirped. After ten seconds of beeping, Vesta stated, "All these events are associated with the city of Los Angeles."

"Very helpful!" Cleo shouted from across the room. Norah sighed and tapped the corner of the whiteboard. The images dissolved, and Norah's green wall of plants came back into focus.

Cleo was stoic, or she looked stoic. It was hard for a wooden crate to display complex emotions.

Norah dug around in her bookshelf until she found a

small notebook embossed with a tarot-card pattern. Frowning, she skimmed the spells inside. The book wasn't a grimoire because none of the spells worked. Rather, it was a lab notebook. Flipping to a blank page, she carefully wrote *Attempt #23* at the top.

"I appreciate the effort, but I wouldn't blame you for giving up," Cleo told her from across the room. The wooden crate sat in her usual spot atop Norah's coffee table.

"No talking from the test subject, please," Norah teased.

With the investigation into Wendy stalled, she had finally set aside an evening to work on her roommate's unboxing problem. First, she had to set the mood.

"How about a little music?" She clambered to her feet.

She approached the old radio her mother had given her, which she'd shoved between two plants. A thin coat of dust clung to the dials. Norah still had no idea if it worked. Plugging in the yellowed cord, she found a switch at the back and turned it on. Static blared.

"At least the power works." When she grabbed the channel dial between her thumb and forefinger, she was unprepared for the force of the magic that surged into her. A destabilizing wave of awareness hit her face and coursed through her veins.

After Norah reclaimed her balance, the room was different. How? It didn't look different. The TV, her plants, and Cleo's rough wooden corners were the same. A new underground river of awareness flowed beneath everything, however.

The energy from her small urban jungle of plants was very clean—green growth and an unconscious striving toward the hot ball of the sun. Sadness touched her heart as she turned to Cleo. The awareness that flowed into Norah from the wooden crate was complicated. Cleo's desire to escape her plywood prison and return to a living body warred with an impulse to shrink and be less trouble, and to refrain from bothering anyone with her condition.

A burst of static caught Norah's attention, and she turned the dial to seventies rock. Soothing licks of an electric guitar filled the room. As she let go of the dial, the awareness drained out of her and back into the radio.

Norah sat on her sofa and put her face close to the wooden box.

"You're not a bother," she assured her. "I'm sorry I haven't cracked the curse, but I like having you here."

The spirals Norah thought of as Cleo's eyes glowed.

"Where's this coming from, doll?" the pixie asked, suspicion lacing her voice. "Did you join a new-age cult? Bad idea. Wave a crystal around all you want, but don't give anyone money."

It was hard to read a plank's expression, but Norah thought Cleo was deflecting. A soft sigh shivered through the crate.

"I appreciate the sentiment," Cleo whispered. " No more moping! Let's show this curse our worst."

Norah grinned. "Always." She put her chin in her hands. There were dozens of spells they hadn't tried. "What if you looked at your reflection in a cursed mirror? Like two negatives making a positive?"

"Where are we going to find a cursed mirror?" Cleo asked.

"Any Goodwill dressing room?" Norah replied. Cleo

chuckled, and Norah considered the problem more seriously. "I'll ask around. Stan might be able to help. In the meantime, there's something I want to try." Norah looked at her. "It's risky."

"I doubt you can make the problem worse," Cleo shot back.

"Risky for me, I mean. I want to try using two wands at the same time."

"A devil's three-way!" Cleo exclaimed.

Norah choked down a laugh. "Sure." She retrieved a wooden cylinder from her bookshelf. The case was a work of art, courtesy of Stan. A six-inch length of polished white cedar nestled in the velvet lining. White cedar trees could grow through solid rock, and the wood was effective at penetrating other magic. Norah planned to break through the curse with the white cedar and restore Cleo's body with the blue gum eucalyptus, ideally without doing a deposit-losing amount of damage to her apartment.

"I'm going to try to crack the curse's protective coating," Norah announced, whipping the white cedar through the air a few times. Her eucalyptus wand stayed in her pocket. One thing at a time.

The white cedar would take some getting used to. The magic from the blue gum eucalyptus was like water. It washed and flowed. This new wand produced jagged white power that moved with the imprecision of lightning. With a flick, Norah crafted a spear of light barely bigger than a toothpick and sent it hurtling toward Cleo.

The terra cotta base of her aloe plant exploded in a burst of white sparks.

"Shit!" Norah exclaimed. The curse had confounded her spell, misdirecting it three feet to the left.

The leaves of the big fiddle leaf fern sitting next to her aloe rustled, yellowing at the edges in disapproval.

"It was an accident," she told the assembled foliage. She apologized profusely to the aloe, which she'd denuded to treat her burns, and carefully snuggled it into her best mixing bowl, patting dirt around the edges. The aloe turned to the sunny window in a stiff huff.

Okay, so she couldn't send a spell directly at the box.

"What if I send the spell everywhere?" she blurted. "Create a three-dimensional grid of magical points…"

The plants behind her rustled uncomfortably. After a moment of silence, Cleo spoke up. "I hope you have more mixing bowls."

A few practice runs with the white cedar later, Norah was ready, or as ready as could be. She inhaled deeply, allowing the magic beneath her feet to fill her body.

Drawing small runes with her left hand, Norah filled the air around Cleo with needle-sharp white spears of magic dispersed at even intervals like wicked snow. Clenching the blue gum eucalyptus in her right hand, she sent its magic flying.

Norah felt a surge of satisfaction as three of the spears hit hard magic. Her heart beat faster as she closed her eyes and abandoned her rational ideas of space. She urged the engaged spears onward and coaxed them as they burrowed into the malicious coating of the curse. The dark magic pushed back, snapping one spear, then two. The third spear cracked through the protective spell, and a thin, unstable hole opened.

"Something's wrong!" Cleo shouted. Norah clenched her eyes tighter and ignored her. She didn't have much time. Her right hand thrust forward and blue magic rushed into the hole, a typhoon of energy that broke against the knot of the old charm inside in a thundering wave and pulled it out.

Yes! The turbulent spell eroded the curse's protective shell and Norah poured herself into it, becoming the torrent, pulling and pulling until there was a pop. The magic spilled over and subsided.

Norah opened her eyes. On the coffee table in front of her was Cleo.

She was still a wooden crate.

"What the fuck was that?" the cursed pixie shouted. Norah frowned. Something had happened. She would have bet Leaf's life on it. If she hadn't broken Cleo's curse...

Acrid smoke filled her nostrils, and Norah heard a spark as the lights in her apartment went out.

On the sideboard, the antique radio was smoking.

"No, no, no, no, no." Norah rushed over and grabbed the artifact in gentle hands. It was dead. The wires of its guts were melted in a hot puddle, and the wood was black. More than that, there wasn't a drop of magic left inside.

"This is bad," Norah stated.

The plants around the radio were worried about the fire danger in their midst, so Norah unplugged the cord and moved the smoking mess to her kitchen sink. Cleo was quiet on her coffee table when Norah returned.

The pixie was going to tell her to stop her experiments. That it was too dangerous. Did she think Norah was going to give up so easily? When Norah was about to protest, there was a knock on her door.

Norah knew it was Stan, and she knew he wanted to help. *What the fuck is happening?* Trying to shake off the weird energy surrounding her, she invited him in.

Stan glanced around the room, blinking when he saw the smoking radio.

"Electricity's out," Stan stated. That was an understatement. His ice-blue eyes bored into her. "What have you been up to?"

Destroying ancient magical artifacts?

"Not much…" Norah's voice trailed off unconvincingly. Stan wasn't angry. She was certain of that.

"How about I look at the breaker?" he asked. Norah led him down the hall, trying to shake off the feeling that something extremely weird was happening.

CHAPTER NINETEEN

Madge was not happy with the Cafe Gratitude menu. "Who would eat something called *I Am Liberated*? What even is a raw kelp noodle? Is it going to liberate me to sit on the toilet all day?"

A woman whose body fat percentage was probably a negative number glared daggers at her. Norah looked away. Truthfully, she forgave Madge's foul mood. The pixie had been grounded with a bum wing since the incident at the safe house. It would heal, but her current circumstances were a struggle.

Norah couldn't blame her. She wouldn't want to wade through the mystery gunk on the LA city sidewalks, either.

A petite server walked over, silver hoops dangling from his ears.

"Do you ladies know what you want?" he asked, trying not to stare at Madge.

"There's actual sugar in the smoothies, right?" Madge crossed her ankles in front of her as she leaned against the potted succulent in the center of the table.

"They're sweetened with raw date syrup," he explained.

Madge growled. The sunlight slanting through the open sides of the breezy patio twinkled threateningly off her sharp acrylics. Over the past few days, she'd filed them even sharper out of boredom.

"Fine. I'll take the blue spirulina coconut sludge," Madge stated.

The server's fingers quivered on his small notebook. "Would you like to say the affirmation?" he asked, his voice shooting up into a higher register.

Norah gave her friend a warning look. Madge rolled her eyes. "I am stellar." She gritted her teeth. The server beamed and trotted away as Norah ordered her pizza with a resigned "I am jolly."

Madge peevishly kicked the spoon at her feet.

"I know we're not affirmations people, but the food here is good. It's full of nutrients. It'll be good for us," she whispered. "Besides, one time when I was here, I watched Beyonce eat oatmeal!"

Her given reason for going to the famous vegan restaurant was to provide Madge with nourishing, wing-healing food. In truth, she was more worried about herself. She'd been off since she'd broken the radio. The weird initial burst of...*whatever* had faded, but something strange was biding its time in the back corner of her brain.

Norah glanced around, desperately hoping to catch sight of a sufficient celebrity to take Madge's edge off.

Crash!

Norah looked down, ready to scold the pixie for causing even more of a scene. Madge sat quietly, arms crossed and eyes closed. A faint snore escaped her lips.

"*Corbin Smythe owes ten million dollars to the IRS!*" someone shouted. Norah spun.

A woman had climbed onto a table in the corner of the patio. Slamming the overhanging ceiling with her fists, she shouted the accusation again while kicking over a tumbler of iced tea.

Corbin Smythe was famous. Rumors about bad financial decisions had trickled down to her, but nothing that explicit.

"*Marilyn Cooper had post-partum psychosis!*" the woman shouted. Her arms flapped at odd angles as her mouth moved, and her toes thudded up and down with thick, uneven stomps. As her boot slammed on the table, it snapped the wand next to her salad fork in half.

The woman was a witch. More than that, she was exhibiting the classic signs of a curse. The weird jerky movements were one tell. The public airing of dirty celebrity laundry was another. No one sane shouted gossip at noon on the Cafe Gratitude patio. Self-respecting show biz types reserved that kind of gossip for midnight calls to TMZ from a burner phone.

"*Silver Lion Productions pays female execs half as much as men!*"

That was public information. Norah pushed her chair away from the table and grabbed her wand. She peered at the other diners on the patio, who were edging away.

The witch jerked again. Her body might have been out of control, but her eyes were alert and terrified.

Norah looked through her magical sight at the energy around the witch. The curse was the color of snot and had knotted itself around the witch's wrists and ankles.

"Candace Crawford got butt implants!"

If Norah didn't stop this soon, the witch wouldn't have a career to return to. She drew a long, slow spiral with her wand and sent a cone of silence across the patio. It fit over the witch like a party hat over an action figure, and the words coming out of her flapping jaw cut off mid-sentence. She might still be yelling, but no one on the patio could hear it.

Half the diners sighed, relieved. The other half, who had leaned forward to catch the hot gossip, slumped in disappointment, enthralled by their phones and menus.

Norah started to understand the outlines of the curse. It was a twist on a spell for revealing. Typically, such spells were used for showing a witch or wizard secret doorways or hidden writing. This one had been gruesomely cast on the woman's memories. It was as if someone had punched a magical hole in her head to spill her secrets.

While maintaining the cone of silence, Norah drew two small circles in the air and connected them with a rune. A cork-sized cylinder of dense blue magic emerged from her wand, floated into the air, and accelerated into the witch's flapping mouth, where it corked the spilling secrets. The magic spread into a fine net, shoring up the witch's integrity and forcing the curse out of her body.

After Norah dropped the cone of silence, only the crackle of the melting ice on the table at the woman's feet escaped. She swayed, rubbed her head, and slumped.

Norah made a mad dash and caught the witch as she toppled off the table. Grateful she'd been using her free weights lately, Norah slipped one arm under the woman's knees and eased her down onto a chair.

The server wearing silver hoops hovered in Norah's peripheral vision.

"Ma'am?" he whispered. "We're going to have to ask your friend to leave."

"Give me a second," Norah snapped. A groan escaped the unconscious woman's lips. She opened her eyes, frightened until she saw Norah.

"Can you walk? Norah asked.

The woman leaned on her heavily as they inched through a gauntlet of staring diners and found a shady spot to sit on a concrete barrier outside. She pulled a bottle of Floe out of her purse and handed it to the woman, whose hand hesitated as she grabbed the bottle.

"Are you sure you want to waste the good stuff on me? Isn't this shit like twenty dollars?"

"Not if you refill it from the tap and reseal the caps," Norah whispered. The witch laughed and drained half the bottle.

"I'm surprised you'd trust me with that little life hack. I'm not so good with secrets. I'm Laura, by the way. Laura Preston."

They shook hands. Norah took the bottle of Floe back and drained it. "If you're feeling better, I would love to know if you have any idea who cursed you." Norah watched her carefully.

Laura's tea-stained ballet flats tapped nervously on the concrete. "I don't want to get you mixed up in anything."

"Please. I'm like an organic smoothie. I love getting mixed up."

Laura sighed. "Do you know a guy named Harry Bing?"

Norah's eyes widened. She sure did.

"I don't have evidence," Laura explained, looking around to ensure they were out of earshot of the cafe. "At least, I don't have proof. I know Harry Bing tried to buy my company two weeks ago. When I said no, he kept calling. First he sent flowers, then a fruit basket."

"What an asshole!" Norah exclaimed.

Laura chuckled. "Here's the thing. It was full of kiwis. I'm allergic to kiwis, which only a few people know. Even in LA, it doesn't come up that often. That viper is the only person on Earth who could make fruit menacing."

"A hundred and fifty people die from falling coconuts a year," Norah told her. The witch returned a soul-withering glare.

"Anyway, after the inedible arrangement, things started going wrong. Our office got robbed. I sprained an ankle while running in Griffith. The calls from Bing got less and less nice. 'Wouldn't things be much easier if I sold him the company? Dangerous out there for a small business. Dangerous out there for a single woman.' That kind of thing. Now this."

"What's your company?" Norah asked.

Laura patted her pockets and fished out a business card. *Dailies Distribution* was written in twelve-point courier on the front. Norah felt a surge of interest. Something clicked in the corner of her mind dedicated to deals. Glowing lines connected names, and she beamed.

"You know, I've been looking to partner with a distribution company," she mused.

The witch handed her two more cards.

"I'm sure I won't be getting much use out of these after

the scene in there." She jutted her chin to the cafe. "Give them to your friends. Use them as bookmarks."

"I bet you twenty bucks that Candace Crawford has an endorsement deal with a plastic surgery clinic by tomorrow morning."

Laura stood cautiously. "The woman does have a great butt. God. I still haven't paid my bill. Maybe I'll dine and dash for the first time since I was an impoverished film student. That was a new wand, too!"

"You know what? Lunch is on me." Norah smiled.

"Are you sure?" Laura's voice was laced with uncertainty.

"You can get the next one," Norah bargained. "I'll have my pixie call you about lunch next week. A friendly chat is all I ask."

"Fine, but no affirmations," Laura countered. "I am *not* liberated."

"Neither am I. How about pizza? I've also got a great wand-maker I can connect you to." She started to tell Laura about Stan. When they said their goodbyes, some color had returned to Laura's cheeks.

In the cafe, Norah found Madge sitting on the edge of a bright blue smoothie, shoving mouthfuls of frozen juice into her face with a doll-sized spoon.

"This is delicious." The pixie glared at the drink. "Is that how the vegans get you? With their untrustworthy healthy milkshakes?"

"Laura is fine," Norah replied. "Thanks for asking. She works in distribution."

Madge's wings fluttered in unthinking excitement, and she yelped.

"Let's get our food to go. We might have the last nexus for our magical whiteboard."

Madge grinned. "Great. I could use a good crockpot soak."

CHAPTER TWENTY

Norah knew she should be with her client, but she struggled to pull herself away from the on-set food photographers. So far, a bowl of oats had been covered with white glue instead of milk, and a dwarf was going at a raw chicken with a blowtorch and brown shoe polish.

Now the food styling team, a mix of humans and magicals, was loudly debating the merits of magical versus analog ways to make the bowl of Oriceran sunfruit on the table before them pop for the camera.

"I'm still way over-exposed." The camera operator shielded his eyes with his hand as he tried to look at the table.

Sunfruit looked like miniature pears. They were called sunfruit because they emitted a thousand watts of light when they ripened. They were a traditional food of the light elves.

Sometimes Norah wondered if that was where Stan got his weird taste for lemons. According to Stan, the light elves celebrated a holiday in the late summer after the sunfruit ripened but before the weather got cold, a solstice with drinking and dancing in the orchards at night under the light of the fruit. Christmas lights had always reminded Stan of the holiday, and he applied blinding wattage to the complex's citrus trees every December.

A dark elf on the photography team held up his hands, and a disk of magical darkness appeared over the camera's lens.

"Little darker," the camera operator commanded. The light dimmed. "Stop! That's it right there."

There was a gravelly greeting near Norah's left hip. Her client Winston was about three and a half feet tall and looked very dashing in a red and white striped beanie.

"Maybe the sunfruit was a mistake," he mused. "I should have eased into magical produce. Ruby apples would pop."

"Ruby apples would break people's teeth," Norah countered. Winston was a young gnome who had gotten his start on a TikTok channel called "Gnome at Home," spouting lifestyle tips and cooking with Oriceran produce. He had been the first-ever magical competitor on *Iron Chef*. However, the episode he appeared in, *Battle Unicorn*, had sparked so much outrage that he'd briefly been driven off social media. A meme of him serving a unicorn carpaccio handroll in a glittering horn made the rounds every few months.

Norah had hired a crisis management PR team and was slowly reintroducing Winston to the country in a series of soft-focus cooking channel guest spots. It was going well. She'd even gotten a few feelers from the *Martha Stewart Living* bookers.

"What's our motto?" she asked the gnome.

Winston sighed. "Keep it light. Keep it fun."

"With the sunfruit, the light is a gimme. All you have to do is bring the fun."

"You got it, Norah," Winston agreed as a chipper PA pulled him away to hair and makeup. Norah peeked out from behind the kitchen set. Out in the stadium seats, young people in black clothes and headsets ushered audience members to their seats. A good number of people had been lined up outside the soundstage when she pulled in. That was good. Shows that had to use too many seat fillers lost their energy.

Norah entertained herself for the hour before the show started by watching a stylist slip pieces of cardboard between a stack of pancakes and cover the whole thing with motor oil. The smell was acrid, but it looked amazing. Norah's stomach twisted, then emitted a noise between a purr and a growl.

This is what I get for spending an hour staring at food.

There was another twitch and another noise. This one was deeper and weirder. She didn't think it had anything to do with hunger. The third time, she recognized it. Static. The noise grew louder, moving from her stomach up her spine and into her head. Blue sparks flashed in her vision.

A grip holding a gold bounce looked up, and his jaw dropped. The camera operator glanced up from his monitor.

"Who the fuck is holding that sparking blue light?" he yelled.

"Fireworks just came out of that lady's eyes." The grip pointed. His face was white.

Norah moved back. The sparks hadn't just been in her vision, then.

"Stick a bag over your head or get the fuck out," the cameraman ordered. Norah mumbled an apology and fled deeper into the soundstage. A warm spot in her stomach grew and expanded into her limbs, loosening her skin. Another burst of abdominal static traveled upward, and her eyes flashed blue again to the alarm of the twenty-something working the crafty table.

Norah pulled out her wand in time to cast a containment spell before another burst of static started. The magic from her wand constricted around the static, forcing it into a dense ball in her stomach. Between her high-waisted jeans and her cropped blouse, she saw a quivering lump. The magic inside her pushed against her spell. Through a faint ringing in the ear, she heard the director call, "Places."

She touched the lump. It jiggled like she had swallowed a balloon full of pop rocks.

Norah gripped her wand and poured more magic into the constricting spell. The more energy she used, the more the knot inside her pushed back as it tried to wriggle free of the bonds. She felt another burst of static pulse, doubling the pressure. Her spell wouldn't hold much longer.

Whatever was happening hadn't felt bad. The static hadn't hurt her. It was like she was a dial being tuned.

Like the dial on that old radio.

Another pulse of magic spread through her guts and the constricting spell shivered, stretched tight.

"Quiet on the set," someone shouted through a megaphone. Norah clamped down on her closed lips, and the iron tang of blood spread across her tongue. With a barely audible whisper, the dam of the constricting spell burst. A thunderstorm of blue light coursed through Norah's body, and sparks of blue light flowed out of her fingers and eyeballs.

The strange sensation she'd felt the night she had melted the radio returned. This time she understood.

She hadn't destroyed the spell inside the artifact. Instead, she had transferred it into her body. The light flowing through her eyes and fingers dimmed, and currents of information rushed to fill the space. Fragments and impulses.

The woman working crafty wanted to build a relationship with the show's producers that would leapfrog her onto the network's creative team. The assistant director was angry, partly because that was his job and somewhat because he had only taken this gig to flirt with the head of hair and makeup, and she was gone. Norah had heard one of the food stylists mention earlier that someone had left to do prosthetics on a prestige fantasy drama.

Norah caught sight of Winston's pointy hat and felt a burst of emotion from the small gnome. He wanted to get through this apology tour and go back to making videos at home. He didn't want to disappoint her.

The trickle of information from the surrounding world was becoming a flood. It might overwhelm her if she didn't find a way to control it.

Norah ran through the stage door and found a line of people waiting for a game show. Their intentions ranged from wanting to make their sixty bucks as seat fillers to wanting to convince their parents that music was a viable career choice.

After shooting down the hallway while batting away errant emotions, Norah locked herself in the bathroom. A feeling bludgeoned her from the nearest stall: a woman wanted to "make them all pay," whatever that meant. Norah edged closer to an exec in red whose desires were blissfully limited to perfecting her cat-eye makeup.

"It looks great," Norah complimented her, and the woman blinked in surprise. Oops. She had played her hand too early.

She could figure this out. The radio had only been on intermittently. It had a dial. That meant somewhere inside her, there must be a dial. Norah poked her belly button, then giggled madly when nothing happened. She closed her eyes and felt the shape of the magic inside her. An outline resolved, and the enchantment pulsed like radar. Later, she would have to check its range. For now, she followed the pulse to the old magic knot, exploring the twists.

She didn't know what all the intertwined spells did, but she found a small loop of magic near the bottom above her right kidney. With her hand on her wand, she sent blue magic into her guts and tugged on the loop. The roar of feelings and emotions faded.

Norah sighed, relieved. She wasn't prepared to be a satellite dish for every deranged emotion in Hollywood. She tugged the magic loop again but felt a pang as it caught against another part of the spell. The enchantment was turned down, but it wasn't off. She'd have to settle for being a small satellite dish, like a ham radio.

Back in the hall, the door she'd pushed out of was locked. When she tried to go in the main doors, a large man in black pointed at a glowing sign that said: "ON AIR." Norah sighed, plopped down on a bench, and pulled up a live broadcast feed. Whatever the magical food photography team had done, it was working. Winston was chopping sunfruit, the light reflecting off the whorled blade of his Damascus steel knife.

"Now we're going to add a little mint. This is regular mint, mind you. You don't have to go all-Oriceran. It's okay to try one or two new ingredients..."

A woman sat on a bench across the hall, and Norah winced. The woman's silk blouse was yellowed with sweat stains, and worry creased her face. More than that, Norah's new magical radar picked her up. She needed a romantic lead for a new film, a fresh face.

"I have an elf you might want to look at," Norah ventured. "His name is Frondle. Classic love-interest looks."

The woman's eyes widened, and she rose to her feet with such alarm that she almost snapped a stiletto.

"What the fuck?" She kept her eyes on Norah as she backed down the hall. When she reached a safe distance, she turned and ran, heels clicking.

Oh, right. People don't like having their minds read. Did it qualify as telepathy? She didn't hear full-formed thoughts. It was more flashes of emotion and currents of desire. Norah tugged on the magic in her guts until she progressed on the loop. The enchantment wasn't off, but the signal was so low that she'd have to stick a finger up someone's nose to know what they wanted.

They'd probably want me to remove my finger.

She fiddled with her inner workings to kill time before the taping ended, turning the enchantment up and down. She started testing the range and sent it out in a wider arc through the building but almost lost control as the desires of a large studio audience hit her in the face. She couldn't feel specifics with that many people, just a draining well of need. She turned the dial down again. Range testing would have to wait for somewhere less crowded. A trial run, for instance.

The broadcast ended. Norah fiddled with the loops of the enchantment until she was sure it was off and went to congratulate Winston.

Madge fluttered two inches above a large throw pillow that Norah had placed on her desk. The timer on her phone counted down.

"Fifteen more seconds." Norah tried to sound encouraging.

"Fuck you." Madge was breathing hard.

"You can do it. Five seconds. Annnnd....done."

The pixie collapsed onto the pillow, then tumbled down the side onto the desk and sprang to her feet.

"How did that feel?" Norah asked.

"Hey, missy. You can't deflect all my questions about your new 1930s radio powers by asking about my wing. Which is healing fine, even though flying feels like being licked by a fire elemental."

Norah raised an eyebrow. Madge flapped her wings

and, grunting in pain, flew up far enough to poke Norah in the nose.

"Ow!"

"You can't put me off forever. Tell me about the radio."

Norah sighed and described her effort to break Cleo's curse. Then she told Madge what she'd felt at the soundstage. "I ran in Griffith this morning and tested the range. It maxes out at about a hundred feet."

"How's your control coming along?"

"I'm getting the hang of it. Ugh. I tripped the dial this morning and got a brain full of that creepy old guy who always hits on me at my coffee shop. You do *not* want to know his intentions. It made me want to Windex my gray matter."

"Yikes."

"Yeah." Norah nodded. "Enough about me. How was your meeting with the distributor?"

"It took an hour for her to stop apologizing." Madge sounded peevish. "First Arret landed the distribution deal! This one's big, Norah."

Norah gazed at Madge's grin. "Madge! That's amazing. We should celebrate!"

Norah rolled her chair over to the mini fridge in the corner and retrieved a bottle of champagne—the expensive stuff that she usually saved for clients.

"Whoa." Madge whistled. "We can't refill that one with tap water."

"I don't care. We deserve it," Norah countered. Madge frowned. Weighed down by stress, the pixie still hadn't recovered her *va-va-voom*.

"I'll let you ride the cork," she added, pulling off the foil and giving the bottle a little shake. Madge's wings flapped wanly, and she huffed her way onto the cork. The subsequent pop launched the pixie into the air. A small "Woohoo" reached Norah's ears from the shooting blur.

Norah found a coffee mug from her brother's cafe and filled it to the brim. Then she retrieved a sawed-off test tube from a pink jewelry box in Madge's office, filled it, and handed it to the pixie, who had glided elegantly down from her extreme sports adventure.

"We still have a lot of work to do." The warning was undercut as she drained the test tube and handed it to Norah to refill.

"Nothing goes with champagne like a thousand emails," Norah replied. "I'm ready."

Madge started reading messages off the smartphone she used as a computer, and they both got a little tipsy as they worked their way through the list. Several mugs later, there was a long pause. Norah hiccupped, then felt guilty when she saw the worry on Madge's face.

"This is weird," Madge's face was lit by the phone screen. "Are we involved in a gritty Mother Goose reboot?"

"No. Ooh, that's a good idea. Do you think we could do *The Old Woman Who Lived in the Shoe* as an erotic thriller? Call Tarantino!" Norah sprang unsteadily to her feet.

"I'm cutting you off," Madge deadpanned.

"Wait, why do you ask?"

"One of these messages is weird. It says Hickory dickory dock, and then the number 872."

Norah dropped heavily back into her chair as Madge tipped the champagne bottle over and climbed inside the neck with a tiny straw.

A minute later, she emerged.

"Well? Any ideas?"

"I don't have any," Norah replied. " I know who would."

It was hard to hear her mother over the goats bleating in the background.

"Let me go into the shed," Petra shouted. A second later, a wooden door slammed, and the background noise faded. "Eight hundred seventy-two, you said?"

"Yeah. Ring any bells?"

"Sure. A big one. Are you okay?" Petra's voice was laced with caution.

"What does it mean?" Norah asked.

"It's a call sign for an old friend of ours, Ignatius Dunne. He was a movie producer before he was an agent. The Silver Griffin kind, not the Hollywood kind. He's older than Dad and me. He is a whiz with a wand, though he must be frail at this point. 'Hickory dickory dock' is the old Griffin code for trouble."

"What kind of trouble?" Norah asked.

"I'm not sure. That's what worries me. Do you want us to come down there? We can be on the road in twenty minutes."

"I can take care of it. Besides, the goats need you."

"What they need is to stop chewing on wasps' nests. We've had the vet in twice this week."

"Where can I find this guy? Mr. 872?"

The wooden door re-opened, and the bleating from the goats almost drowned out her mother's voice.

"Try the Mark Twain Library. Before the internet, we used it to send messages back in the seventies. When we didn't want to leave a magic trail, we resorted to old-fashioned pen and paper."

"The horror!" Norah exclaimed. Several decades prior, her third-grade teacher had described her handwriting as "minimally legible."

"I hope you know how to read cursive," her mother told her.

"I'll struggle through."

CHAPTER TWENTY-ONE

As it turned out, cursive wasn't her biggest problem. She found the secret magical room of the Mark Twain Branch Library fine by tapping a glass display case of summer-reading fantasy novels under the big mural stretched across the room near the ceiling. After she had slipped through the shimmering glass into the magical pocket room, she realized she had no idea where to look.

The collection of spell books was smaller than the one at the Fremont branch. If someone had planted a message here, they had done it without magic. There were no guiding spells or traces of magic other than the one she'd used to open the door. In the end, she went shelf by shelf and book by book, trying not to get distracted by reading any words.

Two hours later, she yelled triumphantly as a slip of paper fluttered to the ground.

She had found the code inside an art deco grimoire of herbal remedies from the 1920s. When she thumbed through the pages to ensure she hadn't missed any other messages, the remedies mostly consisted of gin. Juniper and mint hit her nose from a beautiful black ink illustration of a bottle stuffed with herbs. Norah stuck her nose between the pages.

"Oh, my God! It's smell-o-vision."

She flipped to another page, this one a toothache remedy. The illustration showed a clove tree. She took in the spicy tropical aroma.

The beautiful book had a jade-green cover, and Norah enjoyed its sensory pleasures until she was smacked in the nostrils by a page titled *Bogwife's Stinking Tincture,* made with three parts weasel bile and one part tar. Eyes watering, she slammed the book shut and sniffed fresh air into her nose before retrieving the slip of paper from the floor.

Two sets of numbers were scribbled on it in spidery ink. She flipped it over several times and cast a revealing spell to check for hidden messages. Nothing, just numbers. Norah's phone couldn't work in these library pockets, so she moved back into the sunny library and sat in a chair designed for a child rather than a grown woman.

The numbers were probably a latitude and longitude, and when Norah typed them into her phone, it spat out the location of the Old Zoo on the eastern edge of Griffith Park. It was an hour away in traffic. Norah sighed and headed to her car.

Griffith was packed this Sunday afternoon, and Norah had to park down the road and walk. After winding through picnicking families and ascending a grassy slope, she saw the dark mouths of the caves.

The Old Zoo hadn't been in service for more than fifty years, but the manmade caves that had once housed lions and polar bears still stood. They were vaguely threatening, jagged holes that contrasted sharply with the bleached trees and sunshine.

About half of the area had been taken over by a group of muscular men in West Hollywood Gym tees carrying laser tag guns. They were engaging in simulated warfare between mimosa breaks.

The other half of the area was full of clowns. Two were in full white face paint, five wore *commedia dell'arte* masks, and for the rest, who could tell? Also, a posterboard sign on their picnic table said SPLATURDAY CLOWN WORKSHOP. Her feet slowed, refusing to take her any closer. She heard one of the clowns round everyone up and introduce himself as Dr. Boing.

A small figure in black-and-white stripes on the outskirts stared at Norah. At least, she thought he was staring. It was hard to tell under the grinning green mask.

She was almost on top of the red location pin on her phone.

Please let the location be in the laser tag half of the caves. She crossed her fingers and brought the screen to her face, then spun in a circle to orient herself. Her stomach sank as it pointed her directly at the clown. *It must be my lucky day.* Norah trudged to the group.

"Are you here for Splaturday?" Dr. Boing asked.

"Maybe?" Norah's real mission would take too long to explain.

A tall clown made his way through the group and pushed his spiky devil mask onto his forehead.

"Norah?"

It was Frondle. She gaped. The young elf's body was

barely covered by a sequined wrestling onesie and he was drenched with sweat. He looked great and inexcusably comfortable.

"Everyone! It's Norah! My agent!"

Norah cringed as the word "agent" tore through the clowns like wildfire. Spines straightened left and right, and guts were sucked in as the assembled performers jockeyed to appear in her line of vision.

"Are you here to watch the workshop?" Frondle asked.

Norah inhaled deeply. If only she had a wizard with five or six wands to fight instead. She coaxed a smile onto her face. "Absolutely!"

A wave of excitement rippled outward, and someone produced a lawn chair and a champagne bucket full of mango wine coolers. Emergency provisions. She cracked one open, chugged it in one go, and leaned back.

Norah had braved improv, sketch, standup, one-man shows, live podcast recordings, monologue showcases, and outdoor Shakespeare. She'd never had twenty people clown directly at her.

Half an hour later, she was devastated to discover she was having a good time. Even though their eyes tracked her like a creepy Victorian painting, watching for her reaction, the clowns were talented.

"Stop fucking looking at the agent, Ambassador Trashcan!" Dr. Boing shouted from over her right shoulder. "Sorry," he mumbled to Norah. "They're good kids but painfully overeager."

"I appreciate the enthusiasm."

Dr. Boing slipped a card into her cupholder.

"You wanna take a look at anyone, I'll put you in touch.

Or if your kid has a birthday or something." Norah tried to imagine Leaf watching *commedia dell'arte*. To be fair, there were a lot of fart jokes.

The show ended, and after an unending line of handshakes, Dr. Boing chased off the last of the clowns loitering around her and started stuffing props into duffle bags. Frondle trotted over.

"Do they have clowns on Oriceran?" Norah asked offhandedly. "Crystal people smashing watermelons with their fists? Anything like that?"

Frondle scratched the point of his ear. "The light elves have a form of poetry called… I guess the best translation would be 'a thousand follies.' Each poem is a thousand rhyming couplets of insults disguised as compliments. Some are quite humorous."

"Sounds like high school." Norah laughed. "Get back to your friends. Call Madge next week if you want to catch up about any auditions."

Frondle nodded cheerfully and went to help Dr. Boing with his bags.

Alone at last, Norah slipped into the cave. It didn't smell good, but not in the urine-and-rotting-food way she expected. The energy was foul, and the whole thing smelled like a battle. A loveseat with sawed-off legs reeked of burned chemicals. The stained upholstery was still hot, with wispy smoke curling from the stuffing. A nearby IKEA dresser someone had been using as a table was newly splintered, with one corner smashed in.

Grabbing her wand, Norah searched for magical trails while coughing from the vapor rising off the sofa. Bingo. Glowing magic zigged and zagged across the dirty concrete, and there were wide, uneven splotches where hexes had hit the walls.

Norah picked a mud-brown magic trail to follow. It originated outside near the picnic tables, then moved into the cave before ending in a splashy patch near a locked gate. Norah rattled the bars and saw that a padlock had been blasted off its chain by ferocious kinetic magic. The metal was still burning-hot, and she yanked her hand back.

This witch or wizard had abruptly stopped casting magic. Or been stopped. Norah picked another trail. This one, a rancid yellow, was similar. Whoever had cast the spells had come into the cave and then...stopped. The rust-red trail was the same.

Finally, Norah noticed a trace of sewage-gray magic. Unlike the others, this one led out of the back of the cave. Pulling her sleeve over her hand, Norah opened the metal gate and climbed the narrow staircase. This was how zookeepers must have accessed the cages back in the day. The trail faded before she reached the top.

A magical four-way battle would have been quite a fireworks display. It must have happened late last night when the park was empty. Norah climbed back down and reassessed the room. She pulled on a knob of the broken dresser. It was stuck and took all her muscle power and a little magic to open.

She dumped out the drawer's contents near the mouth of the cave. Half-squeezed toothpaste stuck to cheap gossip mags tumbled onto the dirt, and a small bottle of linseed oil. That was the type of oil Norah used on her wand. She squeezed a drop onto her palm. The oil was infused with protective magic, which confirmed her suspicions that a witch or wizard owned it.

Norah was sure she had missed something. The dark hole where the drawer had been beckoned, although Norah's stomach turned at the thought of putting her hand in there. When she was about to suck it up and do it anyway, she had an idea. Closing her eyes, she felt for the radio magic lying dormant inside her. She tugged gently at a loop of the spell, which crackled to life. Her fingers tingled, and her eyes sparked. Norah shivered. She would never get used to the eye sparks.

She allowed her awareness to flow to the box. What was she looking for, a raccoon intent on violence against anyone near its home? A squirrel bent on destroying the zoo industrial complex?

There were a few signals inside the dresser, but they were very small and strange—more like chemical compulsions than human desires. Norah suspected they were insects or spiders. Hopefully, not poisonous ones.

Reasonably confident that nothing with teeth would bite her, she plunged her arm up to the elbow into the dark hole, stretching to feel around the base. The rough plywood abraded her fingertips, and a splinter dug into the flesh of her forefinger. When she was about to pull her hand out and run for the nearest tetanus shot, it brushed the corner of a book.

As Norah walked into the light with her find, the sun revealed cracks in the book's chocolate-leather cover. It was old and dry, without any embossing or marks other than age.

Something moved on the spine. Norah almost dropped

the book before realizing it was a yellow-and-black striped caterpillar. A pulse of chemical impulse flashed into Norah's mind from the little insect, and she quickly turned her internal radio dial off. What a caterpillar wanted out of life wasn't anything she could understand.

Norah held the book to her face. The caterpillar was beautiful. Its soft body was striped with clean, bold colors. Sensitive black antennae turned to her as it crawled onto her index finger. The striped body undulated up her hand. Careful not to fling her new friend onto the lawn, Norah opened the book to a random page.

She couldn't read it. The writing swam, and try as she might to latch onto specific symbols, her eyes refused to focus. Was it in a foreign language? When she looked across the busy park, English words appeared on the page in her peripheral vision. When she looked back, the words blurred again.

She swiftly flipped through the book, searching for anything readable, and found a dog-eared page near the middle. Was it paper? A sick feeling in her gut suggested it might be animal skin. Either way, it was drenched in old magic. Instead of dissolving into words, the ink spiraled across the page, twisting into a series of increasingly complex magical runes. Sucking her in.

Stop looking at it.

This inner warning was reedy and faded into nothing as the writing on the page curved into a tunnel, stretching out into the darkness. The center of the pages filled with darkness, unbroken ink blacker than black. All she had to do was walk into it.

A massive solid shape slammed into Norah's shoulder

and sent her tumbling onto the grass. The book flew out of her hands and launched into a wide arc before landing face-down in a bush.

She clutched her wand, ready to fight. Above her, the man who had hit her blocked out the sun. *Oh shit.*

He had a gun. It was matte-gray, with an orange tip and the words Zappers Home Laser Tag scrawled on the side. Norah slumped again in relief.

"Oh, my God, sweetie! I am sooooo sorry." The man's abs rippled through his thin pink tank top.

"It's okay." Norah gasped. It was true. Without that tackle, she would still be looking at that creepy cursed book.

A willowy twenty-something ran up and slung his arm around the shooter's waist. He raised an eyebrow. "Did you thank him for tackling you? Girl, you need to work on your self-worth."

Norah allowed herself another blissful few seconds on the ground, then allowed the men to pull her to her feet. The caterpillar, undeterred, was still on her hand. Noticing it, the smaller man smacked his companion on the shoulder.

"You covered her in bugs! That's gross. Also, we need to pick up our game, or we'll have to pay for brunch."

The guy in the pink tee retrieved his gun and brushed errant grass off it.

"Come to the West Hollywood Gym for a free smoothie anytime," he shouted over his shoulder as he ran away and shot up into the trees.

As air filtered back into Norah's lungs, she gingerly plucked the brown leather book out from between prickly branches and slammed it shut the instant it pulled.

The leather was warm in her hands, and she desperately wanted to re-open it. To stroke its pages. To explore the world that lay in the darkness beyond the ink.

"I'm not falling for that again." She glared at it sternly. "Don't even think about it."

The magic on the dog-eared page had grabbed her attention and hung on for dear life. Norah shuddered. Although it screamed evil energy, she still wanted to open it. *I never thought I'd say this, but thank God for laser tag.*

She pulled off her thin windbreaker, wrapped it around the book, and wound a protective spell around the bundle. Better to be safe than sorry.

CHAPTER TWENTY-TWO

The second Norah arrived in the loft, Leaf took charge of the caterpillar. He retrieved a large glass jar from the cabinet, poured its contents down the drain, and took cuttings from his parents' houseplants to assemble a small terrarium. He covered the top with cheesecloth and secured it with a rubber band.

Several minutes later, Norah saw Jackie staring into the garbage disposal, her face drained of color.

"He poured out thirty-two ounces of Erewhon soup. Thirty-two, Norah."

Erewhon was where you shopped when you were too good for Whole Foods. Norah had once purchased a small bottle of hot sauce for twenty-five dollars, then let it go bad because none of her food had seemed worthy of it.

The remains of expensive tomato bisque dripped down the drain.

"That's a lot of soup. Did you take out a second mortgage or something?"

Jackie laughed, then softened when Leaf walked carefully into the kitchen with his caterpillar jar and his dad's meat thermometer.

"I have to keep it in my bedroom," he announced. "The internet said caterpillars do best in warmer temperatures. The kitchen is seventy-two degrees, but my room is seventy-five."

"I need to borrow the jar for our family meeting, sport," Norah replied. "Afterward, I will return him to your room's perfect microclimate. Deal?"

The caterpillar wiggled its way up an aloe leaf.

"Deal." He handed the jar to Norah and ran off.

Jackie shook her head and poured herself another cup of herbal tea. "A goat is sleeping on a little dog bed on his floor. Are we screwing him up?"

Norah grinned. "Oh, yeah. You're looking at years of psychoanalysis."

As if on cue, Pepe walked into the kitchen and stared Jackie down until she handed him a carrot from a red enamel colander on the kitchen counter.

"We had to get a farm share," Jackie informed Norah. "Although he has been a good influence on Leaf in the eating-vegetables department."

The goat's knowing glance unsettled Norah, and she retreated to the living room. Cradling the caterpillar jar in her lap, she lounged on the sofa while her mother inspected the windbreaker-wrapped spell book.

"Be careful, Mom. That thing took me for a ride yesterday," Norah warned.

Petra made a disapproving noise. "I was avoiding dangerous curses before you were born, young lady."

"I know, I know. This one was a doozy."

Wand moving in careful circles and lines, Petra removed the blue protective magic around the bundle and gingerly unfolded the windbreaker. The brown leather book was placid on the glass top of the coffee table.

The leather was beautiful—a loamy brown, full of life. Surely the page that had enthralled her had contained critical information? Norah's hand stretched to the book. She would only look for a second.

Petra slapped her hand away. "Don't even think about it," her mother scolded. "It got you once. It'll be easier to get you again."

Norah stuffed her hands in her pockets and scooted to the other end of the sofa. Her mother's face was serene as she shot tendrils of magic at the book, testing and exploring. What worried Norah was her father, standing far away from the book near the loft's tall windows. His eyes followed his wife's every movement, and his knuckles were white on his wand. He was ready to spring into action at the first sign of danger.

Lincoln breathed a sigh of relief when Petra flipped the corners of the windbreaker back over the book and tied it with a protective spell so strong it left burn marks on the nylon.

"That was my favorite windbreaker," Norah grumbled.

"Buy another one," Petra replied.

"It was vintage."

Someone knocked on the door, and Andrew appeared in the living room with Quint in tow.

"Now that the gang's all here, let's get to work." Lincoln was uncharacteristically worried, maybe afraid.

They sat down.

"This is serious stuff." Lincoln gestured at the jar in Norah's lap with his wand. "Leaf's new buddy is a monarch caterpillar. In its larval stage, the species acts as magical amplifiers. This one must be hardy. I'm surprised the book didn't kill it."

"Is it dangerous?" Jackie asked, glancing nervously at her son's bedroom door. "Leaf has already fallen in love with it."

"It's a caterpillar," Lincoln replied. " Leaf shouldn't do magic around it. Not without a lot of practice."

"Poor Ignatius. I doubt he's still alive." Petra stared at the book.

"He must have known he wouldn't be able to deliver his message in person," Lincoln mused.

So many magical trails had dead-ended in the Old Zoo cave. "Are you sure it was him?" Norah asked.

Petra nodded. "He had an affinity for caterpillars. That was his handwriting on the note."

"What about the book?" Andrew asked. The mermaid on his bicep was covered in goosebumps.

"It's a very powerful grimoire dating back to 1500s France. The spells inside are old and mostly illegal."

"What about that dog-eared page?" Norah asked. She looked down and realized she had edged unconsciously closer to the book.

"It's a control spell," Lincoln informed them. "You said you saw the ink inside transform into a tunnel? If you had gone through it, you would have been in the power of the person that book belonged to."

"Whoever used this book is dominating other people," Petra added. "The basic control spell has been fortified with two others. The first works strongly on shifters. The second siphons magic. That might be why you're still attracted to it, Norah. It sucked out some of your magic."

Norah's heart beat faster. The mermaid on Andrew's bicep gasped.

"The book wasn't open that long. You only lost a tiny bit," Lincoln added when he saw the expression on Norah's face. "Magic is like fingernails. Give it time, and it grows back. Try to take it easy for a few days."

The living room was suddenly very cold. Norah felt a strong urge to cast her most powerful spell to see if she still could. To ensure she hadn't lost her mojo. That probably wasn't what her father'd had in mind when he told her to take it easy.

"What do you know about the spell book?" Norah asked.

Lincoln and Petra exchanged looks. "It's one of only two copies in the world."

"Who has the other one?"

"When the Silver Griffins were destroyed, there was massive chaos," Petra replied. "A lot of errant magic and more loose ends than a broken loom."

"Most of the artifacts in the Silver Griffin vault were destroyed," Lincoln added.

"Not all?" Norah asked. The enchantment lodged in her guts twitched. "I guess you looted that radio."

"I like to think of it as historical preservation rather than looting. I'm still not sure it was the right move." Petra's hazel eyes pierced Norah's tough exterior. "We'll see."

"Who else might have engaged in light historical preservation? Who has the other grimoire?" Norah asked.

Lincoln rubbed his chin. "They'd have to be extremely powerful. A lesser wizard would have read the book and had all their magic sucked out."

"I guess that narrows it down." Quint put down a half-empty cup of coffee. Norah felt queasy. Her brother always finished his coffee.

The mermaid on Andrew's bicep quivered and pulled the clamshell she was sitting on shut.

"Great. I guess we're looking for a powerful evil wizard." Norah swallowed. Fantastic.

The family sat silently for a few moments, fidgeting with their wands. Finally, Norah looked at Jackie and Andrew. "How does Leaf feel about clowns?"

CHAPTER TWENTY-THREE

Jasmine Miller gathered the knot of production assistants around her in the corner of the building. It was their first time on set, and they shifted excitedly from foot to foot as she handed out plastic-lidded coffee cups. If they noticed their boss's blank expression and twitchy puppet-like movements, they chalked it up to the stressful environment and the general weirdness of people who chose to make their living from wall-to-wall sixteen-hour days.

Watching the young people sip their coffee, Jasmine zeroed in on a twenty-something with dark skin and hair who was holding her coffee cup gingerly without drinking it.

"Something wrong with your coffee, Carolyn?" she asked.

The young woman was suddenly interested in her worn-out tennis shoes.

"I try not to use disposable cups," she confessed.

Jasmine took two quick steps into the circle. "Oh. I'm

soooo sorry." Anger rumbled in her voice as her volume increased. "Let me take it back to Starbucks and have them put the paper back into the fucking tree!"

The young woman wiped a drop of spit off her cheek.

"Drink the fucking coffee." Jasmine huffed. "I don't need my PAs falling asleep in the middle of the goddamn day."

The young woman drank her coffee. The other overeager young people in the circle started chugging. Jasmine stared at them until they were finished. Then, one by one, cups slipped from their hands onto the concrete, glassy filters sliding over their eyes. Any faint creases of worry on their faces smoothed out into empty placidity. They stood like statues, arms limp, under their boss's attentive inspection.

"Good. Very good. Now, get to fucking work. Jeremy, stay on the cast's asses all day. I want to know everything they say and do. Every secret. Every fucking fart. Got it?"

Jeremy nodded. Jasmine turned to Carolyn. "You. Clean up these coffee cups and find me in my office. I have something special for you."

The young woman nodded.

Norah was pulling into the small parking lot behind her office when her phone rang. The caller ID said it was Frondle.

Norah grinned. She'd worked hard to get the young elf a part in a new action movie about underwater cave diving. It was a meaty speaking role, too, for someone with his experience. He was playing a surf instructor. Typecasting, maybe, but everyone had to start somewhere. Most importantly for Norah, he played the part of an elf rather than in human drag.

His first day of shooting had been scheduled for the early morning. She picked up the phone. "Frondle! How's my Hollywood star doing? How was your big scene?"

There was a long pause, then a woman spoke.

"Is this Norah Wintry? You're listed as Frondle's emergency contact."

Norah felt the earth drop out from under her. "What is it?"

"He's fine, but there's been an accident. I'm a nurse at Providence St. John's. Can you get down here?"

Norah peeled out of her parking space and screeched out of the lot, then made a wild left turn onto the street as cars moving in both directions left skid marks from braking and laid on their horns.

"I'm on my way. Where is he?"

For the first time in Norah's memory, Frondle wasn't smiling. His face was pinched and even paler than normal. As Norah approached his hospital bed, he shouted, "My life is over!" and flung himself onto his pillow. Alarmed, she went for her wand and was about to shoot a healing spell through the elf's body when a severe-looking nurse in incongruous teddy bear scrubs tapped her shoulder.

"Don't bother. One of our nurses is a wizard, and she knitted him up fine. He was more shaken up than injured."

In other words, he was having a tantrum. That was okay. Tantrums were Norah's bread and butter.

"What's going on, buddy?" she asked, patting his shoulder.

"They re-cast my role. They said they didn't have time to stop shooting while I recovered."

Norah winced. Film shoots were disaster magnets, and something always went wrong. She liked Frondle, and something like that was a big blow for a young actor. "Slow down and tell me what happened."

Frondle curled up on his side. "We were shooting underwater in the ocean, doing the scene where my co-star and I get knocked over by a wave, and she saves me. There was a water elemental there doing the waves. I cast a breathing spell before I went under. When the wave knocked me down, something on the beach sucked up my breathing spell. I freaked out and inhaled a lungful of salt water, then bumped my head."

He pointed at a faint red mark above his eyebrow. Norah squinted. The nurse rolled her eyes.

"They insisted I go to the hospital. I tried to argue with them, but they were very threatening. Someone started yelling about worker's comp. On my way out, I saw them putting my costume on a *human*. The surf instructor is supposed to be an elf, Norah! Someone has betrayed my people!"

Norah stroked Frondle's hand. "Hey. Most actors would kill to be cut from a major Hollywood movie. I'll get you more roles. Just try to keep your chin up."

She took her hand away and slung her purse over her shoulder.

"You're leaving?" Frondle's lip quavered.

"I'm gonna go find out what happened. Straighten this out." Her features grew stern.

"There was something wrong with the sand. I know it. Sabotage!"

"I'll take a look. No promises."

"Avenge me, Norah! Avenge me!"

The words echoed down the hall as she headed back to her car. After she dialed a number, she put her phone to her ear.

"Hey. Madge. How do you feel about doing a site inspection?"

CHAPTER TWENTY-FOUR

When she and Madge arrived on set, the production had moved away from the water and was clustered around a lifeguard stand. A tight knot of screaming people was wielding expensive equipment. Security had let Norah past the caution tape. The producers were probably trying to make nice out of fear that Frondle would sue the studio.

With Madge flying surveillance, Norah combed the beach for traces of magic. She took off her tennis shoes and waded into knee-high waves. Under her feet, a few faint specks of magic glittered in the sand, blurred by the ocean water.

One of the trails was from a light elf, almost certainly from the breath spell Frondle had cast. The other spell was inscrutable, especially through the water, but it had probably come from a magic well. It was just big enough to disorient the elf by sucking up his magic while he was underwater.

"You think another actor sabotaged him?"

Madge snorted. "It wouldn't surprise me. Jealous understudies are LA's apex predator."

"Wanna go check him out? Try not to get hit by a drone."

Madge whirred away, and saltwater licked the blisters on Norah's heels. She needed information. In a time-honored Hollywood tradition, she decided to find the least powerful person on set and yell at them until they coughed it up.

A production assistant shuffled by with a coffee caddy, and Norah hooked her sleeve.

"Hey!" she called. The PA's face turned to Norah, but her eyes looked straight through her at the horizon. A seed of unease popped up inside Norah.

"What's your name?" Norah asked.

"Carolyn." The young woman's voice was remote.

Norah frowned. "What do you know about the accident on set earlier today?"

The PA shrugged. "Sorry. I have to take these coffees..."

Something was wrong. Carolyn shuffled away almost in slow motion, and Norah caught her.

"They replaced the elf playing the surfer, right?"

For an instant, the haze covering the girl's eyes cleared, radiating fear. Her pupils narrowed to pinpoints.

What was this PA's deal?

Following a hunch, Norah inhaled deeply and reached inside for the 1930s spirit radio that lived in her guts. This wasn't going to be fun. The set was overflowing with artists, who were not known for their rational, straightforward desires and intentions.

Turning the magic onto its very lowest setting, she

approached Carolyn. It took a few seconds for a clear channel to establish itself. When it did, Norah's suspicions were confirmed.

The PA's intentions were buried deep under a thick control spell. The young woman had a singular desire, faint but decisive. *Out.* Someone was pulling her strings, and she desperately wanted a pair of scissors.

The PA's body shook, and the coffee caddy tumbled out of her hands, cups separating from lids as coffee drained into the sand.

"Carolyn! Are you all right?"

The PA's eyes rolled back in her head, and the gurgle in her throat became a scream. "*Magic always rises to the top!*" she shouted. In a testament to the chaos of movie sets, not a single person looked over.

The current of intention flowing into Norah dropped to a trickle. The spell controlling Carolyn was growing stronger.

Norah grabbed the PA's shoulders. It was like touching an electric fence. Her muscles clenched as the magic inside her crackled into Carolyn's body, ricocheting between them as it began to punch through the foreign enchantment.

The radio was stronger than the control spell, or it would be. She just had to hold on. A million electric pins pricked her skin as she dug her fingers into Carolyn's shoulders. If she let go, this horrible feeling would stop, but the PA would be lost. Maybe forever.

Norah gripped tighter, the crescents of her fingernails breaking Carolyn's skin. The control spell on the young woman was eroding under the onslaught of Norah's spirit radio. It grew thinner and thinner until finally, the control spell cracked open. The burning pinpricks on Norah's skin dissolved as the magic flowed into a channel between them, peeling off the control spell like the skin of a tangerine.

Their connection was strong but confused. The PA's intentions were an incoherent jumble. All she wanted was to know what was happening. Norah held on as the magic washed away the remaining traces of control. When Carolyn slumped, Norah eased her to the ground, feeling horror at the rips in the shoulders of the PA's t-shirt. Blood dripped over her collarbones.

Carolyn made a choking sound as if to talk, and Norah leaned over her. The young woman croaked. "My boss… Jasmine. I think she put something in my coffee. Before that, this morning by the beach. She was doing something with…"

"With whom?" Norah asked. Carolyn shuddered, eyes fluttering closed and chest heaving. She was losing consciousness.

"Please. Carolyn. You'll be okay. Tell me who you saw."

The PA's groan was barely audible. Breathing with some difficulty, she rasped one more word. "Saxon."

Triumph warred with fear. The trail she'd followed had led her straight into the lion's mouth. Below her, Carolyn's eyes went blank, and her body sank into the sand.

"*Get the set medic!*" Norah screamed, retrieving her phone to dial 911.

Norah told the cops a version of the truth. She had visited the set after her client had an accident, noticed a PA acting strangely, and called 911 when the young woman collapsed.

Norah had kept her spirit radio turned on while the cops questioned her, and soft channels of intention flowed to her. One of the cops was a human. He was itching for a reason to arrest any magical he could find. As he questioned her, his fingers stroked his gun. No magic was needed to see that.

The other cop wanted to hide something. That was interesting. Norah raised an eyebrow at him, and he broke eye contact. *What's your secret?*

Norah glanced down. The blue fabric of the officer's pants stretched across a thin eight-inch rod. *Is that a wand, or are you just happy to see me?*

He was a wizard, and his bigot of a partner didn't know. Interesting. Norah waggled her eyebrows at the outline of the wand, and the officer's eyes went wide and darted around in fear. She smiled.

"Is that all?"

"Er, yes." the wizard cop sputtered.

He pulled his partner away to chat with the paramedics, and Norah went to find Madge.

CHAPTER TWENTY-FIVE

A fierce tornado of noise ricocheted around the room from Madge's office, even through the closed panel over the shelf. Inside, sturdy plastic clattered against wood, rising to a crescendo occasionally interrupted by a gravelly shout. The pixie was having a fit, and Norah was half-tempted to join her. From the moment Norah had turned on the lights, a parade of crises had slammed First Arret.

There was another dull crash. Norah, wincing, tapped on Madge's office panel with a fingernail.

After a sudden silence, the panel slid open. Norah bent down. The Barbie Dream House furniture inside was in disarray but unbroken. Madge's tantrum had been thwarted by the sturdy bubblegum plastic. The chaos hadn't been entirely harmless, though; a spidery crack ran into the middle of Madge's smartphone from a smashed corner.

"Another one?" Norah tried to keep her voice casual, but the pressure had started to balloon in her head.

"Duncan is leaving."

"Shit. What did he say?" Norah asked.

"Some mangled word stew about pursuing new opportunities elsewhere. Almost word for word what we heard from Carlisle. If he gets that FX show about angels, he'll still have to pay us." Madge crossed her arms.

Norah shook her head. "Whoever's pulling the strings here will pull that one too. That's our two highest earners now that Duncan has that ketchup campaign. I'm going to go over there."

Madge's jaw dropped so hard that Norah was surprised the pixie didn't plummet from the sky. The Dunker lived in an influencer house in Beverly Hills that smelled like rotting protein powder and 20-something boys who preferred cologne to showering. The boys had named it Fuckingham Palace, and only the threat of bankruptcy could drive Norah there.

Madge dove in front of the doorknob, blocking Norah's exit. "A house call won't help. Duncan's not angry with us. He's afraid of someone else. At least we'll still get the ketchup residuals."

"Like a McDonald's wrapper." Norah flung herself into her chair. "We're getting fucked around."

"You think Garton Saxon is involved?" Cleo had begged to come to work today to test a new invention she'd gotten with her friend Stellan's help. The old prop master had come by to say hello and met Cleo. Yesterday evening, he'd swung by with a gift. Said he'd had a hankering to tool around in his fabrication studio.

What he'd produced was a musically activated skateboard on wheels.

Cleo whistled a short melody, and an electric whir

kicked in. The low-wheeled platform she sat on sped to Norah, crashing into her desk as the enchanted pixie whistled the note for stop.

"Sorry," Cleo apologized softly.

"You're getting the hang of it."

Norah realized with embarrassment that she'd been too intent on breaking the spell to help Cleo improve her life in the meantime. With a cheerful melody, the pixie reversed, accelerated, and promptly dented the other side of the desk. *Hopefully, she won't need that platform for long.*

Wisely moving away from the furniture, Cleo did a few donuts on the carpet. Norah was too stressed to enjoy the show.

"To answer your question," Norah paused, "yeah. I think Saxon is stage-managing our downfall."

Madge's phone rang, and Norah winced. She held her breath as Cleo whirred to a hard stop. "First Arret talent, this is Madge. Laura! How are you healing?"

A muscle below Norah's ear unclenched. Laura was solid. She had to be trustworthy. Norah had saved her from a curse. Plus, their names rhymed. Only a monster would break up Norah and Laura.

Madge chattered on. "How's that live oak from Stan working out? That man can perform miracles with seven inches of hardwood, hahaha..."

The dead quiet of the room grew deader, and the muscle in Norah's jaw clenched. Something was wrong. One look at Madge's expression and the pressure in Norah's temples increased. Stars of pain pulsed at her eyes' corners. Norah rubbed her face. Fuck. Not Laura too.

Her careful web of connections was fraying, swept

away by malicious currents. Norah thought about the number on the little slip of paper Harry Bing had given her. Her company would be worth less than grit in a sandbag if all her clients abandoned ship at once.

If I sold out for pennies, he might still hire me. Hell, he might prefer it. Seeing her every day would give him more opportunities for gloating.

Working for Bing was a curdling thought. The man's gaze was disgusting, full of greasy calculation. He was an undeniable success, and in a couple of years, she could claw her way out of the swamp and take another crack at starting her agency.

"Laura. Please. Can you at least come in? As a courtesy for the de-cursing... Mm-hmm... Okay... All right. I understand."

Madge pressed the disconnect button with such force that the spidery crack on her screen crunched wider. Norah held her breath, watching for signs of a second tantrum. *Maybe this time, I'll join in. My mugs could use a good shattering.*

Instead, the pixie met Norah's eyes, shook her head heavily, and closed the panel over her office with heavy, trudging steps. There was a finality to the blocky *clink* of wood on wood.

Norah's feet tingled, and she tapped them on the floor, breathing rapidly. The puzzle she had been carefully assembling wasn't falling apart. It was being blow-torched.

She clomped over to the bookshelf and flung open Madge's office. The pixie was inside, lying face-down on the floor. Norah pinched the back of her silky black blazer, pulled her out, and flung her into the air.

Madge's wings flew open in surprise, flappingly wild. As she regained her balance, she made a red-faced beeline at Norah's head, somersaulting at the last moment to kick both feet into her earlobe.

"Ow!"

"I don't appreciate being woman-handled." Madge huffed, genuinely angry.

"Sorry! I refuse to let us sulk ourselves out of business."

Nurturing a germ of an idea, Norah went to yank Madge's phone off the shelf, swearing as the cracked screen sliced her fingertip. Retrieving a tissue, she waved the phone at the fat pixie.

"Call every single person on our roster," Norah demanded. "If Saxon hasn't contacted them, warn them. If he has, get them back. If there are real problems in our client relationships, we will ferret them and cover them with fucking dwarven superglue. We'll lower our cut to eight percent. Fuck, make it five if you have to."

She slammed into her chair, then tapped the edge of her magical screen with her wand and pulled up their roster. A list of names glowed green in the air.

"Who have we lost?" Norah asked.

"You can't save a sinking ship with a pep-talk," Madge told her evenly.

A *thunk* interrupted the steely silence. Cleo ran into a wall.

"Give me the names." Norah drew her words out like taffy. After a *hmmph*, Madge read them off. As Norah tapped the name of each client they had lost, it blinked red. When she was done, they stared at the board. It looked like a fucking Christmas light display. Norah's cheeks puffed out as she exhaled through pursed lips.

"Maybe you're right. Maybe we're dead, but I want to poke the carcass with a stick to make sure." Norah righted Madge's overturned pink plastic desk and placed the cracked phone on top of it.

Flapping her wings with exaggerated sarcastic movements, Madge flew back into her office and pulled up the red and green list of names. Norah smiled encouragingly, and Madge returned a rude pixie gesture. Norah had only seen her use it in rush-hour traffic.

Wheels rolled over the wooden floor, and something bumped Norah's ankle softly. She looked down. Cleo was there. She repeated the soft bump. Norah opened her mouth to snap at the box, then closed it as runes scrawled across it.

Cleo glowed a comforting gold. The bump was Cleo's best effort at patting her on the shoulder. Norah patted the crate, then drew her hand back as a disorienting crackle of magic pushed back against her. *What the hell?*

A crackle of static bloomed and burst in Norah's guts, and she straightened in surprise. If she wanted to keep her clients, she would have to give them something worth standing up to Saxon for. She was going to have to serve them their dreams. Norah spun her chair to Madge's office, watching the pixie type peevishly.

"Can you get them here in person?" Norah ventured.

Madge froze, then waggled her head uncertainly. "Maybe."

"I want to look them in the eyes. If they're in California, I want them face to face."

"I'll do my best. Half of them are scared and starry-eyed from lapping up Saxon's bullshit. How am I supposed to herd them here?"

"Your charm!" Norah slid Madge's office door shut with a bang.

They would stay if they thought she could give them what they wanted. *Might* stay.

Norah pulled a tote bag of empty Floe bottles from the back of a cabinet and trudged to the bathroom down the hall, letting the mindless chore of filling and re-sealing soothe her. As she walked back, the bag dug an irritating red line into her shoulder.

Soon, clean lines of translucent bottles marched across the small desk in the waiting room. Norah fished in a drawer for some high-end keto lamb bars and arranged them on a table. They tasted like Slim Jims, but they cost four times as much and were therefore fancy.

"Time to break out the good stuff." Shivering, she tapped the bottom drawer of her office desk with her wand, releasing the magical lock, and removed a large rectangular black ceramic box. Fantasy scenes were painted on the lid in dark gray relief—beautiful drow workmanship.

Would that be workelfship? She shook her head and carried the box to the waiting room, then opened the hinged lid. The ceramic was so thin that the overhead lights passed through it, clearly illuminating the beautiful illustrations on both sides.

Inside, wrapped in silk and tied with cloth-of-silver ribbons, were spheres the size of cherries. Norah pulled off a string and flicked open the wrapper. If she was pulling out all the stops, she had to ensure the snacks hadn't gone bad since being imported from Oriceran two years ago. At least, that was what she told herself. *Another of Stan's many gifts.*

The beauty of the dark chocolate sphere shivered Norah's skin. The candy reminded her of the black opals in the Natural History Museum's gemstone exhibits. There was a richness to the voids, but unlike black opals, the flawless ebony surfaces of these chocolates were uninterrupted by tawdry colors. Unable to hold off any longer, Norah popped the sphere into her mouth.

The chocolates tasted like the comforting dark before the end of a good night's sleep. Sweetness turned to bitterness. Bitterness turned to budding warmth.

The dark elves who lived in very cold places, Stan said, ate these candies in midwinter. They promoted joy, empathy, and communal feeling, which usually staved off the temptation toward cannibalism during lean freezes. Norah had chuckled, taking it for a cheap shot at the dark elves, and Stan had looked at her with disapproval. He was serious.

If my clients want to eat me alive, I can at least force-feed them a reason to feel bad about it.

She was as ready as she'd ever be.

"Who's coming in?" she demanded, flinging the panel over Madge's office open as the last notes of Oriceran cocoa and bitter orange dissolved on her tongue.

"Most of them. Today and tomorrow. The first one should be here in...two hours."

Norah's game-day enthusiasm dipped. "Keep calling. I'll take another crack at Cleo."

The robot skateboard did a quick donut in the middle of the office. "Lucky me." She was unusually peevish.

Norah cracked her knuckles and closed her eyes. She would need to push her new radio powers to the max over the next two days, so she might as well warm them up.

Leaning over Cleo, Norah rested her chin on her fists. "This enchantment embedded inside me...it detects people's intentions. When I un-cursed that production assistant on the beach, her deepest intentions were buried, but they weren't gone. I felt them through the curse.

"If my new powers can pass through a curse, maybe they can weaken it. That's what I want to try. Turn them on to full strength and try to feel what you want. See if the current between us creates a weak spot. I need your permission. It might get...intimate."

"Because you're going to be reading my mind? Or my...woodgrain?" Cleo asked.

"Sort of," Norah confessed. "I can't hear your thoughts. The power goes deeper than that. It picks up feelings, wants, and impulses."

"I don't know if that's better or worse," Cleo mused.

"Neither do I," Norah admitted.

The box drove back and forth across the room on its robot skateboard. Pacing. It occurred to Norah that the pixie hadn't been able to pace in a century. Finally, Cleo skidded to a stop at Norah's feet.

"Fine. No calling *TMZ* if you learn anything weird."

"I would never do something so tacky." Norah glared with mock offense. "You deserve at least *The Hollywood Reporter.*"

Cleo snorted, and a collection of runes glowed on the

box. Somehow, the crate looked like it was sticking out its tongue. Norah opened her tarot-card lab notebook and flipped past the page labeled *Two-wand solution.*

"Don't worry, you're my favorite," she murmured to her blue gum eucalyptus as she retrieved it from her desk.

She had convinced her mother to skim the dangerous brown leather grimoire for anything that could help Cleo, dog-eared page excepted. Petra had delivered, and Norah pulled a spell scribbled on a piece of notebook paper from her purse. She memorized the whorls and lines of the wand movement and formed her lips into the silent words of the spell.

"Okay! Let's turn it to eleven and crack this thing open." The crate's planks expanded and settled slightly as Cleo emitted a small sigh.

Preparing to pick up a broad field of emotions, Norah accessed the radio magic, turning it up, up, up. Information flooded in from the neighborhood around her, crashing against the bulwarks of her heart and mind and mixing into indistinguishable channels.

Two people sleeping under a portico outside wanted decent coffee and somewhere to charge their phones. A woman must be walking a dog a few feet away because there was a bright ball of energy at the level of her ankles that craved pats and treats. The dog's owner didn't know what she wanted, and Norah felt bittersweet sympathy for the pulse of formless craving that reached her through the radar.

Downstairs in the pizza shop, Ji-woo's dad wanted to get out of the heat. There was also an ache for his son, a desire to kick him out of the restaurant to something brighter and greener.

Ji-woo was thinking about a girl. The image reached Norah's mind, a sparkling daydream of a woman with long brown hair, glowing tennis shoes, and...

Oh, my God, it was her. She almost slammed the radio magic shut, embarrassed. Only the steady square of Cleo in her peripheral vision stopped her. She had a curse to break.

Still, it was interesting. She'd always had a friendly rapport with Ji-woo. He lived nearby, which was an important bonus. She'd seen relationships in this city destroyed by crosstown commutes. Ji-woo was tall, impeccably courteous, and had a dreamy swoop of silky hair across his forehead. He also smelled like pizza. Maybe they could bottle that smell for cologne as a side hustle...

She was getting distracted. Norah re-read her scrap of paper and let Ji-woo's wandering desires flow out of her, focusing instead on Cleo. The current flowing into her from the cursed pixie was muffled like a scream through a wool coat. Norah pushed at the radio magic inside her, urging it past its limits and opening herself to maximum information.

She pressed her palm against Cleo's woodgrain, and a river of visible sparks flowed around the crate. Norah focused her attention on a single spot, a paisley curlicue rune carved into the corner of the box. That was where she would strike.

Cleo's voice wasn't getting louder. The curse gummed up the channel.

The last time Norah had used her radio magic on Cleo, the pixie had emitted a distinct desire to get out.

Now, the outlines of Cleo's desires had changed. She wanted to talk to Stellan about adding an antigravity spell to the robot skateboard to boost the vertical potential.

Norah saw a hint of optimism there, but not for a cure. Cleo wanted to stop the curse-breaking attempts. Shocked, Norah almost drew her hands away.

Please don't give up on me, Cleo. I can fix it.

Norah started tracing the new spell's outline, drawing decisive lines and circles. She carefully pronounced the Light Elvish words, which were something along the lines of "release us from the earth."

There was a swell of magic as the box floated into the air. *Yes.* Norah imagined the crate blooming like a flower, its planks rolling out into petals to reveal the pixie inside. Cleo would see then that Norah wasn't useless and she didn't have to abandon all hope.

A smooth edge bumped Norah's butt. The seat of her office chair was also floating in the air. So was she.

Norah had been so distracted by her daydream that she hadn't realized an antigravity spell had taken effect. Everything not nailed down was in the air. Books floated off the shelves. Norah's abandoned lukewarm coffee was a brown golf-ball glob, wobbling over her new computer.

Shit. What goes up...

There was a yelp from Madge's bookshelf office, and something banged against the wood. Poor Madge. Zero gravity was probably even weirder if you *could* fly. Maybe NASA would send a pixie into space someday to learn about it.

Cleo hadn't changed. The crate hung in the air, the

mechanical platform floating six inches below, wheels spinning fruitlessly.

Apparently, all I released her from was gravity. She needed to bring them all down gently.

Suddenly, the door to the office rattled and opened. A figure popped inside.

"Hell, yeah. Sick float party!" Duncan complimented her.

Norah brightened. "Madge talked you into a face-to-face!" She winced at the silk-wrapped balls orbiting the room behind him. Hopefully, they'd make it through the inevitable descent.

The sight of an empty silk wrapper floating away from Duncan's pocket cheered her up considerably.

"What did you think of the chocolate?" she asked. He gave her double thumbs-up. Power from Norah's wand was still flowing around the box and through the room.

"Um. Would you mind giving me a hand? More like a wand."

Red-enameled bamboo appeared in Duncan's hand. "How can I help?" he asked, eyes compassionate.

"Bring us down gently when I release the antigravity spell."

A current of intention flowed into her from the young wizard. He wanted to help. There was a gleaming black tint to the current he was throwing off, which Norah suspected was an effect of the chocolate.

It wasn't just the chocolate, though. He wanted to help because he liked Norah. She could tell he wanted to stay with the agency, but he was afraid of losing his income. Trouble at home. Norah blinked. *Gravity first, deals later.*

"On three?"

Duncan nodded.

Counting down, she drew a circle over the spell and slashed it with a quick diagonal line. Her stomach somersaulted as she plummeted a foot before Duncan's counter spell caught her. Moving quickly, Norah snatched her floating coffee cup and scooped up the globule of coffee an instant before it cascaded over her laptop.

On her feet again, she went to greet Duncan properly. He shied away.

"What's up with your eyes?"

Oh, right. Emit one tiny spray of sparks from your eyes, and suddenly, everyone has questions.

Norah closed her eyes, reached inside herself, and turned the radio down to a diameter the size of her desk. The eyeball sparks died to an occasional attractive sparkle.

"Thank you so much."

"Can you put me back on my platform?"

Duncan turned, saw Cleo, shrugged, and carefully replaced her on her robot skateboard. Cleo circled the room to reclaim her bearings, then zoomed out the office door.

"I need a breather. I'll be in the waiting room, convincing one of the young hunks you represent to use me as a coffee table."

Duncan choked down a laugh. Norah righted both their chairs and offered one to Duncan.

"I don't want to waste your time." His brow furrowed. "Your assistant is very convincing."

"She could talk a hat off a gnome," Norah agreed. "So let's get straight to it. Leave with my blessings if you're not getting what you need from First Arret. If it's something else… If you're being threatened—"

"Someone sent me a message," Duncan replied. "Like, a physical email with a little portrait of a flag in the corner?"

"A stamp?" Norah ventured.

"Yeah! So old-timey. It said I'd get kicked out of the Palace if I didn't find a new rep."

A current from Duncan flowed into her awareness. Norah tried to understand its shape, then it clicked.

"You want to move out?"

Duncan looked around the room, dropping his voice to whisper, "Yeah, I *want* to, but my whole thing is being the single funny guy in the party house. My Romaz deal has social engagement bonuses, and I get a lot of cross-traffic from the other bros."

"What do you *want?*" Norah asked. He looked at her again, serious this time.

"My mom has been too sick to work, and my little sister just started college. I can't throw them under the bus. That paper email…"

"Letter?"

"Yeah, that letter made it sound like even worse things could happen. The agent I've been talking to…I don't know. He's fine. Bing's got a lot of influence..."

That one was a needle to the heart. He'd gone with Bing, although not willingly.

Norah rolled the new information around in her mind.

"Are you happy with Bing?"

The radio said *No!* An image reached her of a man in a suit who was ninety-five percent haircut.

"He knows everyone," Duncan observed cautiously.

"Not a ringing endorsement."

"He says I'm a good-looking guy, and I should stick with that. He says the wizard thing is alienating. He wants me to do full non-magical drag. I'm auditioning for a CW show next week."

Norah's nose wrinkled. "Is that what you want?" she asked. Duncan rubbed his eyes with his palms. He'd lost weight, and his hair was limp.

"He doesn't get me. If I get that show, I could move into an apartment that doesn't smell like chlorine and feet. I've been seeing this girl, or I was until she saw my bathroom. She called it an affront to human decency."

"Is it?" Norah asked.

Duncan distracted himself with a glum wand twirl. "Most definitely."

A path through this tangled thicket began to reveal itself.

"If you stay with me, I will keep you in that house," Norah promised. Duncan deflated and started to climb to his feet. Norah stopped him with a glance. "I will connect you with this town's best business manager, who will set up a trust for your mom and sister. Figure out how much money you need to get them straightened out for good. Have you ever made a budget?" She looked at his tennis shoes, limited edition Jordans.

"I got these for free." He held up his hands defensively. Made sense.

"How much extra crap do you get from TikTok collabs?" she asked.

"We have a six-car garage with piles full of skateboards,

espresso machines, and unwearable streetwear. Don't ask me about the jockstrap avalanche of 2021."

"I absolutely will not. What I *will* do is connect you with a reselling service. And a housekeeping service. There will be light at the end of the tunnel. Okay?"

"Okay," he replied cautiously. An ember of hope flowed to her.

"Then we will figure out what you want to do. Do a few open mics and see if a live performance is a fit. A tour? I'll get you auditions with people too powerful to cross. We'll figure it out. If you stay."

She pushed a bottle of Floe to him.

"Can I have tap water? That stuff tastes like the Fuckingham Palace pool," Duncan mumbled. Norah grinned.

"You can have whatever you want."

She almost danced as she lifted her wand and shot a thin stream of water into a clean coffee mug. She had gotten him back; she could feel it. As he contemplatively drank his water, their conversation devolved from big life questions to pleasant chitchat and his cautious agreement to return to First Arret.

When he opened the door to leave, rowdy noise hit Norah. There were eight people in the waiting room. They'd all been eating chocolate.

"You're next, Winston," Madge shouted over Norah's shoulder.

The gnome trekked in, and Norah shut the door.

The drive home from the office only took two minutes, but exhaustion stretched it out interminably. Every driver on every street was out to get her today. Cleo was good company, however, more enthusiastic than Norah had seen her in ages. With her planks vibrating, she looked alarmingly bomb-like.

"Spill the beans," Norah demanded. "You met someone. Work? Romance? You meet a buff fairy transformed into a saw? A were-termite?"

Cleo gasped. "Is that a thing?"

Norah, who enjoyed seeing the box exhibit a range of emotions other than watchful placidity, admitted, "No. Shifters tend to be mammals, although once I met a Weretoad. He was a standup comedian, always telling women he was a prince so they'd kiss him."

"What a turd." Cleo huffed. "No, I didn't meet a were-termite. I talked to a witch whose brother is a whiz with enchantments. Antigravity enchantments." A glow of enthusiasm pulsed across Cleo's engravings.

"You think he can break the curse?" Norah asked excitedly. *That's supposed to be my job.* Cleo went dark and quiet, and Norah had to slam on the brakes as a dented sedan cut into her lane. Even as they turned onto their much more peaceful street, Cleo remained silent.

"What?" Nothing. It was like trying to talk to an end table. Norah parked and, sighing, chucked Cleo under her arm. There was a muffled squeal.

"Put me on my platform. I'm going to drive around the courtyard," Cleo retorted stuffily. What had gotten into the pixie? Norah held the box in front of her face.

"What if something happens? What if someone...I don't know...*takes* you?"

"My platform has a maximum speed of twenty-five miles an hour, and I'm perfectly capable of yelling for help."

The grimoire-slash-lab-notebook dug a sharp corner into Norah's hip. She winced. It was up to almost a hundred entries. "I know I've failed you, Cleo, but I'm not giving up. We'll solve this."

"I'm not a failure!" Cleo barked so sharply that Norah dropped her. Her hands clawed the air to catch the box, which banged onto the concrete and rolled once so that the side with the eye-like runes was facing up. " I'm not a project. I'm a...person with corners. Put me on my platform!"

Norah jerked the robot skateboard free of the car and put it down. Wheels whirred behind her as the crate followed her through the gate and into the courtyard. Norah ignored the box until the noise split away. Cleo had turned toward the pool.

Good. Let her cool off. Would the chlorine hurt her wood, though? Norah debated hauling the pixie bodily back to the apartment where she would be safe. Instead, she kicked the wrought iron railing of the stairs up to the second floor.

She'd been sitting all day, listening attentively to clients. Her brain had been vacuumed out by a succession of desperately needy creative types. Her butt had started to go numb at the end, and she was filled with formless energy, her brain unable to conduct it into useful activity. She didn't want to think about what she needed. She didn't want to think at all.

Inside her apartment, she flipped on the A/C and stared briefly at the Hermes sneakers, which flapped around inside a large gilt Victorian birdcage she'd purchased from a prop shop south of Thai Town. As she approached, the shoes flapped eagerly, banging against the wires.

"Not today, boys," she told them. She needed exertion, not exhilaration. Pulling on workout gear and stuffing her feet into dirty sneakers, she was out the door in minutes. Cleo was nowhere in sight as she jogged up the gentle slope to Griffith Park.

CHAPTER TWENTY-SIX

Ultimately, they held onto most of their clients, clawing First Arret back from the edge of insolvency. Only a few scattered wisps of blinking red glowed on the board of names. She didn't think it was over, though. Sure, she was stubborn, but so were her enemies. The atmosphere in the office grew thick, and she and Madge waited for the other shoe to drop.

When the call finally came, it came after hours to Norah's cellphone as she hit the steepest hill of the three-mile loop she'd been burning off her jitters.

"Norah? It's me, Duncan."

She slid across a patch of gravel to a stop and patched the call into her earbuds.

"Hey. Did that business manager get in touch?"

There was a long pause. Norah took slow breaths and walked out to a small overlook. Over the hillside to the west, miles away, a thin column of smoke rose into a general haze. Sirens echoed in the distance.

"Um, yeah. There's a problem."

"You didn't get kicked out of the house?"

"Sort of."

"Shit. I'm good for my promise, you know. Whatever it is, I'll get you back in. Who's the house alpha?" she asked.

"Bro, we're all alphas. None of us are in the house anymore. It burned down."

Another siren rang, slightly distorted. She realized it was coming from her phone and not the city below her.

"My lucky ring light is in there," Duncan continued. "Should I go back for it?"

"What? No! Just...hang tight."

She pulled up TikTok and checked Duncan's feed. It was live. In the blurry video, he held his phone to his ear, backlit by flames. The video had over a million live viewers.

Norah frowned. "It's not a publicity stunt, is it? You don't think one of the guys did it?"

"What? No! All our Jordans were in there."

A stream of sympathetic emojis washed over the live feed.

"Don't do anything stupid," Norah demanded. "I'm going to cut this problem off at the source." The figure on the video nodded, and Norah hung up.

The flying shoes were a risk, like strapping the jet engine of a 747 to a golf cart, but Norah didn't want to waste an instant arguing with gate guards at the Universal backlot. After lacing the shoes so tight they cut off her circulation when she wasn't actively moving, she'd activated them and hoped for the best. Now she was five hundred feet in the air. She didn't have time to be afraid as long as she kept moving.

She'd made fantastic time from Griffith. A personal best, she suspected, although she hadn't timed herself. There had been an accident on the 101, and the sun had gone down by the time she'd turned down a side street near the working entrance. She debated ditching her car for good and flying, but visions of hitting a pigeon with her face deterred her.

The dark was an excellent cover, however. Daylight would have made her an obvious intruder, but the velvety haze of night provided the perfect cover. It was too dark to see anything interesting, like the *Jaws* lagoon or the *War of the Worlds* plane crash.

People were still around, but Garton Saxon's production had moved into one of the massive gray warehouses below the Universal Studios theme park. New Yorkers had the Statue of Liberty. An oversized yellow minion watched over Angelenos.

Norah flapped jerkily down, less a predatory bird than a desperate chicken, and alit on the warehouse roof with an errant crash. She winced, then relaxed as the metallic roar of heavy machinery filtered through the sheet metal below her. It wasn't quiet on the set, at least. She drew a small circle with her wand and sent a burst of blue magic into it until the metal roof glowed red-hot and melted her a peephole. When she could touch it without burning herself, she looked inside.

The set was palatial, with several reconstructed interiors of European palaces. A wide array of art directors, builders, and stunt coordinators were working on rigging the collapse of a wooden staircase crawling up a lavishly painted wall. This must be Saxon's awful Henry VIII project, which suggested his many spousal decapitations were justified because demons possessed the women. *What an asshole.* The thought encompassed Garton and the long-dead king.

The far corner of the enormous space housed a greenish object. Norah squinted at a row of glowing frosted windows. A train car? That's right. This was Garton Saxon's famous office. That was supposed to be on the Silver Lion lots. *Maybe he pays to have it towed around town.*

Keeping an eye on the pair of security guards circling the warehouse perimeter, Norah flew unsteadily over to the corner that housed the train car, used her wand to cut a large rectangle in the warehouse wall, and climbed inside. As she stood, a flap of her left shoe sent her sprawling to the floor.

Norah's pinkie bent backward as she caught herself on the floor, and she swore inwardly, fixing her feet with a glare she hoped conveyed, "I've always wanted to try fried shoe, so don't give me a reason, you hand-stitched assholes." Picking up on the psychic message, the shoes folded their wings demurely. *Better.*

There was a foot of space between the warehouse wall and the shining green train car. Norah cast a quick glamour over the punched-out rectangle so the guards wouldn't raise the alarm the next time they walked past it and edged around. Filigree iron steps at the end of the car marched up to a stained-glass door. It was too late for a complicated plan, so Norah opened it.

"I told you not to—" Saxon's snarl took a U-turn into calculating silence when he saw her. "Miss Wintry. To what do I owe this trespass? Unless the gate guards let you in, in which case I should thank you. I'm in the mood for a little severe discipline."

Saxon sat stiffly on a carved antique chair. It was very delicate, the kind that would splinter with a slight weight shift. Everything in the office was beautiful, mostly undersized antiques with careful patterns and decorative finials. The exception was a brass lantern on the corner of Saxon's desk, whose blocky bulk contrasted with its surroundings.

"You blew up the Fuckingham Palace," she informed him evenly.

Garton's mouth slid greasily into a smile, lips curling back from large white teeth. He picked up a peony-painted teacup from his desk and sipped, pinkie out. "You can't possibly be surprised," he purred. On a teak stand in the corner behind him was a filigree birdcage not dissimilar to the ones she'd bought for her unruly flying shoes. *Maybe we shop at the same place?*

"I'm not surprised. I'm pissed off." Norah put her hand on her wand. "Do you have it out for witches? Or women? Both? Magicals should stick together."

A growl grew in Garton's throat. There was a predatory amusement in his expression, as if he were a lion listening to a long list of gazelle complaints.

"We don't need to stick together. You need to fall in line. Have you looked at my hall of trophies? Well, the one in *here*, anyway." He flashed her a quick, remote smirk and swept his hands across the photographs on the wall. *Garton Saxon, this is your life.* The frames captured over a century of the old elf's escapades. Mostly in photographs, but here and there were old newspaper clippings with black ink illustrations.

"I saw my first motion picture at the Chicago World's Fair in 1893. Lord, but Thomas Edison was a ratfink. A barely literate technician, not a visionary. I grasped the potential. A camera is not a tool for observation. It's a tool for control. Who decides what people see?"

"Very Orwellian," Norah remarked.

"Orwell was a ratfink, too." Saxon vibrated so tensely on his wooden chair that his teacup rattled against its saucer. "While your great-great-grandparents were curing warts in some forsaken bog, Miss Wintery, I was building a moving pictures empire. It wasn't even hard to reinvent myself every few decades. Tell people a good enough story, and suddenly you're back on top."

"You've had quite the career," Norah agreed.

Saxon set a florid orange china cup on the table beside him and leaned back. "Whatever devil or brain aneurysm told you you could scoop my empire out from under me gravely misled you."

"I'm not taking anything from you. I'm building my own...well, not an empire yet. Call it a city-state. Why don't you stop scrabbling over crumbs and bake a bigger pie?"

"Your naïveté would be charming if it wasn't a pulsing thorn in my eye. What you're describing is impossible. Cooperation leads to arguments. Argument leads to weakness. Weakness leads to destruction. A film is not a machine with interchangeable parts. It's an anthill."

"You're the queen?" Norah rolled her eyes. "Give me a break. You're making a dopey gritty reboot of Henry VIII with a lead who's as old and out of touch as you are. Why would I get in your way when you're doing such a good job of destroying yourself?"

Garton's fingers clenched, crushing the cup and saucer in his hand into neat pieces. These he launched at a nearby yolk-yellow velvet chair, then wiped his hands on a silk handkerchief on the edge of his desk.

"I'm bored now," he muttered, looking through her as he reached for the brass beacon on the corner of his desk. Norah activated the radio magic inside herself with a crackle, desperate for any edge.

Growing up in the dark days of the Silver Griffins' downfall, Norah had seen plenty she was too young to see. There had been so much recent action, from the burning Vince to the triple threat Gus and, most alarmingly, that evil brown bear trap of a spell book.

She still wasn't prepared for Garton Saxon's intentions to hit her. The old elf wanted absolute control. Over her, over everything. Fed by a fetal terror, he wanted to destroy what he couldn't control.

Norah gasped and stumbled backward but failed to create any distance between her and the tsunami of black intent washing over her. He didn't want her death or for her to pack up and move to a state without a coast like many Hollywood failures before her. He wanted her to be so terrified and tortured that no one would ever cross him again.

These apocalyptic needs were connected to an image that bobbed in the current of emotions. A flower? Why was

Saxon thinking about a flower? It wasn't a real flower, being only loosely botanical. No, it was some craft woven from loops and twists of a dark thread. Not thread, hair? From whom?

Norah wondered if she'd made a terrible mistake as Saxon effortlessly slid the brass lantern on his desk to him and arranged his fingers on the symbols that had started to glow on the glass. *This is not good.*

Saxon murmured something at the beacon, and it filled with mesmerizing white light, flattening the shadows in the room. A wide white beam burst from its center and hit Norah straight in the heart. She screamed, less from pain than from Garton's lip-licking anticipation of her agony.

He wanted her to hurt, but he hadn't, and her scream trickled away below the oscillating hum of the beacon. No, she wasn't feeling pain. The sensation was stranger than that, loose static inside her. It filled her like firecracker energy in her chest. *The radio magic... It's doing something to protect me.*

It wasn't enough. As the beam from the beacon widened and brightened, the radio magic filled her body in a scramble of blue sparks. She realized there wasn't enough of it, and some sank into the intricate hand-knotted silk carpet at her feet. Here and there, it left holes. The beam broke through one such gap, patchy blue static in her left hand. Her fingers curled and shot forward against her will, pulling her to the antique desk. Saxon laughed. "Good. That's it, little marionette."

She needed more of the static. How much more of Saxon's twisted intentions could she take? What if the onrush of evil somehow eroded her?

The beam broke through at her right knee and hurtled toward her chest, pulling her onto one foot like an unbalanced Karate Kid. She turned the radio magic up with a fierce twist and blue static ballooned through her, pushing out Saxon's light beam.

Now that she was on two feet, she would have to do something.

Saxon banged frantically on the side of the beacon, muttering Elvish curses that crackled with hints of the actual curse. While he was distracted, Norah's eyes flicked around the room.

Whatever the beacon was, it was failing. Or at least, it was failing to work on her. When Garton gave up and twisted the beam to the chittering birdcage in the corner, Norah jumped.

Not jumped, flew. There was no unsteady handwaving as the powerful magical wings on her feet shot her to the rail car's glass roof. The rate of acceleration dropped her stomach to the level of her shoes, and she didn't get her wand up in time to spell the glass away. She did, at least, break the smoky glass with the tip of her blue eucalyptus wand rather than her face. As glass fell around her, she wished she *had* gone face-first. Crashing through the sunroof had snapped her wand in half.

There go Plans A, B, and C.

Some brain stem instinct kicked in, and she managed to snatch the second half of the wand from the rain of glittering shards. Blue energy bled from the splintered ends.

No. No, no, no, no, no, no. At least her flying shoes weren't wand-powered.

A single "Hey!" from a crew member carrying a c-stand

escalated into a flurry of activity as people and magicals raced to the sound of the breaking glass. They found Norah frozen in the air ten feet above Saxon's office, wings flapping steadily at her feet.

Run, Wintery. Or...fly.

She looked into the gap between the rail car and the wall where'd she'd cut her way in. *Quickest exit is the entry.* Diving, she was forced to divert at the last second as a burly security Kilomea poked her head through the hole. The glamour must have broken with her wand. Norah shot around the warehouse's perimeter and back into the sky, scanning for another exit. Fifteen feet below, a wizard carrying a pile of ruffled velvet dropped it and shot a weak stunning spell in her direction. She easily dodged.

"Don't stun her! She'll die if she falls from up there." The unnerving admonishment faded as she zigzagged along the warehouse perimeter.

There. A huge loading dock in the distance was open to the outside, the concrete inside stacked with piles of fresh-smelling wood. Someone watching from the floor saw her eyes zero in.

"Close that loading dock and get that witch!" Garton Saxon's magically amplified voice boomed so loudly through the warehouse that the sound wave knocked Norah a few feet off-course. Saxon's employees were highly motivated by the anger in his voice, and the rolling metal door creaked and began to descend.

It was going too quickly. If she accelerated, she might be able to make it. She also might hit a metal wall at full speed. *"Fly, my pretties,"* she screamed, and the shoes picked up their pace, slinging her forward.

White blurs streaked across the warehouse floor below. Mice? No, mice shifters, she realized as the streaks grew in size, and the dots became sinewy, aerodynamic masses of white-furred muscle. Somehow, they were moving faster than her.

"Fly like...something much faster than the wind," she ordered. "An experimental naval aircraft? A UFO! Go!" The shoes pushed against their upper limits of speed, their leather creaking and their laces flying.

If she didn't get out now, she wasn't looking at a simple arrest for trespassing. Blue static crackled a warning inside her. She could feel the desires of hundreds of people beneath her. Most of them wanted more than anything in the world to avoid attracting Garton Saxon's attention. *Join the club.* He had terrified these people. She could still pick out his signal among the chaos, a swamping onrush of evil.

The door was half-closed and rolling even faster.

"I will rub you with exotic oils," Norah whispered breathlessly to her shoes. "I will buy you bulletproof laces. Please, go!" The wings folded into a final desperate dive.

Another spell shot up to block her, this time a pooling snare of dark elf magic. Norah ducked it and cried as it yanked out a clump of her ponytail that had brushed against it.

There would only be a few feet of space by the time she reached the door.

When she was twelve, she had gotten to the final round of a birthday party limbo contest. Unable to decide between going headfirst or feet-first, she had attempted a sideways split. Not only had she fallen spectacularly, but she had also ripped out the seat of her stiff new jeans.

Some of her classmates had called her "granny panties" until her high school graduation. Those were her friends.

Headfirst or breach? Vowing not to repeat the birthday limbo fiasco, Norah opted to attempt a feet-first slide into home base. She angled down between clumps of the frightened crew, who were making a lot of noise but appeared unwilling to take a witch to the chest. Norah's shoulder thudded into the ground and her shoes tugged, pulling her to freedom. The garage door creaked down.

Daggers bit into her shoulder, drawing Norah's attention away from her feet. A mouse the size and shape of a greyhound had buried its rotten teeth in her shoulder and was attempting to drag her back inside. Norah screamed at the second white shape at its heels. *These must be the denizens of Saxon's cage*. The mice weren't evil. Like the PA at the beach, they were under Saxon's control. Real power banged against a stolid layer of the curse.

"PULL!" Norah screamed, larynx burning, then gurgled with pain as the command spurred the mouse holding her shoulder to bite down. Its claws scrabbled on the smooth concrete, unable to find purchase, and the nearby crew seemed unwilling to approach the snarling rodents.

As the shoes pulled, Norah stabbed the broken end of the wand into the mouse shifter's shoulder, murmuring a silent apology. The rodent emitted an eardrum-piercing trill of pain as its jaw released.

She slid under the aluminum door as it slammed shut, losing several more strands of hair. The shoes pulled her into the air upside-down, and the last thing she saw before she passed out was a sloppy brushstroke of blood from her shoulder streaked across the concrete of the loading dock.

Few places were ideal for regaining consciousness. If a soft bed in a sunlit room was at the top of the list, hanging upside-down in the dark a thousand feet above the ground had to be at the bottom. Only her tennis shoes' steady, measured flapping brought her around from blank-brained terror.

She forced her lungs into slow, steady breaths before she passed out again. So much blood was pooling in her head that that might happen anyway.

Her phone, miraculously, was still in her pocket. *Anyone who says skinny jeans are out doesn't own flying shoes.* After wiping the sweat off her fingers, she meticulously slid it out.

Stan picked up halfway through the first ring.

"Norah? Where are you?"

Pushing down manic laughter, she asked, "Can you meet me at the In-N-Out off the 101 by Universal Studios? Maybe bring bandages."

"Of course. Are you okay?"

"I...I'm alive. I'll be down in a minute. I hope."

"Down? Are—"

Norah cut the call.

Norah begged Stan to look at her wand immediately, but he ignored her attempts to bribe him with unlimited double-doubles, focusing instead on her bare feet and bloody shirt. Sanitizing her shoulder with healing light, he ordered her to keep pressure on the wound, bundled her into his Thunderbird, and raced home at about a hundred miles an hour.

At least three cops ignored their scofflaw speed, and Norah wondered again about the magical composition of Stan's dashboard hula girl. Norah had tried to leave the sneakers in the In-N-Out dumpster, but they had fluttered out and followed her dejectedly into the car.

Stan ushered Norah into his apartment and flung the sneakers carelessly into his entrance hallway. Not content to lie around, they preened and flew over to the doorway, where they parked themselves in a neat pair. Norah shivered as she looked at them. She'd half-hoped they would fly away when she'd taken them off on the In-N-Out curb. *Give me a broomstick any day. I refuse to be hauled bodily upside-down through any more nights.*

After pulling out a decidedly Oriceran first-aid kit, Stan treated the bites on her shoulder with an antiseptic anti-curse salve that smelled like burned rubber. He tried to make her some tea but finally relented to her pestering and inspected the broken halves of her wand.

"How's the patient?" Norah asked after a minute, her brows scrunching.

Stan glanced at her shoulder, then followed her eye line to the table. "Oh. You mean the wand. Did you know that sometimes broken bones can heal stronger than before? If the wood trusts you, it's the same with wands."

She stared at the pieces, and Stan left the room. When he returned, there was a small plastic bottle in his hands.

"Wood glue," he announced.

"You're fixing a *magic wand* with wood glue?" Norah felt uncertain, but she trusted Stan.

"Don't ask me what it's made of." He squeezed a small drop onto the end of the wand.

"What, ground-up unicorn hoof?" Norah shot back ironically.

Stan's gray eyes slid off hers. "Er..."

Norah inspected the iridescent glue more closely. "Oh, shit. Don't tell Twitter."

Stan held the first two fingers of his hands a foot apart, and molten light ribboned between them. He placed the halves of the wand together and made a complicated series of twists and turns with his fingers like a cat's cradle master. When he was finished, the center of the wand bulged brightly, wrapped in glue and connective light. Stan offered it to her gently.

Norah met his eyes. "I love this wand." She wanted him to know how much it meant.

Stan nodded enthusiastically. "Good! That's very good. Keep it up over the next twelve hours. Tell the wand that it's a good wand, that it has done very nice work, and you want it to heal."

Norah's eyebrow quirked into a question. *Really? Hmm.* Stan had an incredible talent for saying absurd things that turned out to be true. Norah patted the undamaged tip of the blue eucalyptus with one finger.

"You've been very brave," she told it gravely. "Would you like some nice almond oil?" Maybe it was a trick of the light, but the glue at the center of the wand brightened. "Okay, beautiful." She stood up to tend to her patient and moved to the door. Stan caught her in a nervous stare-down with the flying shoes, which had risen into the air to block her exit.

"I don't think I was built for three-dimensional travel, Stan," she told him. "At least not outside of a comfortable airplane. Preferably first class."

The tongues and laces of the tennis shoes drooped, and Norah felt guilty. The shoes *had* saved her life.

"Hey, Stan." She didn't take her eyes off the translucent wings. "Would you take a sculptural commission? I have an idea."

CHAPTER TWENTY-SEVEN

The delicate ceramic head of a shepherdess statue exploded into a fine powder between Garton Saxon's fingers. Before him, Heberd winced. He had purchased the statue for his boss a year earlier on Saxon's birthday, and his boss had placed it on a shelf in his green train car—a rare spot of approval. Now, Heberd suspected Saxon had been setting him up for a higher fall.

The shepherdess' crook snapped, and Saxon began to break off small chunks and fling them in Heberd's direction. Somehow, his destructive jetsam always hit Heberd's eyes as if they had a magnetic pull. He wished he could buy a pair of work goggles without drawing further ire. Saxon was magnificently attired, as always, in an embroidered black silk robe and a silver bolo tie in the shape of a glowering female elf.

Saxon's train car was being repaired by a team of nineteenth century-stained glass experts. Not the first time they'd been called in. However, it was usually Saxon who'd done the smashing. Heberd had been forced to dig up an old circus tent from the prop warehouse and set it up as a makeshift office. He had transferred all the furniture himself.

The pieces were still standing after Saxon cooled down from his blind rage. In the end, it hadn't taken very many trips. There wasn't much extra space in the large tent. Most of the square footage was taken up with cages. After buying all the antique bird cages in the city, Saxon had been reduced to shopping—or at least, sending Heberd shopping—at regular pet supply stores. The mountain of cages loomed impressively.

Saxon tented his fingers. "We're two days behind on *Six Devils* because of that Wintery slag. I swear, Hebby, I'm going to grind that witch into a fine paste, use that paste to fill a witch-shaped jelly mold, hire a necromancer to revive her, and grind her stupid revived body into an even finer paste!" Saxon's voice hopped hysterically between high and low ranges.

"Want me to produce a list of suitable necromancers?" Heberd ventured. He ducked his head as the dismembered remains of the shepherdess whizzed over his shoulder, taking off a chunk of his earlobe. Heberd allowed himself to look pitiful, stifling a whine and adjusting his position so the light would catch the dripping blood. Maybe that would distract Saxon from further organic destruction. The elf's eyes did liven at the deep red drops hitting the knotted silk carpet below the dwarf's feet.

A shadow passing over the blood broke Saxon's reverie and startled Heberd. Quickly, he spun. The door flap was still closed.

"We're in a tent, idiot. They're coming under the walls!"

Saxon hissed. As Heberd spun, a clawed pink paw slid like liquid over the edge of Saxon's desk, and an antique enamel inkwell disappeared.

"Uh-oh," Heberd muttered.

Saxon was on his feet. He yanked the brass beacon off his desk and swung it as a bludgeon at the claws reaching for the glittering silver bolo at his throat.

The swing missed and the hand retreated, but somehow, the bolo disappeared.

"Who let the bloody willens in?" Saxon screamed as a rampaging low-slung shape toppled him off his feet. Clutching his beacon, he hastily arranged his fingers and lit the beam, aiming at the nearest cascade of pink flesh.

The creatures were too slippery. The targeted willen bent into an arc that was either cartoonishly balletic or balletically cartoonish, and the ominous beacon beam did nothing but illuminate a patch of canvas.

"Keep them away from the cages!" Saxon screamed, blasting raw light out of his hands at the willens oozing under every edge of the tent.

This was bad. Saxon was an elf of cautious planning and tight-fisted control. A schemer. He wasn't a great improvisational fighter.

Heberd kicked at the nearest rodents with no real plan other than hoping that Saxon would see him doing *something*. This worked until his first kick landed, a solid blow to the haunches that sent a willen corkscrewing over the layered carpets. Snarling as she recovered, the willen conscripted two of her friends into full-toothed retribution. Heberd grabbed a standing candelabra, relieved as the dancing flames extinguished on his first swing at the trio of attackers.

Across the tent, an avalanche of cages sloughed off the pile, pulled down and cracked open by nimble pink paws. Skittering mouse-sized shadows escaped through the gaps between the floor and the canvas.

Not all of Garton's pets fled. Shadows from the candlelight flickered grotesquely as the mice shifted, ballooning ferociously. One mouse the size of a greyhound leapt onto Saxon's desk. Heberd watched in horror as a ropy pink tail whipped a red line across the light elf's face.

A second willen jumped onto Saxon's arm and knocked the brass beacon onto the ground. The elf howled, and the willen snatched the artifact and tucked the shiny metal into some secret skin fold. After a moment, however, the rodent shook and flung the lump of brass away like a succulent-looking fruit that had turned out to be full of spiders. That was some curse.

Heberd had never understood more than a few phrases of the willen language, but he was sure the complex high-pitched chitters echoing through the room were a warning. Unlike the tent's gleaming metal, the beacon lay untouched on the ground, fleshy bodies flowing aerodynamically around it. Garton, bleeding and knocked down, clawed his way torturously over the carpet to the artifact until a willen whose yellow buckteeth had been filed into fangs hissed him away. Another hopped onto his back, pressing the elf's small body into the carpet.

Is that willen wearing a golden crown? Heberd thought so. The creature on top of Saxon was fat, approaching the size of a small hippo, and the self-satisfied look on its face was unaltered by the squirming underfoot. Heberd batted away a paw going for the brass buckle on his work boots. *Never allow a war to spoil a little petty larceny*. He briefly mourned his pocket change.

A dim corner of Heberd's mind devoted to self-preservation emerged from hibernation. It was possible that the willens would kill him, although their violence seemed incidental to the smash-and-grab that was their higher purpose. If he lived and Saxon died, he'd be out of a job. Whoever cleared out Saxon's estate would quickly begin asking tough questions, particularly about some of the hidden compartments in the Beverly Hills house.

If both he *and* Saxon lived, the elf would be enraged. More than enraged. He'd be quivering nitroglycerine. Heberd backed away from the battle before him, humbled by the thought.

He had never seen Saxon out of control. Even his casual destruction of objects or, more often, people, was tightly wound and calculating. Saxon unleashed would be a truly awesome apocalypse.

The dwarf turned to the door flap, pushed it open, and sprinted away from the chaos as fast as his stubby legs would take him.

CHAPTER TWENTY-EIGHT

Stan texted Norah on Saturday afternoon. Killing time by watching one of the ballroom dances from *Top Hat*, she perked up at the alert.

It's ready.

For once, Norah had to look for Cleo. The pixie was luxuriating in a sunbeam in the kitchen, wheeling slowly to follow the afternoon light's progress across the floor. A cornflake crunched below her wheel.

"Do you ever mop?" she asked Norah.

"Hmmm... Mop? Mop? It's like a wand with a wet bit on the end. Can't say I know much about those." Norah grinned and pulled her wand out of the leather holster on her belt.

Cleo snorted and scooted forward an inch. "A *wand holster*? I thought only total losers wore wand holsters?"

"Ignore her," Norah whispered to the blue gum eucalyptus.

"I believe your words were, 'If you ever see me wearing one of those, shoot me with a vaporizing spell,'" Madge said. Her impression was uncanny. More alarmingly, she pulled her toothpick-sized wand out from between her cleavage. Norah nervously moved behind the nearest doorframe.

"It's padded. It has an anti-termite enchantment. My blue eucalyptus doesn't have to roll around inside my purse while recovering. Have you seen the inside of my purse?"

Madge narrowed her tiny eyes. "Unfortunately, yes."

Norah waved Madge away and turned to Cleo. "I'm taking you on an errand!" she announced.

Wheels whirred, and Cleo inched backward. "Norah, I...appreciate everything you've done for me. I do. The curse-breaking is exhausting..."

Norah hesitated. Cleo had always submitted willingly to her craziest plans. The runes on the side of the box glowed, and the pixie continued, "I've been so wrapped up in getting my body back that I forgot what I've gained. For instance, my wood hasn't aged a day. No chips. No scratches, even. Remember when you tried taking Stan's saw to me back when you thought I was trapped *inside* the box?"

Norah remembered. "Stan was very upset with me for breaking his saw."

Cleo glowed eagerly. "That was *dwarven* metal. Plus, as you have so ably proved on a near-infinite number of occasions, I'm spell-proof."

"You're a tank," Norah agreed, wondering if she should be insulted. "Actually, this isn't about breaking the curse."

"Hmm," Cleo said. The rune that looked like an eye glowed twitchily.

"Please?" Norah asked. "If you hate it, I'll...never take you anywhere again."

Cleo tsked disapprovingly. "Let's not get ahead of ourselves. Ugh. Fine. I want to drive."

Norah paused in alarm.

"I'm *joking*." Cleo groaned and zoomed into the doorway.

The Barnsdall Art Park occupied a hilltop between Los Feliz and Hollywood and had a nice view of Griffith Park. The last guy Norah had dated briefly had brought her up here for a picnic. How long ago had that been? Norah pushed the thought out of her mind. She had taken a weaving class in one of these buildings when she'd first moved to Los Angeles. Her mother still had the wool mat she'd made.

The place was busy for a Saturday afternoon, forcing Norah to park near the bottom of the hill. Cleo allowed herself to be carried under Norah's arm, and the two of them made their way up a graffiti-covered concrete staircase.

On the crest was Hollyhock House, a tan building complex that Andrew Lloyd Wright had designed in the early 1920s. Norah boosted herself over a hedge near the back with a quick antigravity spell. Inside the perimeter was a courtyard with a shallow fountain ringed by a circle of concrete steps. A small iron cherub statue danced in the center of the pool.

Norah faced the cherub. "I'm a pretty girl, and I like pretty things."

Cleo snorted, about to make fun of her, when she was interrupted by a rush of pouring water. The shallow circular fountain was draining rapidly through some hidden pipe. When it was dry, the concrete bottom broke into sunburst sections along thin lines and dropped away to form a large spiral staircase descending into the hill.

The concrete ended after a full spiral, and carved wood took its place. As they descended, the concrete went back into place, concealing the secret entrance.

"These carvings look familiar," Cleo observed as Norah carried her past the intricate birds and lizards that made up the curving balustrade.

"I sometimes wonder if Stan ever sleeps," Norah agreed. The staircase would have taken a human craftsman years of work. She nodded sincerely at a life-sized carved heron holding up the rail. Her wand shivered in its holster.

An airy arch at the bottom of the staircase let them out into a large workshop.

For being windowless and underground, the space was cheerful. Smooth parquet in warm wood stretched below their feet, and the air smelled pleasantly of sawdust and aromatic oils. The workshop occupied the entire hollowed-out hill. It was circular, the walls rising for fifteen or twenty feet before curving into a domed ceiling. The room was illuminated by a large chandelier or a very small sun. *Or maybe a very bright jellyfish.*

The center of the...chandelier...was an undulating glass bulb, as thin and transparent as air. Tendrils of pure light flowed out of it, rippling gently as they floated near the ceiling, dispensing with anything as crass as wires or bulbs.

Cleo whistled. "They're not called light elves for nothing."

"No," Norah agreed.

Sturdy workbenches circled the room. These tables were attractive with nice lines but dispensed with intricate carvings. Norah guessed that the ninetieth or hundredth time you banged your hip on a sharp wooden beak, you started to see the benefits of minimalism.

Stan was behind one of these. He nodded at Norah, who placed Cleo on the floor on her platform. The pixie zoomed over to Stan.

"Hullo, Cleo. Have you met Stellan?" Stan asked. The dwarf next to Cleo nodded. Even when Stan greeted her, she could not look away from the dwarf's beard. The dwarf looked ordinary in rolled-up black jeans and a death metal shirt, except for one thing.

Stellan had gotten a beard blowout. The roan tresses that flowed from his chin shone like liquid metal, coaxed into the kind of perfect beachy waves that Norah had stopped attempting years ago with her hair.

Stellan ran a smug calloused hand through the waves, which rippled under the room's magnificent lighting.

"Impressive, huh?" The dwarf grunted.

It took Norah a full four seconds to recover her voice. "You have to give me the name of your hairdresser. Or is it a barber?"

"Or a sorcerer," Cleo whispered.

The dwarf snorted. "I'll try to think of a big enough favor you could do me to trade for that tasty tidbit, but it might take me a few days."

Norah wanted to swim in those shining copper waves.

"I admit he did sharp work on the beard, but he refused to do my armpits," Stellan grumbled.

This aside snapped Norah out of her reverie. Stan suppressed a smile.

"Ah. I guess you'll have to find a braver barber." Norah batted away the vivid images attempting to find footing in her imagination. Fortunately, the dwarf was wearing long sleeves, which kept her curiosity from getting the better of her.

Stan cleared his throat. "While I find the range of aesthetic choices available to the local glitterati fascinating, there's business at hand."

Cleo squeaked as Norah hauled her up on the worktable, where something with square edges that was about the size of a table lamp awaited beneath an embroidered silk cloth.

"You want to do the honors?" Stan asked. Norah grinned, and Cleo's runes glowed as the silk fluttered softly.

Norah stared at her friend. "I'm sorry I wasted so much time trying to fix you. I've been thinking more about my magical prowess than what was right for you. I hope this gift will compensate for it." With her heart beating faster, she yanked the silk cloth off.

Under it was a platform made of polished mahogany, with raised edges and a shallow square well Cleo's size. Braided leather straps dangled from the sides of the square, clearly waiting to hold something Cleo-sized safely inside. The platform stood on two carved wooden feet that were more realistic than Norah had anticipated.

Cleo's runes glowed uncertainly. "Is there a wooden

wart on that toe?" she asked. Norah couldn't blame her for the faint note of disgust.

"I worked from a live model," Stan replied. "Poor Stellan here had his boots off for hours! I can sand the wart off if you want."

"It gives my feet character!" Stellan exclaimed before realizing that Stan had been talking to Cleo.

Norah chuckled.

"It's...impressive in a shark-in-formaldehyde way, but I prefer my wheelie platform for everyday use. More mobile, you know." Cleo's runes dimmed in disappointment.

"We're not done yet," Norah replied. Stan grinned and whistled a four-note sequence. A wooden cubbyhole across the room popped open, and the winged Hermes sneakers flew over, ruffling their feathers in excitement as they landed near the carved platform.

"Once we lace these bad boys on, you should be good to go," Norah told her. The wings flapped in agreement.

Cleo glowed so brightly that the light elf chandelier above them looked dim. "Ooh, ooh, strap me in!"

Norah got to work lacing the sneakers onto the carved wooden feet, and Stan secured the leather harness around Cleo's top. There was a small pouch near the base, not quite wallet-sized.

"Are you sure those straps are sturdy enough?" Norah asked, looking at the bands.

"Most certainly. You'll never guess what kind of leather I used."

The brown braids sparkled faintly, and Norah sighed. "Don't tell me! Please."

Stan waved a hand in assent. "Anyway," the old light elf

said, "I tested them myself. Flew to Santa Monica to have oysters on the beach with an old friend."

Norah raised an eyebrow, but Stan declined to provide additional information. The picture of him dangling from the leather straps, waving in the wind as he beat the traffic across town, was anxiety-inducing.

"Oh, but Norah, these are *your* flying shoes," Cleo protested. "I...suppose you could still wear them. When you need to. We could share."

The image of a city seen upside-down from a thousand feet in the air rose unbidden in Norah's mind. Shuddering, she replied, "Don't even think about foisting these hellions on me again. They're your problem now."

"So, what now?" Cleo asked.

Norah shrugged. "I always used to say 'Fly, my pretties,' but that was mostly for dramatic effect."

Cleo's runes glowed and dimmed. "Fly, my pretties!" the box requested, and the pixie rose into the air.

Runes sparkling up her sides like racing stripes, Cleo whooped and tentatively ascended to the ceiling. Norah cringed as the pixie overshot and careened to the glass chandelier, but two soft tendrils placidly caught her and spun her back to the floor.

"Sorry!" Cleo called cheerfully, swooping forward at breakneck speed. Watching the pixie's trajectory with alarm, Norah moved aside before she got cubed.

Cleo ascended, flew across the room, and attempted a hairpin turn that decapitated a statue of a marine iguana. Norah looked at Stan nervously, but he smiled serenely.

"Don't worry. I loaded up on wood glue. How's the

wand?" He raised a judgmental eyebrow at the padded leather wand holster.

Norah ignored him and pulled out the blue gum eucalyptus. It glowed faintly where the splintered crack had been glued.

"It's been very brave." Norah had pitched her voice so the wand could hear her.

"Keep taking it easy," Stan directed. "If you cast anything too crazy, it might never recover. No show-off-y dual-wielding, either.

Norah gave him a half-salute. "You got it, boss."

A thud drew their attention. Hitting the floor with her right toe had sent Cleo tumbling end-over-end, and she hit the wall with a terrific crash before collapsing on one side. When Norah threaded her way through the workbenches to help, Cleo was upright, hovering at eye level.

"This is amazing!" she squealed. "High five!"

She flipped backward, pointing the soles of her feet at Norah, who laughed and tapped her palm against Cleo's right foot.

"I'm glad you like it."

"I can't decide what I want to do first. I haven't been to the beach in so long. Do you think I can swim?"

This last question appeared to be directed at the winged shoes and not Norah. They ruffled uncertainly.

"Then take it easy for a while. One thing at a time."

"Hmm." Cleo flew a reasonably stable figure eight around Norah and Stan, then landed competently on a nearby worktable. Stan bent to inspect a fresh scratch on the floor.

"Anything else we should know?" Norah asked. Stan

shook his head. "Other than oiling the straps regularly," he corrected. "At least every ten or twenty years."

"I'll set a phone reminder," Norah replied sardonically and turned to Cleo. "What do you think? Should we head home?"

"You know what? I think I'll fly." Before Norah could protest that it was too soon or too dangerous, the translucent wings gathered speed, and Cleo shot up the staircase. There were only two crashes before Norah heard the stairs telescope down.

It was very quiet. Norah poked a decapitated wooden lizard head with one toe.

"Do you want help cleaning up?" she asked.

Stan shook his head. "Nah. You go on. If you want to stop by later, Millie is coming over after sunset. I know she'd love to see you."

Norah beat Cleo home. At first, she tried not to worry. The pixie was probably living it up. Stretching her wings. After an hour, she paced in the living room, subtly agitating her wall of Oriceran plants.

When she couldn't stand it anymore, she knocked on Stan's door. A pale woman in a silky jumpsuit the same color as her alabaster skin opened the door.

"Hey, Millie," Norah greeted her.

"Come on in. We're sitting down to dinner."

Norah pictured the range of possibilities this might entail for a vampire. When she walked into Stan's open-concept dining room, she half-expected to see a personal assistant sprawled on the table, neck eagerly bared. Instead, a small plate of spaghetti shared the table with two wine glasses. Only one of the deep garnet liquids was a cabernet.

"Drink?" Millie asked, pulling out a chair for her. "I'd offer you dinner, but there's no pasta left, and I don't think you'd care for my leftovers."

"I'd love a drink," Norah answered. Stan joined them as Millie handed her a full wineglass.

"Have you seen Cleo?" she asked.

Stan and Millie exchanged nervous looks before Stan sighed and slid a cream-colored envelope across the table. "She asked me to give this to you." *NORAH* was scrawled across the front.

"How did Cleo write a letter?" Norah asked.

"She flew into a gift shop, bought a card, and dictated it to the cashier. She's very resourceful."

"How did she pay for it?" Norah asked, panic rising.

"I tucked a twenty into that little zippered pouch on the harness. Bad luck to give a purse without money in it, you know. I'm not sure it qualified as a purse, but I decided not to take any chances."

Norah's protests died in her throat. "I can't believe she didn't say goodbye."

"I think she thought you would stop her." Millie smiled sadly. There was a subtle note of approbation in the vampire's voice. *They think Cleo was right.*

"Of course, I would have stopped her! She's not equipped for...for..."

"Independence?" Stan asked. "That might have been true yesterday, but thanks to us, it's not anymore!"

"I can't believe you had a part in this." Norah stabbed her index finger at Stan. Leaving her wine half-finished on the table, she stormed out the door. The moon was bright, and Norah stopped under the string of fairy lights on the lemon tree. The envelope tore under her shaking hands, and Norah pulled out a card featuring a rectangular English bulldog. *Tank you very much*, the card read. Norah opened it.

Dear Norah,

Thanks for the new kicks. I've been a pixie, and I've been a box. Now I'm something unique. Sorry I chickened out on saying goodbye. I have decided to go on a fly-about. I'm going to catch up with a few fairies I know in Palm Springs, then hit the open skies. Please do not follow me.

Yours cubely,

Cleo

Norah crumpled the card into a ball and flung it on the ground. After a few seconds, she picked it up, smoothed it out, and shoved it in her pocket. *I should at least recycle it.*

Back at her door, she stopped dead. Her door was ajar, creaking in the light breeze. She had locked it when she left. She was sure of it. Norah held her hand near the knob, and radiating heat warmed her fingers. Someone had melted off her lock. Her *dwarven* lock.

Wand in hand, she nudged the door open with one toe.

Something clattered in the kitchen. Creeping through the dark apartment, Norah finally made out a small shape illuminated by her open refrigerator. A dwarf. Norah held her breath as he slathered cream cheese over a piece of deli ham. *What does he want? Oh, wait. I don't have to guess.*

Norah closed her eyes, reached inside, and turned up her radio magic, extending her awareness slowly past the plants in her living room. *There he is.* Greasy, half-shrouded intentions flowed to her. The dwarf didn't want to hurt her.

She pulled out her wand, hoping she wouldn't have to strain the green break, and shot the dwarf with a medium-strength stunner spell. Crackling blue lines bounced off the dwarf's torso and dissipated in the air. *Shit.*

He was wearing spell-proof clothes. He was either a very powerful craftsman or rich enough to hire one. Or he was working for someone who was.

The dwarf popped a second ham roll into his mouth, sucking it down like a spaghetti strand. Norah's nose wrinkled. She didn't understand the emotions he was emitting. *He wants to run?* Why was he plopping on a stool behind her kitchen island with a hard seltzer if that was true? *When magic fails, try small talk.*

"Make yourself at home," Norah told him.

The dwarf glanced at her. "Don't mind if I do. Want some ham?" He slathered another slice with a generous dollop of cream cheese.

"I'm okay, thanks."

The dwarf shrugged. "Nice to see a woman invest in good-quality ham. I'm usually stuck with tofu slices and vodka."

"Do you break into many houses?"

The dwarf shrugged. Norah moved closer and shot another stunning spell at the dwarf's head. His forearm darted up like a coiled viper to block the shot. This time, it bounced back at Norah, and she stumbled as she ducked it.

"Did you come here to raid my refrigerator?" she asked, irritation creeping into her voice.

Another ham roll disappeared. The dwarf swallowed it, then shrugged. "Nah, I came to warn you."

Norah walked to the fridge, cracked open a hard seltzer, and slid onto a stool across from the dwarf. "What's your name?"

The dwarf chewed noisily, possibly to avoid answering.

"Heberd," he finally replied. Norah nodded.

"Okay. What can I do for you, Heberd?"

The dwarf chugged his seltzer and belched. "I would love it if you killed Garton Saxon."

Norah snorted in surprise, and vodka-infused bubbles tickled her nose.

"Is that all? You don't have anything easier like breaking into Fort Knox? Stealing the Declaration of Independence? Inventing a perpetual-motion machine?"

The dwarf laughed without much emotion. "Don't worry, my expectations are low. If I warned you he was planning to attack, you might be able to distract him long enough for me to find the boltiest bolt hole in Oriceran and hibernate until he cools his heels. Should only take a millennium or so."

Norah reviewed this amazing statement. "What do you mean, he's *planning to attack*? Attack where?"

"Here." Heberd waved his hands around the room. "You know the financiers almost pulled out of his film after that little stunt you pulled on set. He thinks that little butterball you use as an assistant helped someone rob him."

Good for Madge. She would have to ask the pixie about that. "Someone had to confront Saxon about his brainwashing problem," she answered.

"Better you than me, sweetheart. I don't know what happened between you two, but if you're immune to his beacon, you might have a shot."

"When is this attack supposed to take place?"

"I don't know. After that fiasco with the willens, he'll speed up his timeline. He'll need a win."

Heberd shivered, apparently considering what "winning" meant to Garton Saxon.

To Norah's disgust, the dwarf finished the last slice of ham and licked the cream cheese tub clean. After snagging her last hard seltzer from the fridge, he headed to the door.

"Good luck!" he called. "Try to die reaaaaal slow as a personal favor."

"Wait!" Norah yelled and ran after him. She needed more details. When she got to the front hallway, her door was open again, and the dwarf was nowhere to be seen.

CHAPTER TWENTY-NINE

Norah had underestimated the size of the crowd she had gathered in her apartment, and when her third plant got knocked off a shelf by someone attempting to make room where there was none, she drove everyone outside.

"You too." She glared at the black and white goat nibbling eagerly on the melted antique radio in the corner of the room. It was an empty husk now, but Norah couldn't bring herself to dispose of it. Pepe yanked off a piece of melted plastic and bleated.

Outside, Norah stopped alongside her mother. "I can't believe you brought the goat."

"She didn't bring the goat. I did." Jackie joined them. She sipped soda water from a plastic cooler someone had hauled onto the lawn. *This is supposed to be a magical defense militia, not a party.* Norah had done her best to warn everyone, and Stan had talked all the non-magicals in the complex into finding hotels for a few days, citing a termite problem.

"Leaf could tell something was wrong and insisted on sending Pepe with us for protection," Jackie answered.

Pepe puffed up his chest and huffed.

"Are you sure you're up for this?" Norah asked, not sure if she meant Jackie or the goat. She chuckled when both nodded enthusiastically.

"Andrew wanted me to stay home, but it's not as if I'm on bed rest. Besides, I'd do anything for your parents. They treat me like a daughter."

Jackie's voice caught on the last words. She had been adopted as a baby, and they hadn't reacted well to the news that Jackie was a witch. She once told them that they'd tried to exorcise her at bible camp, and Norah still wondered if it was a joke.

"I wanted to send them to a silent meditation retreat in Big Sur, but they knew something was up," Norah confided. She'd asked Madge and Stan for help with Saxon, and the defense force had quickly ballooned.

"You can't get rid of us that easily." Petra proffered a plastic tray with goat cheese canapes. "Now, if you'd care to finance a five-star vacation on the French Riviera, your father and I could be convinced to lay low."

Norah considered calling this bluff before a mental review of her latest bank statement jerked her back to reality. Stan, sitting in the shade, bit down on half of a lemon and tossed the other half to an eager Pepe.

"Who's ready to party?" a young male shouted. *I can't believe Madge invited Duncan.* The shirtless young wizard hopped off a yellow scooter and unstrapped a large wooden barrel from the back.

"Is that a keg?" Norah's father asked, suddenly cheerful.

"It's a *dwarven* keg full of *dwarven* beer," Stan replied, amusement in his voice. Duncan rolled the keg briskly down the sidewalk to the shade.

"What's a dwarven beer like?" Jackie asked.

"I don't know," Stan mused. "I've only used it to strip paint."

This is getting ridiculous. Norah strode over and stopped the rolling keg with a boot.

"Let's save this for the, um, post-battle afterparty." She diverted him to her apartment.

"The Dunker is at your service." Duncan hoisted the keg onto his shoulder. "What time do you think we'll be done? Some guys from the Palace were thinking of coming by later."

"If our powerful evil enemies give us an ETA, you'll be the first to know," Norah replied dryly. Oblivious to sarcasm, Duncan disappeared beyond her door, and Norah took stock of the courtyard.

Andrew was sitting at one of the wrought iron tables near the apartments, discussing a chest etching with a gleaming onyx crystal person. Quint was on the lawn, unpacking equipment.

"Are you setting up an omelet station?" Norah eyed the catering trays, the cast-iron skillet, and the crate of eggs.

"Don't be ridiculous," Quint shot back. "I'm setting up a frittata station."

An unfamiliar woman with dark brown skin stared at Quint with puppy-dog eyes.

"Quinnie makes the *best* frittata." She sighed.

Norah pulled her brother aside. "Did you bring a date?" she demanded. "This is a militia, not a picnic!"

Quint ignored her and returned his date's gaze with a self-satisfied smile. "Will you do the honors, Hazel?"

His date cupped her palms, and a tiny flame between them grew into a ball of fire. She blew on it softly and it leapt into the barbecue, which flared spectacularly to life.

"I think I'll be all right. You worry about yourself, sweetie." Hazel batted her eyes. Norah was too busy to be annoyed for more than a second. Besides, a fire elemental could be useful.

Quint waved a spatula in the air. "Who wants green pepp—"

His voice trailed off in mid-sentence, eyes widening into saucers. The chatter halted as everyone looked at the figure who had entered the courtyard. Every woman in the square gasped in unison.

The tall person striding past the fountain was clad in head-to-toe elven armor, bright scales of some faceted sparkling stone knitted together with metallic thread. Almost skin-tight, the armor was reminiscent of one of Elvis Presley's rhinestone jumpsuits—if Elvis had been a leanly muscled six-foot-five. The light reflecting off the armor was so bright that Norah pulled her sunglasses down onto her face. Madge, forgetting to fly, dropped into the icy cooler water with a splash and a yelp.

Stan whistled appreciatively. *It takes an artisan to know an artisan.* Unless he was mistaken, that was real Light Elven armor. Even knockoff elven armor could bankrupt you. Who was under the silver veil of whisper-thin chain mail flowing out from the circlet around the elf's head?

"Can I help you?" Norah asked, taking a few steps

forward. She hoped this wasn't her enemy's opening gambit.

A bow shone in the elf's hand, strung with light rather than sinew, and a bandolier of biting daggers rested against the scale mail. A hand reached up and tossed back the silvery veil.

"Frondle!" Norah exclaimed breathlessly.

The relentlessly good-humored light elf's face was uncharacteristically serious. He dropped gracefully to one knee, the light from his bowstring dancing across his blonde hair.

"My lady, I offer you all aid and assistance while I have breath to draw," he began. From anyone else, it would have been absurd. Somehow, Frondle lent the gesture gravitas. The festive chatter in the courtyard cooled to something more businesslike. *Good. We have work to do.*

"Thank you, Frondle." Norah nodded at him with a surprising grace of her own. What was that feeling running up her spine? Half-warm, half-tingly? She sucked in her breath as realization dawned. *Pull yourself together, Wintery. This is no time to be horny, especially not for a client.*

"I guess that's everyone," Stan announced.

"Not quite," chittered a low voice. Three pink shapes oozed out of the bushes near the pool. The massive willen in the lead grinned, revealing rows of sharpened, jewel-studded teeth.

"Sick," Duncan whispered so reverently that Norah feared he was getting unfortunate aesthetic ideas. Beside the massive willen were a smaller companion and a greyhound-sized white mouse.

Madge, shaking cold water off her wings, cheerfully flew over. "Hey! You found your cousin!"

As the smaller willen waved at Madge, Norah saw what she was sure was a pair of small pearl-handled revolvers in one of his skin folds. She nodded.

It was time.

"Circle up, troops," Norah shouted. The crowd in the courtyard collected around her, and she inhaled deeply. If Saxon was expecting to take them by surprise, he was sorely mistaken. She launched into the plan she and Stan had spent half of last night on.

"Let's divide into two groups. Anyone with battle experience, go under the lemon tree. Anyone without battle experience, head to the…ugh, the frittata station." Norah sighed as a dapper Quint waved a spatula.

Norah felt sad when her father took her mother's arm and squired her decisively under the lemon tree. They had been through so much together, above and beyond any rational call to duty. Here she was, pulling them back into the bad old business.

She was surprised to find that the group under the lemon tree was much larger than the one around Quint, which included Andrew, Jackie, Duncan, and Stellan. The dwarf had arrived with several dollies loaded with "ingenious traps."

Norah was interested to see Hazel saunter past her into the shade. Nodding at the fire elemental, she lowered her voice. "Nice to see Quint growing up. He usually dates models."

"Didn't you see my Alexander McQueen campaign in Vogue?" Hazel asked, voice sticky with annoyance. A faint memory tugged at the back of her brain. *Oh, shit. I did see that campaign.*

"The one in the active volcano caldera?" Norah asked. "Ooh. I would love to know if you're satisfied with your representation."

Something the size of a toothpick poked Norah's shoulder. "Ow!" She glared as a hovering Madge yanked her small wand out of Norah's t-shirt. Madge had appointed herself second in command.

"Network later over a nice dwarven beer, Captain," the pixie rasped. *Right. Back to work.*

"I want teams of two people on the rooftops there and there," Norah announced. "You'll work in pairs. We'll each take a two-hour watch. The second you see a threat, shoot a warning into the air."

"What kind of warning?" the chief willen asked.

"How about a silver griffin?" Petra suggested, voice steely.

"That might draw attention or expose you unnecessarily." Norah didn't want to make things worse.

Petra shook her head. "We're tired of running away and standing on the sidelines. We're proud of who we are, and we're here to fight."

Lincoln beamed at his wife with ironclad devotion. Norah was sure she recognized his expression from her parents' wedding photos.

"Okay," Norah continued. "When you see an enemy, shoot a silver griffin into the air at their location. We want to know where they are. Don't everyone rush at once, though. Get to your battle stations instead. Stan will assign those after I'm done."

As Stan nodded at the group, the throat of his shirt opened, and diamond scales caught the light.

"Frittata team, you're on defense. Keep the perimeter ward up, run messages, and deliver herbs."

Jackie nodded, the smile gone from her face.

Quint flipped the frittata in his pan into the air and casually caught it. "Don't forget to eat and drink. I'm on crafty. Or witchcrafty, if you will."

A small *baaaa* of enthusiasm rang out from the clutch of magicals under the lemon tree.

"You can't expect me to believe that *you're* a battle-hardened warrior," Norah accused as the crowd parted around Pepe. Looking offended, the small goat clomped back to the tree and stood to his full height.

"Fine. Let's hope our enemies wear open-toed shoes."

She watched her haphazard militia flow to Stan for their assignments. Pepe fixed her with a hard look and snapped a grass stalk in half.

"Norah! We're assigned to a watch together!"

She had to shield her eyes from the glare as Frondle bounded over. In the distance, Stan caught her eye and...was that a wink? Maybe her eyes were deceiving her.

"Your equipment is very impressive," Norah told him.

Someone snorted behind her, and Hazel muttered, "I bet it is."

Frondle, apparently not hearing her, patted his largest dagger.

"I was in the light elf Solar Vanguard for twenty years. Stan says it's like the American military's boat otters."

"The what?" Norah asked, bewildered. Her mother, appearing from thin air, leaned over Norah's shoulder.

"I think he means the Navy SEALs, dear." Petra looked appreciatively at Frondle's armor.

"War isn't as exciting as acting," he explained. "Oh! Did you ever hear back about that laxative commercial?"

Uh-oh. She had forgotten to tell him he didn't get it.

"Nothing yet," Norah lied. Frondle shrugged and strode away, the light from his armor blinding.

"You'll have plenty of time to talk on your long midnight watch!" Petra reminded her daughter cheerfully. "I'll bet that armor looks fantastic in the moonlight."

I'm being subjected to a conspiracy.

CHAPTER THIRTY

The first two pairs on watch trotted off to their stations. Not, Norah noticed, before hitting the frittata station.

She couldn't put it off any longer. Sitting at a picnic table at what she judged to be the center of the complex, Norah closed her eyes and turned her radio magic to full blast, steeling herself for the onrush of emotions from the people around her.

The first layer was what she'd come to expect. Quint wanted to impress his date. Her father wanted to keep her mother safe. Pepe wanted...actually, Norah couldn't quite untangle the bright knot of emotions twisting its way to her from the cheeky goat, although it wasn't the dumb gimme-food-and-love stream she'd detected in passing dogs. The goat's deal was...something to think about.

As Norah increased her internal magic's radius, the common thread in the emotions almost knocked her off her feet. Enthusiastic support. Everyone in the courtyard was here because they genuinely wanted to help. No grudging tagalongs. Even Hazel was happy to be here. Norah scratched a suddenly watery eye.

"Are you okay?" Madge asked, peering at the welling tears. Norah pushed her sunglasses up the bridge of her nose and sniffed.

"I've never been better," she replied honestly. "Who are you paired with?"

"Your brother's date."

"Ooh. Make sure to tell her all the embarrassing stories about Quint."

Madge grinned. "I'm not sure I'll have time. The watches are only two hours." They laughed. Quint, eyeing them warily, flipped a frittata and missed his catch, much to the delight of Pepe, who absconded with the eggy disk.

Norah sighed. "I know we're about to be attacked by one of the most powerful people in Hollywood who is a dangerous light elf. Is it wrong that I'm having fun?"

Madge shrugged. "When life hands you a lemon tree..."

Norah laughed. "Make friends with a goat?"

By the time Norah climbed to the top of her apartment building to take her watch with Frondle, the constant influx of emotions and desires was starting to wear her down. She was eroded, the unending flood picking off the shell of good humor that had lasted most of the afternoon.

Frondle cut a striking figure by moonlight. The crystalline scales of his armor were luminescent in the silvery-orange combination of streetlights and stars. Norah paced around the waist-high retaining wall at the roof's edge, pushing her awareness to its limits. She sensed nothing new. Mostly what she felt was Frondle's blushing affection.

"Whatever happened to that executive you were dating?" she blurted after her sixth or seventh circuit.

As Frondle sighed, his armor emitted a pleasing clatter, like less annoying windchimes.

"She went to her summer home in Italy and didn't invite me. She was tagged on Instagram in poolside photos with some upstart dryad architect. The young man looked very...sturdy."

"Put the *trunk* in swim trunks, huh?" Norah asked.

"He wasn't wearing a swimsuit," Frondle explained glumly, spinning his bow idly on its point. Norah put a hand over her smile.

"Chin up, Frondle. I'm sure she was only the first of many powerful executives who will break your heart."

Frondle's expression warmed as he thought that over. "I guess you're right. I'm an ingenue now!"

Norah's heart fluttered at the good-natured smile. *I could get him a modeling contract.* Norah pictured Frondle on a Calvin Klein billboard, ears poking out of his wheaten hair, rows of abs descending into—

Pull it together, Wintry! She shot to her feet and peered over the edge of the building, scanning the nearby apartments for threats. Frondle joined her with an admirable seriousness of purpose, his bow at the ready.

"I found a free archery class in Pasadena if you'd care to join me sometime. I'd love to learn from your human archers. I think you'd be good at it. You have a very steady wand hand."

"I have a very good and strong wand," Norah replied

loudly, directing the comment to the cylindrical holster at her hip. She pictured Frondle, ex-elf Special Forces, shooting at a target pinned to a haybale, surrounded by giggling pre-teen *Hunger Games* enthusiasts. *That I must see.*

"Once things calm down, I'd love to," she told him honestly. Frondle's high-wattage answering smile boosted her ego to sub-orbital levels.

A moment later, when the light elf wrapped his arms around her and spun her in a wide circle, Norah thought it was a spontaneous romantic gesture. Then an enchanted bullet flew through the air where she'd been standing and exploded into twining black tentacles that stuck to Frondle's armor where they touched. The tendrils wriggled across his shoulder, seeking gaps between the scales.

"*Infernum hexus!*" Frondle's voice was as clear as a bell, and his armor shimmered white-hot, burning away the hex. Norah rolled away from the heat and took cover behind the low perimeter wall.

Now unencumbered, Frondle shot three arrows in succession at speeds NASA engineers would envy. The arrows hit, and three hex bullets exploded harmlessly in the air over the street. Sinking lower, Norah raised her wand and drew lines in the air for an illusion spell, then sent it off with a war whoop.

An enormous silver griffin rocketed into the air, glowing brighter than Frondle and screaming an alarm. Norah directed its ascent to the space above their attacker.

Why hadn't she felt them? She probed the ground beyond the building, searching for any hint of ill intention.

There! Now she understood. The shooter was under the same control spell she'd encountered before. The wizard's true intentions were so muted that Frondle's flood of romantic intentions had overwhelmed them.

That'll teach me to mix business and pleasure.

Now that she knew what she was looking for, she focused her attention. Three blobs of muffled intention popped into her awareness, clustered together along a side street. Norah peeked over the roof wall to orient herself.

"There they are!" she told Frondle, pointing at a red sedan parked in the distance. Frondle nodded and loosed three more arrows, murmuring soft words in Elvish each time the bowstring twanged. Glowing silver arrows raced out, guided by magic on twisting paths that sent them soaring up and then plummeting behind the sedan at precise angles. Norah winced slightly as three channels of emotion went silent.

"Are they dead?" she asked, climbing to her feet.

Frondle shook his head. He'd pulled his elven veil over his face, and she could only read his emotions from the currents flowing out of him. "Those are Sleeping Beauty arrows. They're unconscious."

"For how—"

An ear-piercing shriek interrupted her question. The sky was doubly bright now as a second silver griffin joined the first, shooting up over the other building. She extended her awareness in that direction, but it was too far away for her to feel any enemies. Instead, multiple currents of fear and confusion reached her from the courtyard. Including her father, who wanted... *Oh, no!* Lincoln was desperate to help her mother.

Dread mixed with Norah's stomach acid as she spun to her parents, who had been keeping watch on the other rooftop. Where was her mother? She could still pick out Lincoln, but the current from her mother was a trickle among the streams of emotion.

Going down the stairs would take too long. Norah inhaled deeply and hurdled the low wall at the rooftop's edge. Small figures looked up as she arced into the courtyard, flinging an antigravity cushion in front of herself...

A new current of emotion pierced the noise, churning with so much evil intent that it threw Norah off-balance. Garton Saxon was here, emitting a lightless indigo aura that sucked up the currents of emotion around him. A pure instinct for annihilation had replaced every emotion in the universe.

She came down on hard concrete four feet to the left of her antigravity cushion. There was a crunch and the bones in her ankle shattered, splintered ends scraping tendons at odd angles. The sound was horrible, but the pain that followed as she rolled to a stop was worse. When Jackie raced over, her face turned green at the protruding bone.

"Go help my parents!" Norah screamed. Jackie hesitated, but something in Norah's face turned her toward the far building. Andrew hesitated too, but Norah's throat-burning bellow sent him after his wife. The shattering pain in her ankle and the evil flow of Garton Saxon's intentions twined into a single clear thought.

It's him or us. This was the last stand. There would be no Round Two.

Inside Norah's confused mind, a bright spear of blue light pierced the fear and pain like a glass rod. The light ran down her body into her ankle, filling her like cold water in a bowl. Five words appeared in her mind as the pain disappeared and her ankle floated off the ground, the horrible crunching sound returning as the bones danced into alignment.

LET ME RETURN THE FAVOR.

Her shattered ankle was healing faster than she thought possible. In her right hand, her mended wand lit the air around her with a bright periwinkle glow.

"Is this your doing?" she asked, wiggling her toes as a test. The wand bobbed slightly. "Thank you," she whispered. *Are wands supposed to talk?*

The light around her ankle flashed brightly, then winked out. Norah limped tentatively to her feet, wincing at the pressure on the green break. The fix wasn't perfect, but it was better than having a bone sticking out of her skin.

A scream rose from the roof, and Norah fought through the pain to half-run, half-hobble up the nearby staircase.

The scene on top of the roof was horrifying. Lincoln, Jackie, and Andrew were huddled in a corner, feeding a shrinking green magical shield. Up on the far wall, almost floating, was Norah's mother. Petra's intelligent gray eyes were rolled back to expose glassy whites. *The control spell.* As Norah gained the roof, Petra raised her wand. A blood-red curse sprang at her with crackling fangs. Norah's last-ditch shield spell splintered almost immediately but bought her time to dive into the huddle with her family.

"We thought they'd start slow, but when your mother looked at the first griffin alarm, Saxon hit her with a beam of light from some brass box."

"I've seen it before." Norah shivered as her mother sent

another crimson curse at their shield. Although it bounced off, the green circle shrank a few inches in response.

"We have to cut him off from that box before he turns everyone on our side against us," Norah stated. Jackie was halfway through a curt nod when her eyes widened.

Behind the terrifying non-Petra, two low shapes climbed over the walls. Norah recognized their sleek white fur.

Another curse hit, and their magical shield sputtered out for a full second. Norah threw up her wand and bolstered it, but it shrank faster than she could replenish it.

"Pin down her wand hand while I break the curse," Norah shouted. She raced to her mother, lunging sideways to avoid the mouse shifters. One collected itself and bared its teeth, stalking toward her as she made her way to the edge of the roof. *She'll take us all down if I don't get to her.*

Petra's warm maternal aura made it easy to forget she was an extremely powerful witch. Norah kicked drooling shifter jaws away as she reached for her mother's ankle, and blue magic crackled as her hand wrapped around Petra's calf. The curse weakened almost immediately. Petra was fighting the control spell from the inside like a wildcat and was close to punching through the first weak spot herself.

There was a stabbing pain in Norah's ankle as one of the white shifters bit down. She tried to hold on to her mother, but the creature dragged her backward, and her hand slipped.

Norah screamed, and Quint blasted three stunning spells at the white fur, almost hitting Norah in the process.

The rodent shied away, and Andrew tangled it in a green web of sparks.

Petra raised her wand, and it swirled with bruise-colored magic inches in front of Norah's face. When she was about to release the powerful hex, her arm flew up to avoid her husband's stunner spell. The second shifter knocked him down when Lincoln moved to block her counter curse.

Magic flowed from Petra's wand and tightened around Norah's neck. She coughed until it tightened, then crawled to Petra with the last of her strength. If she could reach–

Stars burst behind her eyes, and the edges of Norah's vision turned to ink. Pressure building at her temples, she crawled one step, then two, then slumped on the roof.

There was a thump overhead. Quint sent a wisp of magic to coil around the choking spell at her neck, and it loosened enough for her to look up and see her mother frozen on the roof's edge, a translucent arrow shaft through her chest. She was breathing but otherwise frozen. Norah glanced back. A small, glittering figure on the other building's roof raised a hand in greeting. Frondle had made the shot.

"It's okay," Norah said. "It's a Sleeping Beauty arr—"

Petra, frozen, swayed to the edge of the roof.

Someone screamed, *"Grab her!"* but it was too late. As Norah's vision dimmed, Petra tumbled over the edge.

Mom! Breath failed Norah's vocal cords as she fought to the ledge. When Quint's counter spell ate through the last constriction, she sprinted.

I'm too late.

Petra's limp body was splayed across the grass, motionless.

Norah screamed. Her eyes adjusted oddly to the dark, sending confusing signals to her brain. *Wait.* Petra wasn't on the ground. She was hovering in the air one and a half stories down. How? There was no visible magic, no anti-gravity column or enchanted net. As she descended, Petra's shadow danced on the ground below, rolling gently onto a waiting bush.

Someone's carrying her. Madge? Madge was tough, but the pixie couldn't haul a load much bigger than a Pomeranian.

Her futile squinting was interrupted by a javelin of light whistling past her ear. Garton Saxon was on the ground, midnight-blue robes rippling under the moonlight and a brass lantern dangling from his right hand. Extending his left, he stole the light from a nearby streetlamp, and the street below plunged into darkness.

Chanting under his breath, Garton waved his hand in a complex pattern of loops and lines. The light he had stolen broke into a swarm of fireflies.

Well, not quite. The back of each buzzing speck of light glistened with a cruel thin blade. Swarming into a V-formation, they rose to the roof. Saxon met Norah's eyes from below, but the beacon didn't twitch. *Your shiny box didn't work on me last time, and it won't work now.*

Her wand was a blur as Norah shot five of the flying knife insects in a row. There were so many.

"Oh, shit!" Andrew exclaimed as he joined her at the edge.

Saxon smiled at her brother's silhouette and raised the

beacon as Andrew shot down the first of the incoming swarm, wand zigzagging precisely through the air. The beacon glowed white, seeking Andrew's outline like a searchlight.

"Not so fast!"

When the beam shot out, something blocked its path. The light refracted, missing the roof by a dozen feet. Norah's radio magic pinged with a new set of intentions as the sharp corners of a box glowing with runes were silhouetted in the beacon's light. Cleo was back, wings flapping at her feet.

"Cleo!" Norah shouted, but her voice was lost in the roar of glowing insectoid daggers flowing over the roof's edge.

Norah sprinted to Quint and her father.

"Mom's fine," she shouted, zapping a bug whose dagger was dangerously to her eye. "Cleo caught her."

"The talking box?" Quint asked, kicking at one of the rats and yelping as a lightning bug pierced his shoulder.

Norah tried to cast a protective shield around them, but the bugs were made of strong magic, and she couldn't protect him. A glowing spear pierced the top of her shoe, and wetness spread from the wound.

"Get off the roof *now*!" yelled someone from the staircase. The nearby metal balustrade glowed red-hot as Hazel bounded up, Jackie following a safe distance.

Hazel's eyes were embers, and flaming braids floated around her head. Before Quint's eyes could register his admiration, Norah grabbed his arm. Dodging the shifters, she pulled him over the roof's edge, casting a wide antigravity cushion as they fell. Lincoln and Andrew followed a half-second later and rolled off their own cushions at a run.

Their shadows sharpened on the ground below as orange flames exploded overhead, radiating so much heat that the hair on the back of Norah's neck was singed. The crispy bodies of lightning bugs rained down around them, bursting into ash when they hit hard surfaces. A tuft of burned white fur wafted onto her shoulder.

"What now?" As Quint spoke, Cleo shouted triumphantly in the distance. Norah pulled him to the sound.

Saxon was in the center of the complex's small parking lot, standing within a protective bubble of light. He was less encased than trapped. The light elf was somehow even angrier now, that impossibility made real by the hurricane-force emotions thrashing against her. Norah staggered as Cleo flung one of her points against the bubble.

"Being spell-proof has its advantages," the pixie shouted as she went in for another dive. The light bubble shuddered but held.

Saxon's knuckles whitened as his fist flexed helplessly around the beacon. Norah smiled. If Cleo couldn't get in, Saxon couldn't get his magic out. Trapped like a spider in a cup, he snarled.

"We need to burst Saxon's bubble," Norah directed.

"Then he'll be able to use his control spell on us," Andrew countered.

"Cleo will block it," Norah stated confidently. The box bobbed in confirmation. "Then we will take down Saxon together."

She, Lincoln, Andrew, and Quint joined wands, and

twining magic raced to Saxon's protective bubble. At first the spell was deflected and flowed around the sides, but it soon gained purchase, corroding the shield underneath. Under the weakening shell, Saxon readied the beacon, a ball of light glowing in his opposite hand.

Smoke streamed overhead. Norah hoped Hazel hadn't melted the roof. The crackle of magic on magic emitted a smell like ozone, and crashes and screams echoed from the courtyard.

Saxon's bubble was shot through with brightly colored cracks before it finally broke open.

"Watch out!" Andrew cried as Saxon lobbed his ball of light and raised the beacon. Cleo, fast on her wings, swooped to block the oncoming shaft of light.

Saxon's scream of rage, piercing the smoke and magic, was nearly inaudible beneath the current of fury pouring out of him. He leapt onto a nearby car and cast a quick light shield. As it deflected Andrew and Lincoln's spells, he ripped open the top of the beacon, revealing an antique lightbulb swirling with chalky gray magic.

Saxon hurled the bulb at them, but its parabola ended in splinters on the sidewalk. The fog smothered the flying shards of glass. Billowing from the bulb, it licked at Norah's feet while concealing Saxon from view.

I don't need to see you. Norah barely had to focus to feel Saxon's murderous anger. His goals had shifted, but his new intentions rang out. Norah leaned onto the balls of her feet. Saxon had decided to run for it and nurture his rage later.

Not so fast. Norah followed the thread of his emotions into the fog. The world disappeared; the mist was so thick that she could feel it press against her eyeballs. Slamming into a car bumper forced her to slow, hands in front of her as she pushed blindly into the fog.

When her pace slackened, Norah briefly feared the fog was poisoned. Summoning an oxygen bubble around her head, she realized the problem was more insidious. She didn't want to track Saxon. She tried to run in the opposite direction and throw hexes at her brother. Watch Petra writhe under a crushing curse. She caught a laugh on her lips.

It's a control spell. Distributed in a fine mist, it was weak but pervasive. Deep breaths helped the evil impulses flow through her without taking hold. Norah fought to keep her legs moving to Saxon's wellspring. Her brother or father shouted behind her, and she prayed that they would resist the fog.

When she slowed to a crawl, so did Saxon. He wasn't in charge of the spell he had released from the beacon anymore, and he was feeling its effects too. Finally, Norah's wand hand flashed in front of her face. The improved visibility meant she was almost on the other side of the fog.

Resisting the fog's suggestion to shoot her feet with a stunner spell, she plowed heroically through the last few yards, gasping as she stepped into the open air. Garton Saxon, looking smaller, was sprinting down the middle of the street. Raising a steadying arm, she shot a clear stream of bright blue light into his neck. The light elf tipped and slid across the asphalt, and the side of his head crunched into a concrete curb.

Norah willed every scrap of power she could force from her body into a stunning spell, which spiraled through the night air into the now-bloody dimple between Saxon's eyes. He was afraid and in pain; she could feel it.

When she rolled his body over, it was very light, and a gash on his head leaked dangerous amounts of blood. Norah went to bind the wound, but her wand shivered and resisted. The blue glow along the splintered break dimmed as she twisted the shaft. He might die. *No. Not yet.*

"How do I shut down Dark Hound?" she asked, her voice rising. Tears glittered in his frozen eyes. "Tell me, and I'll stop you from bleeding out." She tapped Saxon's mouth with her wand, and a grudging blue spark freed the light elf's lips.

"I don't run Dark Hound. Just...easy way to take down the enemy. Like a vending machine for killing Griffins. Put in a name, and boom. Dead wizard."

The stunner spell holding Saxon on the asphalt crackled and dimmed. *Shit.* Norah's wand had done its best but couldn't run on fumes forever. She backed away as Saxon twitched, smiled, and pulled his right hand loose, then drained three overhead streetlights. At close range, he didn't need anything fancy.

Norah dove onto the grass and rolled as shards of light shot toward her. Saxon pulled his arm free and touched his head, light springing from his fingers to bind the wound. He advanced on the crawling Norah, pulling light from a twinkling star overhead. *Was that even possible?* She dodged twice, then reached an exposed stretch of open asphalt. As she scrambled away from the menacing light elf, gray fog licked at her back.

"Duck!" someone behind Norah called. With it came a rush of positive emotion, so eager to protect her that she flattened herself unquestioningly against the ground. A fast-moving object parted the air above her. Turning, she saw Garton Saxon fall, a glowing arrow bristling from his chest.

"Norah!"

She heard the pleasant chime of Frondle's armor before she saw him. Breathless, he enclosed her hand in his, warming her with his light.

"Things were quieting in the courtyard, so I came to check on you," he explained.

Norah squeezed his hand. "Thank you."

They went to inspect Saxon together. More than stunned, he looked comatose. Moving with uncanny grace, Frondle bent over the fallen body and wrapped black gem-studded bracelets around the older elf's wrists and ankles.

"I'm not sure he deserves new jewelry." Norah choked out, staring.

"These bangles are made from black-hole onyx. It sucks in nearby light, so even if he wakes up, he'll be powerless."

Norah looked again. The studs on the bracelets that looked like black gems were lightless voids in the fabric of the universe. Specks of pure nothingness. She shivered as Frondle scooped Saxon's body into his arms.

"Let's go back to the courtyard," she said.

The fog from the beacon had started to dissipate. When she reached into it with her radio magic, no one was left inside. Before they went back, she insisted on scouring the building's exterior for the remnants of Saxon's beacon. The frame seemed inert, but she carried it back to the courtyard.

The apartment complex was chaotic, but the fighting

had resolved. There were scorch marks all over the lawn and a bullet hole in one of the apartment doors. The fire on the eastern building had gone out. Duncan, flanked by the two willens, had six prisoners lined up along the western building's wall. Madge buzzed between the friendly mouse shifter and the rooftop.

In the middle of it all, her family was knotted around a picnic table. When Norah saw them, she ran over. Quint, Andrew, and Lincoln were pale, tending to the body on its side on the table before them. A translucent arrow was still lodged in Petra's ribcage, and she hadn't woken up.

Behind Norah's shoulder, Frondle cleared his throat. "That's a Sleeping Beauty. You'll need true love's kiss to wake her up."

Lincoln's face lit with understanding. "I believe that's my cue." His gruff voice was soft. He bent over the picnic table and kissed his wife. The arrow dissolved in birdsong, and Petra sat bolt upright.

"*Ow!*" Lincoln cried, touching his lip where his wife had accidentally headbutted him.

"Sorry." Amusement flickered in Petra's eyes.

"I'm glad you're back," Lincoln stated. Petra scanned the gathering crowd, relaxing when her three children's faces swam into view.

Norah patted her mom's hand and went to find Stan, who had joined Duncan by the prisoners. Three were the light elves Frondle had knocked out at the start of the battle. The other three were conscious. A witch, a Kilomea, and a water elemental were bound head-to-toe with tight loops of rope and magic.

"Casualties?" Norah asked, jumping as a full branch fell

off the lemon tree behind Stan. "I think Hazel vaporized a few mouse shifters on the roof."

Stan nodded, looking grim. "No permanent damage on our side, but an enemy water elemental was killed. Fell off the roof during the chaos, and by the time anyone thought to check on him, it was too late." His eyes darted to a shadow under the building, a body-sized lump covered by embroidered velvet. Norah walked away and threw up what was left of her frittata beneath an aloe plant.

Saxon would pay for this bloodshed. As she walked back into the light, Frondle laid the light elf's comatose body next to his companions. Four Sleeping Beauty arrows bristled from the bodies, shimmering in the light.

"Does it have to be true love? I'm not sure Saxon has anyone to wake him up," Norah mused.

Frondle shrugged. "It's a feature of the arrows. It doesn't have to be romantic. Anyone who loves him can come forward."

Saxon inspired plenty of emotions. Fear. Envy. Disgust. Invective-laced ill will. Love?

She almost shrieked when Cleo plummeted toward them.

"The flying shoes suit you," Norah told her. "I'm glad they brought you back to us."

"Hey, I've gotten free rent for years. Saving your ass from an evil elf was the least I can do, especially a scumbag like Saxon. You know I knew him back in the twenties."

Norah sighed. "Does he have a long-lost love somewhere? I need to talk to him."

Petra, appearing at Norah's shoulder, grabbed her hand and squeezed. "Maybe he has a mother. She probably loves him against her better judgment." She kicked Saxon's body with a toe to ensure he was still unconscious.

An insistent clomp on metal drew Norah's attention to a small hoof stamping on a drainage grate.

"That goat took out a huge Kilomea," Duncan reported. Something white wriggled between Pepe's teeth. Norah held out her hand, and a small white mouse was dropped into it. It started to grow, and she was forced to put it down as its weight increased exponentially.

When the shift was over, the man in front of them was about Norah's age, with light brown hair. He was also naked and terrified, even more so when he found himself staring at the business end of seven wands and a floating ball of magma, courtesy of Hazel.

"What's going on?" he asked. It took several minutes of questioning and a pair of shorts to get any answers. The mouse shifter had been working on a movie set in February when Saxon had brought him into his office and asked him to look at a brass box. Everything after that had been a blur until he'd woken up in mouse form on the lawn, where he'd promptly found himself scooped up by a goat and unable to shift.

Norah raised an eyebrow at Pepe, who munched regally on a seltzer water can.

"You're okay now," she assured the wizard.

Stan sighed. "These three all claim they were under a control spell that broke twenty minutes ago."

When Saxon broke the beacon.

"Are they telling the truth?" Norah asked.

"You tell me," Stan replied.

Oh. Right. Radio magic. Norah approached the prisoners

and let their emotions flow over her. They were exhausted, afraid, and wanted to go home. None of them wanted to hurt her. However, the water elemental on the left desperately wanted Saxon to wake up and appreciate his undying loyalty. He expected a specific reward. A movie deal?

"That one." She pointed at the elemental. "He was working with Saxon of his own free will."

Stan nodded. Norah decided to let him deal with the brainwashed attackers and retrieved an ice water from the cooler.

Duncan was at a nearby picnic table. "I told the guys not to come over. It's not a party."

"No," Norah agreed.

"Does that mean we can't drink the dwarven beer?"

Norah wrinkled her nose at Quint and Hazel making out across the lawn and decided she wouldn't mind having blurred vision.

"Go ahead, tap the keg."

Frondle clattered over, smiling brightly. "I can help! You know, the last time I drank dwarven beer, I woke up in a fairy circle with no memory of the past six months."

Norah looked around the battered courtyard. A six-month coma had a certain appeal. "I'll be in in a second. I need to talk to my parents."

Frondle led Duncan away, discussing the finer points of magical keg-tapping. Norah stopped listening after he said "pressure," "never indoors," and "catastrophic explosion." It was not like she would get her deposit back.

Petra and Lincoln were under the lemon tree, hunched over a phone. When Norah approached, they reluctantly parted to reveal the Dark Hound website. When Norah saw the two new faces in the grid, her heart sank.

"They chose a terrible image of me," Lincoln grumbled. "I think they made my eyebrows look like that on purpose. You, of course, are as stunning as ever," he told his wife.

Petra looked at the glowing red model of her face. "I haven't done my hair like that in twenty years. I do look ferocious."

"I'm so sorry," Norah began. "You'll have to go back underground until we can shut down Dark Hound. I thought Saxon was behind it, but he used it to take out his enemies."

Petra shook her head, her mouth a firm line. "No, sweetheart. No hiding this time."

"No hiding. No running," Lincoln agreed. "We're going to draw the bastards out into the light."

"Who's a bastard? Are we talking about Quint?" Andrew interrupted. "His new girlfriend is something, huh?"

"I like her," Petra replied.

When Andrew clapped a hand on Norah's back, she saw that the mermaid on his bicep was curled up in her clamshell, black ink ZZZs bubbling from her mouth. The mermaid had the right idea.

"We'll all help protect you," Norah told her parents. "After tonight, I don't think anyone will be eager to go after the Wintery family."

"Guess you're getting into the family business, sis." Andrew poked her with his wand. Norah didn't argue with him, just swatted his wand away and sighed.

"I'm not closing First Arret, but I can't ignore what's

happening to the Silver Griffins. I could do both for a little while. Any dream worth having is worth fighting for."

Madge swooped in and landed on a low-hanging lemon tree branch. It bobbed, releasing citrusy oils into the nearby air. "Besides, if she closed First Arret, I would hire an assassin to murder her. I know a good one, too. Mean little fairy…"

Norah's parents laughed and looked at their daughter approvingly. They all jumped when a boom rang out behind them.

"Stand down." Norah raised her eyebrow at the forest of wands that had suddenly appeared. "Duncan just tapped the dwarven keg. Who's ready for a beer?"

"To victory?" Andrew asked hopefully. Behind him, Jackie rolled her eyes.

"Yeah," Norah replied. "To victory!

"At least for now."

Get sneak peeks, exclusive giveaways, behind the scenes content, and more. PLUS you'll be notified of special **one day only fan pricing** on new releases.

Sign up today to get free stories.

Visit: https://marthacarr.com/read-free-stories/

THE STORY CONTINUES

The story continues in book two, Contract Execution, coming soon to Amazon and Kindle Unlimited.

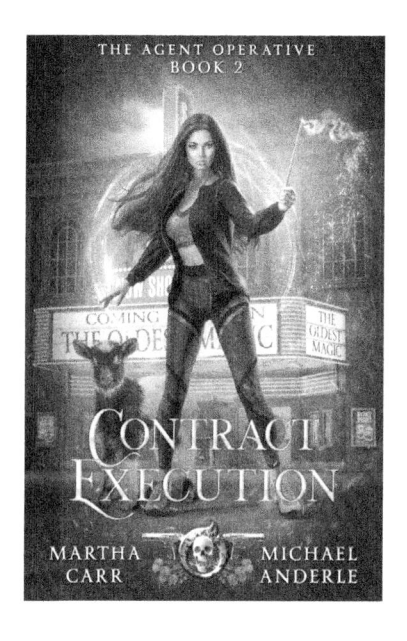

Claim your copy today!

AUTHOR NOTES - MARTHA CARR
NOVEMBER 3, 2022

I've started a project answering questions for my son about my life. I realized after last year's fifth round of cancer, and then chemo this time that he was expecting me to die sooner rather than later. It's been a lot for him to deal with and there isn't much I can do to make it better, except tell him stories that I can leave behind – eventually. Hopefully, a long time from now. I'm going to let you guys listen in as well.

My author notes for this year are going to be answers to questions and all of you can get to know me better, too. Maybe inspire, maybe give you a laugh along the way.

Today's question is: What was it like learning to drive?

I learned to drive in a different era – the mid '70's. No computerized cars, (no computers), and cars with a gear shift between the seats was still a thing. Flyover ramps weren't much of a thing yet and in Washington, DC where I learned how to drive, the Beltway wasn't as jam packed as it is now. Of course, we thought it was and getting anywhere took a while, but in hindsight it was lightning fast.

Woodbridge, Virginia, twenty-three miles from DC, was considered an undeveloped outpost and now rush hour extends to Fredericksburg, fifty-three miles away, which we thought of as a distant city. Like saying New York was close to Delaware. I know, it doesn't seem that far anymore, does it? Times change.

If we wanted to get somewhere around Alexandria, where you know I grew up, we still took the two-lane state highways. They seemed big in those days, lined with restaurants and big, fancy stores, and would eventually become quaint. Most of those stores, like Lord & Taylor, have closed.

However, thanks to the original architect, Major Pierre Charles L'Enfant, DC did have (and still does) four-lane roundabouts that were fast-paced and had multiple exits. You had to be in the correct lane entering the circle to get out in the right spot. And, since DC is a system of one-way roads, choosing the wrong one could take a complicated series of turns to correct. I ended up in Maryland more than once trying to get from DC to Alexandria. Thank goodness I knew the trick that always helped me eventually get home. All the one way streets point toward the Washington Monument and therefore, the 14th Street Bridge, and a straight shot toward home.

But, back to learning how to drive. I started with your grandfather who wanted to save a few dollars trying to teach me in the 1968 Ford Galaxy 500. A behemoth of a car that was taller and longer and wider than a Cadillac and by then about nine years old. It was super modern when Dad bought it - his first brand new car of his life - but by then was showing its age. Limited power steering that only kicked in with a little bit of gas, and no power brakes. When I really needed the car to stop quickly, I literally stood on them, but butt rising off the seat. I marvel at the arm muscles I must have had in those days to parallel park the car and the patience to give just the tiniest amount of gas to get some assistance.

Well, lessons with your grandfather lasted for one very brief session. He started out by barking orders and I was already so nervous that I steered us into the field across the street from our house, leaving tire marks through the grass. Sweat was pouring down his face as he opened the passenger door, half rolled out and walked back to the house to down a few shots of whiskey. After that, he paid for private lessons, thank God.

The lessons were in an old Volkswagen Beetle with a manual transmission. I learned to drive on a stick shift. Who knew that they would become obsolete in this country? Not only was I learning to merge onto a major highway, I was also shifting at the same time, not leaving my foot on the clutch or it'll burn out.

Eventually I got my license (on the second try, which I didn't feel too back about considering a fellow classmate hit a car in the DMV parking lot) and was given that old Ford Galaxy to drive to school and around town, when it was available. I loved it. It felt like freedom with roll-down windows.

My favorite was driving alone late at night when it was just the right temperature to drive with the windows down. There weren't as many streetlights or houses everywhere and there were plenty of back roads with low hanging trees and stars dotting the skies. I would cruise along them with the radio off, listening to the wind rush past the car. Like I said, freedom.

Remember, in those days phones were plugged into the wall and there was no GPS. If I was in the car no one could find me and messages would have to wait, or they could call back again. And I had to pay attention to my surroundings because a phone wasn't saying, "Turn left in one mile." I was much more present all the time with far more nature to look at even in that big metropolitan area.

It's been forty-seven years since I got my license and I've done so much driving since then, I always enjoy sitting in the passenger seat when you're around. I notice so much more on streets right around my house that I miss most of the time. Still, on occasion, there's a back road that just pops up in Texas with a big, wide sky as the sun is setting and I'll put down the window and open up the roof and turn off the podcast and just listen to the wind rush past the SUV. A lot has changed, but sometimes, there's something that stays simple and wonderful and freeing. More adventures to follow. Love, Mom.

AUTHOR NOTES - MICHAEL ANDERLE

NOVEMBER 2, 2022

Thank you for not only reading this book but these author notes as well!

My experience (near) Hollywood

Interestingly enough, my older brother left Texas twenty-five or thirty years ago for the state of California. For a Texan, that was as near blasphemy as you could get.

I had never visited the state, nor was I really interested in the lives of actors or even movies that much, except for the occasional huge action-adventure / sci-fi (think *Indiana Jones* and *Star Wars*–I'm that old.)

Until Darryl invited me for Christmas one year. I got a plane ticket, asked for money instead of gifts, and got on a plane in Houston to head to the rather odd state.

I left my wallet and money on the plane. Never got the money back and learned how you cancel all credit cards.

Welcome to California!

Darryl picked me up from the airport (HUGE!) and drove me to his two-bedroom apartment on a famous street name (that I can't remember). I was suitably impressed by the fireplace that turned on with a light switch.

Sh#t, in Texas, we used *matches*. What kind of black magic was this?

Darryl and his friends were into all sorts of glorious, exciting businesses, including magazines, ad revenue, and even scripts, agenting, and movies.

By comparison, I was truly boring and pedestrian in my life.

I left California with an understanding of why it was so exciting, memories of beautiful weather and glorious mountain ranges, and a weird understanding that pedestrians actually thought cars wouldn't run them over when crossing the street.

I didn't fall for that obvious trap when returning to Texas. In Texas, I made damn sure I didn't walk in front of a car. There was no reason to tempt anyone to clip me to "teach me a lesson."

Car always wins. Period.

Some of the knowledge I've gleaned over the years of visiting California (I did move there for a few years (three?) and the stories I've been told about the state went into the creation of this series.

How pathetic my knowledge was in regard to this series, I shall never divulge.

I hope you enjoy it and all of the shenanigans that will occur ;-)

Ad Aeternitatem,
Michael Anderle

AUTHOR NOTES - MICHAEL ANDERLE

MORE STORIES with Michael newsletter HERE: https://michael.beehiiv.com/

OTHER SERIES IN THE ORICERAN
UNIVERSE:

THE LEIRA CHRONICLES
CASE FILES OF AN URBAN WITCH
THE EVERMORES CHRONICLES
SOUL STONE MAGE
THE KACY CHRONICLES
MIDWEST MAGIC CHRONICLES
THE FAIRHAVEN CHRONICLES
I FEAR NO EVIL
THE DANIEL CODEX SERIES
SCHOOL OF NECESSARY MAGIC
SCHOOL OF NECESSARY MAGIC: RAINE CAMPBELL
ALISON BROWNSTONE
FEDERAL AGENTS OF MAGIC
SCIONS OF MAGIC
THE UNBELIEVABLE MR. BROWNSTONE
DWARF BOUNTY HUNTER
ACADEMY OF NECESSARY MAGIC
MAGIC CITY CHRONICLES
ROGUE AGENTS OF MAGIC

OTHER SERIES IN THE ORICERAN UNIVERSE:

DIARY OF A DARK MONSTER
CHRONICLES OF WINLAND UNDERWOOD

OTHER BOOKS BY JUDITH BERENS

OTHER BOOKS BY MARTHA CARR

JOIN THE ORICERAN UNIVERSE FAN GROUP ON FACEBOOK!

CONNECT WITH THE AUTHORS

Martha Carr Social

Website: http://www.marthacarr.com

Facebook: https://www.facebook.com/groups/MarthaCarrFans/

Michael Anderle Social

Website: http://lmbpn.com

Email List: http://lmbpn.com/email/

https://www.facebook.com/LMBPNPublishing

https://twitter.com/MichaelAnderle

https://www.instagram.com/lmbpn_publishing/

https://www.bookbub.com/authors/michael-anderle

BOOKS BY MICHAEL ANDERLE

Sign up for the LMBPN email list to be notified of new releases and special deals!

https://lmbpn.com/email/

For a complete list of books by Michael Anderle, please visit:

www.lmbpn.com/ma-books/